**Other Bella Books by Kat Jackson**

*Begin Again*

## About the Author

Kat Jackson is a collector of feelings, words, and typewriters. She's a thirty-something teacher/occasional mental health therapist living in Pennsylvania, where she enjoys all four seasons in the span of a single week. Kat's been consumed with words and language for thirty-some years and continues to spend entirely too much time overthinking anything that's ever been said to her (this is a joke, kind of, but not completely). Running is her number one coping mechanism followed closely by sitting in the sun with a good book. SSDGM and snuggle your pets, y'all.

# Across the Hall

## KAT JACKSON

BELLA
BOOKS
2021

Bella Books, Inc.
P.O. Box 10543
Tallahassee, FL 32302

Printed in the United States of America on acid-free paper.

First Bella Books Edition 2021

Editor: Alissa McGowan
Cover Designer: Kayla Mancuso

ISBN: 978-1-64247-228-8

## Acknowledgments

This book will forever remind me of the bizarre lifestyle changes brought forth by the 2020 pandemic, and I am eternally grateful for a job that had me stuck at home for months. An additional thank you to everyone who nudged me along this particular writing journey and was there with supportive cheers for word count reports. Cutting six years down to fifty-three days is a big win in my book (pun intended).

A major thank you to Sasso for being my hype girl and for all the heart reactions to my "you've got email" texts. You are one of the best people I know, and I'm so thankful for our firebox friendship.

I would be remiss if I didn't acknowledge my therapist for doing what she does best and kicking me out of my own head so I could stop thinking and just start writing.

## Dedication

For all of you who have tried to keep it casual...
...and failed.

# CHAPTER ONE

The sound of her thumping heart beat hard and fast in Caitlin's ears. Maybe a little too fast, she thought, and quickly checked her watch to make sure her heart rate wasn't edging toward explosion. 177. Fine. Not at the exploding threshold but still really freaking high. No wonder Caitlin wanted to keel over and unceremoniously die.

She grunted as her breath caught in her throat and wheezed out in an extremely sexy choke. This sucked. She hated running, absolutely hated it. But after gaining thirty pounds during The Divorce to End All Divorces, Caitlin had learned to tolerate the feeling of her feet pounding gravel and pavement. The physical payoff had been nice too, but it was the mental cleansing—the inability to think about anything other than whether or not her heart was going to up and quit—that kept her hooked.

Caitlin wiped the sweat from her brow and dug deeper into her stride. The only way out was to finish the lap because she, Caitlin Gregory, was not a quitter. Okay, that wasn't exactly true, but she didn't *like* quitting, and she had come too far on today's run to give up before hitting her final lap in five…four…three…two…

Just before one, just before her feet crossed over the line that indicated freedom from this physical hell, another body soared past her, kicking literal dust into Caitlin's face. And so it was that Caitlin finished her run—her longest run so far since starting this hellish exercise regimen—sputtering and choking on the debris of someone who just had to be faster than she was.

"So rude," Caitlin muttered, glaring at the other runner as she continued her fast trek on the decrepit track around the football field. Caitlin needed to find a new place to run, but she'd lost her running virginity here, hit all her goals here, and as much as the track sucked and was in desperate need of a total overhaul, she couldn't bring herself to leave the safety and familiarity of her old high school's shitty, gritty oval.

Caitlin reached the bench where her water bottle and keys were stashed and let her body collapse onto the aluminum surface. It was nearing eight p.m. and the sun was doing its delicate disappearing dance. Earlier in the summer, Caitlin had pushed herself to get up early and run before the heat and humidity struck her small town in New Jersey. Lately, though, she'd discovered the joy of evening running. There was something calming about driving one's body to dark, painful places while watching the sun calmly set in the background. It was a juxtaposition Caitlin found she enjoyed, even if it was somewhat masochistic.

The other runner on the track sprinted the final thirty feet before coming to a slow jog in front of Caitlin.

"You were totally checking me out," she said, barely out of breath, which did not endear her to Caitlin.

"That's disgusting," Caitlin replied as she tossed another water bottle at her best friend. "Don't ever say that again."

"Just admit it. You found it unbearably hot that I passed you right before you finished your lap."

"Hot? Seriously? I should have tripped you, sent you flying into the dirt. That was rude as fuck, Lina."

Lina grinned winningly. "You've always been a sore loser."

Caitlin glared at Lina as she stood and collected her things. She started walking away, not bothering to wait for Lina. "And you can't do anything without making it into a competition. Let's go."

Lina jogged after Caitlin and gently nudged her shoulder once she caught up to her. "You looked good out there, kid. New distance?"

It was impossible to stay mad at Lina. Twenty or so years of friendship taught you a lot about a person, and Caitlin would say with bitter honesty that even after having been married to someone else for four years, Lina was still the person who knew her best and vice versa. Of course, Lina and Caitlin's friendship wasn't always smooth sailing; they fought just like any other close friends and had infamously and unknowingly dated the same woman at the same time once, which hadn't ended well at all.

"Four miles. And I don't ever have to do that again."

Lina laughed and bumped into Caitlin again. "You don't have to but you probably will. I warned you about how addictive running is."

"I'm not addicted to the act, but I may be addicted to the payoff."

"And that payoff! Damn girl, you're looking…" Lina paused, the words not coming easily.

Caitlin snorted. "You can't even finish that sentence."

"No, I can! I'm just waiting for the right adjective to come to mind. Sexy? Hot? Gorgeous? Irresistible?"

"Stop. Please. Stop. We both know compliments don't come naturally for you." Caitlin smiled at Lina and patted her shoulder with just enough condescension. "So let's not stress you out."

Lina grumbled something incoherent—she couldn't argue the fact that she was truly terrible at complimenting people— as she and Caitlin walked onto their shared driveway. They'd ended up purchasing condos right next to each other in their hometown even though they'd both sworn in high school that they would *never* live another day in this place. And yet, here they were, both thirty-five years old, living less than a mile from their old high school. They weren't the only ones, either; Seabrooke had a large population of people who simply did not leave the town once they were able to, so Lina and Caitlin ran into their classmates more than either of them desired.

The condo development, at least, was quiet and mostly free of ghosts from high school. Lina had moved in first, after returning from her deployment to Afghanistan several years earlier. Caitlin had spent a lot of time at Lina's over the years, and while she hadn't planned on being Lina's exactly-next-door neighbor, when the condo next door went up for sale during her divorce, Caitlin had taken it as a clear sign that she needed to be as close to her best friend, her rock, as possible. This was proving to have its ups and downs… Especially the fact that the decks off their living rooms were connected, and the slatted wall between them offered very little privacy. In the five months that Caitlin had been living here, that slatted wall had made itself both an up and a down many times over.

Lina dropped her phone and keys in the driveway and began her elaborate stretching routine. She'd been in killer shape in high school, and her seventeen (and counting) years in the Army had only improved her physique. Even Caitlin, though it mildly repulsed her, could admire Lina's impressive muscles.

"So…are you nervous yet?"

Caitlin sighed as she perched on her front steps. She'd known this was going to come up, and she also knew Lina wouldn't let her dodge it.

"No. I'm not nervous. Nervous isn't the word for what I'm feeling."

"Cait, it's okay to be nervous. This is a pretty big change for you."

"It's not though, remember? I've taught high school English before."

"Yeah, and you hated it."

This conversation was like an old record that would not quit spinning: scratches, skips and all.

"I didn't hate the teaching aspect. I hated the environment I was teaching in." Caitlin paused for effect. "Big difference, Lina."

Lina finished her stretches and sat down next to Caitlin. It was annoying, her lack of sweat and how she looked like she'd just come back from grocery shopping, not the six miles she'd run. That effortlessness was part of Lina's whole look. Lina had, as she liked to say, "grown into her butchness" during her twenties. It was true; Caitlin remembered meeting Lina in high school and wondering how hard it must be for a fifteen-year-old to be so wildly uncomfortable in her own skin. Neither of them had been out in high school, and whereas Caitlin had several boyfriends and was generally clueless about her sexuality, Lina was very aware of how gay she was but didn't have the strength to act on it. They'd both blossomed in their twenties and Caitlin had watched Lina evolve: she'd cut her long hair into a faux-hawk, a lesbian rite of passage for many; gotten rid of her mainstream, I'm-only-wearing-this-to-fit-in clothing; and adopted a whole new style that was so butch and so hot—to every woman other than Caitlin, that is.

Even now, in her post-run state, her hair grown out to a shaggy asymmetrical cut with an undercut, in those perfectly fitting running shorts and that tight muscle tank, Lina was undeniably hot.

Caitlin saw it. She did. But it did absolutely nothing for her and she couldn't have been happier about that because Lina was her best friend, and she intended to keep it that way.

"Where'd you go?" Lina's voice crept into Caitlin's thoughts, reminding her that they were midconversation about the major transition coming up in Caitlin's life in, oh, a week.

"Just thinking about how lucky I am to have you."

"Christ, running makes you soft."

"Nah, I think it's the whole 'my entire life has been uprooted in the span of a year' situation that's making me extra thankful for you." Caitlin punched Lina's shoulder, which, thanks to Lina's push-up regimen, hurt Caitlin's knuckles and left no impact on Lina. "But I'm never saying anything like that again, so cherish this moment."

# CHAPTER TWO

Okay. Fine. Maybe Caitlin *was* nervous.

She stood in the quiet classroom and spun in a slow circle. So many desks. So many adolescents who would fill those chairs, slump over those desks, in just one week. There were lessons to plan, meetings to attend, faculty to meet. And soon there would be essays to grade.

*What in the actual fuck am I doing?*

Caitlin set the box of her teaching must-haves on the desk closest to the door. She knew what she was doing—in theory, anyway. She'd earned her bachelor's degree in secondary education. She'd taught for a couple of years at the rival high school in her hometown. There, she'd learned quickly that she hated the politics of teaching, but so many people, including her parents, told her over and over again that it wasn't like that everywhere. The school was the problem, not the profession. Caitlin muddled through a third year and took so many hits that she felt like she never had steady footing in her own classroom. And then, she'd had enough. So, she quit.

She quit for good reason, because Caitlin Gregory is not a quitter who quits recklessly. She quit because she felt like she was never going to be good enough and knew that she could not be the kind of teacher she wanted to be in that chaotic environment. Caitlin also realized in those three years that she had a unique ability to connect with adolescents; she wanted to build relationships with them, not so much deliver grades to them. When she expressed this to Lina, she offhandedly suggested Caitlin think about therapy. Caitlin, naturally, balked at this outlandish suggestion until Lina explained that maybe Caitlin should think about *becoming* a therapist.

It was a surprising leap, that was for sure. It wasn't something Caitlin had ever thought about previously, but once the idea settled into her head, it started to make sense. She researched counseling programs in the area and landed on one that sounded like a good fit. Her parents, thinking they'd finally emptied their nest with Caitlin's younger brother Miles off to college, faked cheery smiles as Caitlin moved back into her childhood bedroom. Three years later, Caitlin had her masters in counseling and found herself applying for an open position where she had completed her internship: Briarwood, a therapeutic school on the border of New Jersey and Pennsylvania.

It seemed like the perfect fit, and for a while it was. Caitlin loved the pace, the surprises, the constant need to stay on her toes and be ready for crises and successes alike. The kids were a lot to handle, but that's what had drawn Caitlin there in the first place: she liked the challenge of connecting with teenagers whom so many other people had given up on. The environment was high stress, for sure, but Caitlin threw herself into her job and thrived.

Seven years later, she burned out. Hard and fast, the fire that had burned so brightly blacked out into a puff of smoke. Caitlin was utterly depleted—and her failing marriage didn't help.

The last year Caitlin spent working at Briarwood was a daze. She vacillated between keeping the kids calm and keeping herself motivated while she watched her marriage take its last plaintive breaths. Even once the divorce was complete and

Caitlin was settled into her new condo, she couldn't muster the drive to put her all into her job. This time, older and a bit wiser, she looked for a new job before quitting. While it wasn't perfect and it certainly wasn't permanent, the long-term substitute position at Vanderbilt High School would tide Caitlin over for a year and give her time to reassess, again, where she wanted to go professionally.

What better time for a fresh career start than when you find yourself newly single after four years of blissfully challenging marriage?

Caitlin took a deep breath and moved through the classroom. She yanked on the cords to open the blinds and felt mildly better once the room was bathed in morning light. She could do this. She had to do this, yeah, but she *could* do this.

Piece of cake.

\* \* \*

"I can't do this," Caitlin moaned, her head in her hands, elbows on Lina's dining room table. "Why did you let me do this?"

Lina slid a freshly made gin and tonic across the table. Neither were big drinkers but both agreed that Lina had a natural talent for making perfect mixed drinks. Tonight, it was just the thing Caitlin needed to take the edge off.

"First off, I had no part in your decision to go back into teaching. And secondly, I happen to think you're an amazing teacher who is incredibly good at psyching herself out."

Caitlin grunted a response before taking a cooling sip of her drink. "Delicious. If I drink enough of these I won't have to go back tomorrow, right?"

"Can we pause the drama for a couple minutes? Cait, you're going to be fine. More than fine."

"I have completely forgotten what it's like to be an actual teacher. I didn't plan lessons at Briarwood. I didn't give tests or assign essays or even have, like, academic conversations."

"Of course you didn't. You were a therapist, not a teacher."

Caitlin chewed the inside of her cheek. It wasn't true but it wasn't false, either. She was labeled as Classroom Support Staff, which meant that she was the therapeutic presence in the room, but she was constantly in and out of classrooms—so much so that it felt like part of her *was* a teacher. Her position at Briarwood was centered around group therapy sessions as well as some individual sessions, but being in the classrooms so much pulled at her natural teaching instincts. For her last three years there, Caitlin was paired with a teacher who was completely checked out, and because Caitlin refused to see the kids flounder academically, she took on more teaching responsibilities than she was required to.

"I didn't expect to feel so much anxiety about going back into the classroom." Caitlin toyed with the straw in her drink as she watched Lina move around the kitchen. "I might totally suck at this, Lina."

"But you won't because you're you and you won't let yourself suck." Lina stared at her phone; her face took on a look that Caitlin didn't often see.

"Um, excuse me, what's happening over there?"

"I'm making you dinner because I'm your best friend in the entire world." Lina shoved her phone into her back pocket. "Have you gone blind?"

"Oh I see the dinner. But I also see the phone that you keep checking. Could it be that there's a lady who's finally grabbed your attention?"

Lina placed a full plate in front of Caitlin with a bit more force than was required. She leveled a steely glare at Caitlin as she sat down across from her. "It's work."

Caitlin knew, she *knew*, to drop the subject. They ate in silence for several minutes.

"I think you're lying," Caitlin said casually.

Lina's silence filled the room. Caitlin waited, mulling over her next attack.

"You know you can tell me about it, Lina." Caitlin held her breath. She knew she was treading in some dangerous waters, but she also knew that sometimes Lina needed a little pushing.

"Caitlin. Enough."

Caitlin nodded and returned her focus to the plate of food in front of her. Sometimes it drove her crazy that Lina refused to even go out on a single date with anyone, but other times it felt fantastic because Lina was truly always there for her. Caitlin wanted to see her best friend happily coupled with someone—she wanted double dates and vacations together—but she also knew the chances of that happening were incredibly slim. Of course, Caitlin mused, she wasn't currently throwing herself into the dating pool either.

"I have a work thing next weekend. One of those annoying formal things. Wanna go?"

Caitlin took the ice breaker and subject change in stride, knowing that Lina had already let go of her prying. "Of course I do. Are we going as friends or pretend looooovers?"

Lina rolled her eyes and pointed her fork at Caitlin, finally meeting her eyes. "Friends. The boys saw right through us last time. If you need rescuing from Sanders and McGinley, you'll have to make up a fake girlfriend."

"Oh good, I can work on my creativity. That'll help with lesson planning."

Lina laughed and shook her head. "You're planning on having your students write about fake partners? I don't recall doing that in eleventh grade English."

"I have a feeling," Caitlin said, leaning forward with a sparkle in her green eyes, "that I'm going to be shaking things up in Vanderbilt High School."

Lina raised her glass and they clinked then sipped. "I expect nothing less of you, Ms. Gregory."

# CHAPTER THREE

The Rachel Maddow poster had fallen off the wall. Again. Caitlin sighed heavily as she retaped the poster to the classroom wall for the third time. She was adamant about giving her classroom, albeit a temporary one, a sense of who she was as a teacher and as a regular human being. She'd hung up several literary posters for the classic teacher flair: *The Great Gatsby* and *The Scarlet Letter* to show she knew what she was teaching; *All The Bright Places*, *I'll Give You The Sun*, and *The Hate U Give* to show she was cool (but she also happened to love those books). Behind her desk was a black poster with the words "Decide what to be and go be it" on it, lyrics from one of Caitlin's favorite Avett Brothers songs.

And then there was the beloved Rachel Maddow poster from the READ celebrity line. This poster had been around since Caitlin's first public school teaching stint and bore tender rips and strained edges from that previous life. Appropriate damage, Caitlin thought. She tried hard not to recall those three years of teaching; it was weird even to her that she was now back in a high school classroom, about to embark on a year of teaching Honors and College Prep English to eleventh grade students. She knew, though, that Vanderbilt was worlds apart from River Valley High School. The stakes here, mostly for students but also for teachers, were much higher.

Certain that there was finally enough tape securing Rachel to the wall, Caitlin focused on the one thing she wanted to get done before the faculty meeting began at ten a.m.: assigning seats. The only way she would memorize anyone's name was if she meticulously organized these kids in seats—alphabetically and front to back.

One of the biggest pulls of this year-long gig at Vanderbilt was that it was in West Grove, a small and wealthy town thirty minutes away from Seabrooke. Caitlin was fairly certain she didn't know a single person who worked here, except for her department chair, Marcy Thomas, with whom she'd been in contact for a couple weeks. Seabrooke wasn't as small of a town as West Grove, but Caitlin hated running into shadows and demons from her past—especially her ex-wife, Becca Horne, who still lived in Seabrooke and knew everyone Caitlin knew. It might have been easier for Caitlin to move away after the divorce, which she'd strongly considered, but it hadn't been what she'd needed. Truthfully, Caitlin hated the idea of moving away and having people think that she couldn't cope with living in the same town as her ex-wife. So, she stuck it out and got stronger every day. And yet, Seabrooke remained full of memories. This little break, a thirty-minute drive to a town and a school full of strangers, was a nice change of pace and scenery for Caitlin, and she welcomed it happily.

"Knock knock!" an exuberant voice called from the doorway.

Caitlin looked up from her seating chart as Marcy Thomas entered. She was probably in her late forties and gave off the unmistakable air of a soccer mom—but the cool soccer mom, the one who had the best snacks and hosted the greatest sleepovers. Caitlin had liked Marcy instantly when she'd met her during the interview.

Now, Caitlin spread her arms out and spun, showcasing her hard decorating work. "Whatcha think?"

"Oh, Caitlin, I love it. You really brightened it up in here!" Marcy walked over to a bulletin board and nodded as she read over the essay writing tips Caitlin had posted. "I had a good feeling about you the moment you walked into that conference room. I think you're going to be a great addition to our team."

Caitlin blushed slightly as she ran her hands through her shoulder-length chestnut brown hair. Compliments from a department chair? Chalk that up under Things That Never Happened at River Valley.

"How are you feeling? Do you need help getting anything situated?"

Caitlin shook her head. "I think I have everything under control. I'm using most of Nicole's things; I made a couple changes to the syllabus but nothing major."

"Good, good. Nicole is super organized so that's a bonus for you! She also told me to tell you to go ahead and email her if you have any questions." Marcy poked at her phone, then flipped it around to show Caitlin a picture of a chubby baby. "Look at this little angel! Nicole's barely getting any sleep so she usually responds to emails and texts right away!"

The only thing Caitlin had learned so far about Nicole Donovan, the teacher whose place she was taking for the year, was that she felt passionately about teaching massive amounts of grammar and punctuation. Caitlin had audibly groaned when she'd gotten to that part of the syllabus and had no qualms about hitting delete several times.

"Oh wow, look at the time! We better head to the big welcome back meeting." Marcy gritted her teeth against her gigantic smile. "You know how these go."

Caitlin grabbed her bag and followed Marcy out the door. "Unfortunately, yes. I certainly do."

* * *

The band room was buzzing with conversation and laughter. As Caitlin followed Marcy into the large room, she was surprised at how small the Vanderbilt faculty was. Briarwood's staff had been small because of the nature of the school, but River Valley's faculty had topped 250. Here, there were barely a hundred teachers and counselors roaming the room.

Caitlin scanned the room reflexively, looking for familiar faces. She'd made it halfway through by the time she and Marcy sat down among the other English teachers, several of whom Caitlin had already met. They seemed like a nice enough group, but knowing this job was temporary didn't give Caitlin a lot of drive to make new friends. Again, Caitlin was surprised at how small the English department was: including herself it was just eleven people.

Marcy sighed. "Okay, which one of you is covering for her? Where's Valerie?"

Two women giggled while avoiding Marcy's stare. A guy who looked like he was straight out of college turned red and purposely looked in the opposite direction. An older man cleared his throat with a sly smile. No one was giving up Valerie, whoever that was.

A clapping from the front of the room saved the rest of the English department from being questioned about Valerie's whereabouts. Caitlin tried to focus on the welcome back lists and reminders but she couldn't stop scanning the room. This was Lina's fault; after she'd come back from her first deployment in Syria, Lina had struggled with being in crowded places. Caitlin had watched her scan over and over again, searching for any possible threat. When they were out together, Caitlin felt safer knowing that Lina was so attuned to everything going on around them. It wasn't until Caitlin got that handy degree in counseling that she'd realized Lina was showing signs of PTSD and suddenly, the constant scanning didn't seem so helpful anymore. Lina refused to go to therapy, and when she came back from her second deployment to Afghanistan, her PTSD symptomology had changed—among other things, she simply refused to be in large crowds of strangers. Caitlin had adopted the habit of scanning the room during Lina's overseas absence, and while she knew it didn't help Lina when she was struggling, she couldn't stop herself from doing it with or without Lina next to her.

And there it was: a familiar face. Bound to happen, right? Caitlin was both relieved and excited when she spotted Drew Garrison, a guy she'd met in her undergrad education program.

Movement at the front of the room took Caitlin's attention away from Drew. She made a mental note to track him down later. A couple teachers were setting up a Google Slides presentation while one of the assistant principals droned on about making timely parent contacts so that no one was ever surprised by a student's grade. Caitlin chuckled quietly; it really was the same no matter what school you walked into.

A commotion at the end of her row diverted Caitlin's attention yet again. A woman about her age was shuffling through crossed and extended legs as she made her way toward the empty seat next to Caitlin.

Marcy let out an exasperated noise and shook her head. "Never a dull moment with this one," she muttered.

The two women in front of Caitlin resumed their giggling as the new woman dropped into her seat.

"Good morning, my friends!" The woman shook out her long, curly, platinum blond hair and tossed a winning smile in Marcy's direction. "Sorry, boss, had a bit of car trouble."

"We're just glad you made it, Valerie." Marcy's tight smile gave away exactly how she felt about Valerie's lack of punctuality.

"You must be Nicole's sub," Valerie said, turning that smile to Caitlin. "I'm Valerie West. I'm sure everyone has told you wonderful things about me."

Caitlin did *not* want to start off the year by being the person who detracted attention from the speaker at the front of the room. However, she liked Valerie's energy immediately despite the fact that she was clearly the black sheep of the English department. Or actually, maybe that was *why* she liked her immediately.

"Caitlin," she said quietly by way of an introduction.

Valerie, clearly not suffering from the same need to fade into the background, rooted noisily through her bag and shifted around in her seat to say hello to someone behind her. While the same AP continued to drone and the teachers finalized their presentation preparation, Valerie made a scene of collecting her massive amount of unruly blond hair and piling it into a wild bun atop her head. Caitlin wanted to laugh but was too mortified by the attention being drawn near her.

"I'm going to turn it over to your colleagues now. They've prepared a short presentation on grading equity, which will be one of our central foci for this school year." The AP gestured toward the group of teachers—two women and two men, how equitable—as he moved away from the center of the room.

"Hey everyone," one of the men began.

"That's Mike Wilcox," Valerie stage-whispered to Caitlin. "Why you'd choose to become a teacher with that last name is beyond me."

Caitlin stifled a laugh. Yup. Valerie was her kind of people.

As Mike welcomed the staff and made terrible jokes about the end of summer vacation, Valerie continued to name the other teachers who were part of the presentation.

"Joe Donnelly is the head of the math department. Nice guy but weird in that math teacher way, you know? I don't think he's ever given a kid below a B-. Gross. Okay, and the woman with the short hair is Bethany Markel. She's fine. Like, boring fine, but nice. She teaches Chemistry and the kids really like her because she bakes for them every week." Valerie snorted. "I've had her cookies. Not that great. And that delightful human being on the end, the one looking like she wants to murder me with daggers thrust from her eyes, is Mallory Walker. Literally hates me. *Hates* me. And for no valid reason."

Caitlin stopped studying the weird way Bethany Markel's ankle-length pants stopped higher on her left leg than on her right and moved her eyes to Mallory Walker. Whoa. Yeah, wow, she was sending a death stare directly toward them. She hoped Valerie was right in thinking that the glare was meant for her, and not Caitlin. There was pure disdain shooting from Mallory's deep, dark eyes—so dark they looked black. Mallory's dark brown hair was pulled neatly and tightly off her tanned face. Even with a look of repulsion on her face, her attractive features stood out: a slightly angular jawline and full lips, downright luscious eyelashes beneath sculpted eyebrows. Caitlin scanned Mallory's body, taking in her perfectly fitting khakis and navy-blue Vanderbilt polo. *Cute*, Caitlin thought. *Very cute.*

As she moved her eyes up Mallory's body to her face once more, Caitlin's breath caught in her throat. No doubt about it, that cold stare was fixed on her now. Even from twenty feet away, Caitlin could feel the drop in temperature.

"See?" Valerie laughed and bumped against Caitlin. "Just breathe and she hates you. Welcome to the club."

Caitlin wasn't about to let Mallory win this glare-off. She could play this game; Caitlin may be nervous and dying to make a good impression, but she would never let herself be intimidated by a colleague. Much thanks to three years teaching at River Valley for that lesson. As she continued to hold Mallory's gaze, Caitlin shifted her expression into genuine warmth with a friendly smile. She watched as the tiniest bit of ice slowly slipped away. Then, before Caitlin could win the battle by fully melting that glacier with just one heated and determined smiling stare, Mallory's glare snapped away and she moved seamlessly into her part of the presentation.

*Gotta keep an eye on that one.*

# CHAPTER FOUR

"Tell me again what you're wearing?" Caitlin tapped her speaker to turn down the volume of the Fleetwood Mac station she was listening to on Spotify. "I don't want to clash like we did last time."

Lina's voice was muffled; Caitlin guessed she was in her closet as they chatted. "Um, so, about that…I have to wear my uniform."

Caitlin nearly spit out the sip of water she'd taken. "Wait, it's *that* kind of event? Lina!"

"I know, I know. I'm sorry I didn't tell you sooner. But you'll be fine—just wear, like, something simple and classic."

"Oh my God," Caitlin murmured as she stomped into her walk-in closet. Prior to moving, she'd coveted Lina's closet, and honestly, this gorgeous, massive closet in the master bedroom was one of the main reasons Caitlin had bought the condo. "Simple and classic. I should check your mom's closet for that."

"And by that you mean…"

"Simple and classic is code for boring, Lina."

"Maybe it is in your twisted little world of double meanings. Look. You know what my uniform looks like. The fancy blue one."

"Ah yes, the fancy blue one. Such technical terminology, Sergeant Ragelis."

"Fuck off. Stop harassing me and get ready. I'll meet you outside in twenty minutes."

Caitlin tossed her phone onto a pile of sweatshirts and looked around her closet. She had a lot of options, but nothing was screaming "Pick me!" Caitlin prided herself on having so much clothing that she could select an outfit within five minutes for any occasion. Army events with Lina were different, though; her outfit had to be classy, dignified, and impressive—and usually she was only able to hit two of those marks.

As Caitlin flipped through her dresses, a soft ball of fur wound its way through her legs. Pepper to the rescue.

"Hey, spicy girl. Why don't you paw at the dress I should wear? Make yourself helpful for once?"

Pepper purred in response, but instead of pawing a dress, she flopped onto her back and made biscuits in the air. Caitlin immediately knelt on the carpet and rubbed Pepper's large belly, cooing to her about what a good, beautiful girl she was. Caitlin had adopted Pepper during the final hellish year of her marriage, and Pepper had made it very clear that she did not like Becca by hiding and hissing whenever Becca was home. Moving into the condo had been transformative for Pepper, and she'd turned out to be the kind of cat who loved to eat her happy feelings and do little more than roll around in sun rays on the floor. She was perfect.

"I'd rather stay here and pet you, you gorgeous little creature, but alas, our girl Lina needs some arm candy tonight and mama has to get ready."

Pepper continued happily rolling around the floor of the closet while Caitlin grabbed a predictably simple and classy black dress and pulled it on. She was all for supporting her best friend at these formal events but she wished she could add a little more excitement to her outfit—like that distressed jean jacket winking at her from the corner.

\* \* \*

"Ditch the jacket."

There was no use in arguing; Caitlin knew she wouldn't win. She shrugged out of the jacket, tossed it into the backseat, and gave Lina an overly bright grin along with a little shimmy.

Lina's face was creased with nerves. She repeatedly ran her hands over her dress blues and walked at a clip that Caitlin struggled with in her heels.

"Dude, slow down. We don't have to race for the best table."

But Lina didn't slow down. She looked over her shoulder at Caitlin and gestured for her to speed up. Typical.

Caitlin managed to get in stride with Lina by the time they entered the Colton County Event Center. Neither woman was a stranger to this building, as it was the only event center anyone in Seabrooke used for events: wedding receptions, anniversary parties, awards ceremonies, even a funeral reception here and there. The center had several different rooms—some, much to Caitlin's amusement, were themed—so it was easy to make any kind of formal event fit.

Tonight they headed to the ballroom. This was the largest and fanciest room, but sadly it was not themed.

"Can I get a head's up as to what I'm walking into?" Caitlin asked as they approached the entrance to the ballroom.

"A bunch of Army people and their spouses," Lina said drily.

"Yes, thank you so much, super helpful. Now tell me what kind of event this is before I walk back to your car and put that jacket on."

Lina took a deep breath. She still looked nervous, and when Lina got like this, there was nothing Caitlin could do to calm her down. "A retirement."

"Holy shit. Lina Ragelis, did you finally throw the towel in?"

"No, of course not." She yanked open the door and ushered Caitlin inside. "Lieutenant Barrows."

Caitlin couldn't help it. She gasped out loud, but thankfully it was lost in the noise of the ballroom. Now was not the time to address the bomb Lina had just dropped, but damn if she wasn't going to hear about it later. Caitlin slapped on her best smile and prepared herself to play the role of doting best friend.

After two hours of military schmoozing and nibbling at surprisingly tasty hors d'oeuvres, Caitlin grabbed another glass of white wine from the bar and sat down at a nearby table. The bites of food weren't cutting it; Lina hadn't properly informed her about several things, apparently, but the biggest issue right then was that there would be no dinner served, and Caitlin couldn't keep hoarding the mini quiches. She'd make Lina stop at Steak 'n Shake on the way home; it was the least Lina could do.

While sipping her wine, Caitlin looked around the room. Army events never failed to amaze her: all these uniformed people who willingly put their lives on the line had a funny way of letting loose. As she glanced around, Caitlin's eyes found Lina. And then they found Lieutenant Barrows, who happened to be standing in front of Lina, talking with her quite intensely. Caitlin's best friend alarm sounded loudly in her head. She muted it and observed the interaction between Lina and Barrows. It didn't look volatile. That was good. Oh. Oh no. Lina's face was turning that weird shade of purple it took on when she was biting back words she wanted to say but knew she couldn't. Now her shoulders were doing that funny twitching thing they did right before Lina—and Caitlin was already out of her seat, making her way across the room—lashed out.

"Lieutenant Barrows! I hear congratulations are in order!" Caitlin nudged herself right between the two women, not caring who saw or what they thought. Lina absolutely could not blow a gasket. Not now, not here.

Candice Barrows had a twisted look on her face, pain layered with sadness touched with anger. But she was a professional even in the moments preceding retirement. Her face sealed itself up into a mask of placidity as she offered Caitlin a tight smile. "Caitlin. Nice to see you again."

"Really a great party you've thrown here. Those snacks! Amazing." Caitlin didn't dare look at Lina but reached back and grabbed her forearm. "Unfortunately, we need to take our leave now. Lina promised she'd accompany me to my parents' dog's birthday party."

Deciding it was best to avoid giving Lina an opportunity to say anything at all, Caitlin waved at Barrows and dragged Lina away before either woman could interject or even say goodbye. Lina dutifully followed Caitlin even after she released her death grip on Lina's arm, and the two made their way silently to the car.

Caitlin gave Lina five minutes of sitting in silence in the parking lot before she announced, "I'm starving and I need a stiff drink. Take me somewhere."

Twenty minutes later, Caitlin, once again wearing her distressed denim jacket, took a satisfying sip of her vodka tonic with extra lime. She was eagerly anticipating the quesadilla she'd ordered and impatiently waiting for Lina to stop being mute. After watching that tense interaction between Lina and Barrows, Steak 'n Shake wasn't going to cut it. Lina had brought them to Porter's, a bar outside of Seabrooke. In typical Lina fashion, she'd yanked off her formal jacket and thrown on a hoodie before coming into the bar. It was a strange outfit, but once they were seated at a high top table in the corner, no one could see anything but the hoodie.

"I don't want to talk about it," Lina said firmly. She took a long sip of her IPA to punctuate her point.

"Fine. We can talk about how excited I am for the first day of school."

Lina stared at Caitlin, cartoonishly wide-eyed, before barking out a laugh. "You're not serious."

"About which part?"

"The being excited part. I don't believe you."

"Okay, maybe excited isn't the right word. But I don't know, I feel good about it. I'm comfortable with the material I'm teaching, and the school is small—there's only twelve people in my department, oh, and this girl Valerie is pretty cool. I think you'll like her. She seems like a loose cannon, but she was super helpful—she shared a ton of her stuff with me." Caitlin frowned. Lina was staring across the room and obviously not listening. "Anyway, I was thinking I'd show up naked on Monday, just to start the year off right."

Caitlin waited a couple beats. Lina was so focused on something that she hadn't even taken the naked bait. On one hand, Caitlin was happy to see Lina distracted from The Barrows Incident, but on the other hand, she didn't love that her best friend had dipped out while she was sharing her very important thoughts about starting school in two days.

A friendly punch to Lina's shoulder brought her back immediately. "Yeah, wow! Sounds like things are going to be great on Monday, Cait."

"Including the part where I'm showing up naked?"

Lina's expression shifted to disgust. "Please don't do that."

"I would never. But nice to know you weren't actually listening to me." Caitlin spun her glass around the table. Where was her damn quesadilla?

Lina suddenly got up and moved into the seat across from Caitlin, effectively blocking Caitlin's view of the front of the bar. Caitlin creased her forehead. She was confused—Lina always liked to have her back to a wall. Now she was totally exposed.

Caitlin opened her mouth to question Lina's move but couldn't get a word out before Lina started talking.

"I was thinking we should do some landscaping in our backyards next weekend. Definitely plant some mums because they look so good in the fall. And we should consider getting pavers to make that path you want from the deck to your garden. Great idea. Let's check out prices some night this week."

Lina was horrible at hiding things. Something was up, and that something had to be on the side of the room Caitlin could no longer see without awkwardly leaning. As she leaned to her right, Lina mirrored her action, still blabbering about their backyards. Caitlin quickly leaned to her left but Lina had cat-like reflexes and continued to block Caitlin's view. Fine. Caitlin moved like she was leaning to her right again and Lina followed, but Caitlin snapped back to her left before Lina, now pontificating about tulip bulbs, realized what was happening.

"Sit still!" Lina commanded, thumping her fist on the table for emphasis.

Too late. Caitlin saw her.

There, in the corner of the bar, nestled quite closely with a dark-haired woman, was Caitlin's ex-wife, Becca. Bile rose in Caitlin's throat. It was inevitable, this moment. But she still wasn't ready for it.

As Caitlin unabashedly stared, Lina intercepted their waitress and asked for their meals to go and for the check. Caitlin wanted to look away. There was no point in continuing to ogle Becca and her apparent new girlfriend, but Caitlin found herself unable to blink and move on. When Lina reached across the table and grabbed Caitlin's wrist, she looked away only because Lina's grip was so hard that she thought her circulation was cut off.

"Knock it off!" Caitlin yanked her hand away.

"Stop staring," Lina said. Her voice carried an authoritative tone that was usually reserved for soldiers under her command. "You don't want her to see you, do you?"

No. Definitely not.

But while Lina signed the check, Caitlin snuck another look, this time at the woman with Becca. There was something vaguely familiar about that dark hair and those strong yet feminine shoulders, but Caitlin couldn't place it. Probably some annoying person she'd gone to high school with.

Lina gestured toward the boxes of food. "Don't forget those. Are you good to go out the main entrance? We could leave through the back if that's easier for you."

The sincerity in Lina's voice softened Caitlin. She loved her best friend for many, many reasons, but it was Lina's protective nature that had sealed the deal on their friendship. Caitlin had a way of getting herself into situations that required some assistance in getting out, and Lina was always there for her with multiple exit plans.

"The front is fine," Caitlin said with a determined nod. Fuck Becca. Fuck Becca *and* her date. Caitlin was wearing a classy dress, and she would walk out of this bar like she owned the place.

"Lead the way," Lina said proudly.

# CHAPTER FIVE

The early morning jitters and rush to get out the door on time weren't things Caitlin missed from her old teaching days. It didn't help that she hadn't slept well the night before; her mind had raced for hours, digging up old teaching memories and sending Caitlin's nerves into a panic. She'd tried every deep breathing technique she'd taught her kids at Briarwood, but nothing had helped and she'd lain awake until almost two a.m.

Now, as Caitlin merged onto the highway that would take her directly to Vanderbilt, she worked through a variety of feelings: relief for having a shorter commute than the one to Briarwood, pure anxiety over meeting and proving herself to roughly seventy-five adolescents, slightly manic exhaustion from barely sleeping and the racing thoughts, and some anger for never having acquired the taste for coffee, which she imagined would be really helpful right about now.

"We can blame Becca for that one," Caitlin muttered. She turned up her music—a running playlist to get energized—and settled into the remainder of her thirty-minute drive.

Caitlin didn't want to belabor the whole Becca situation, but it still bothered her how things had gone down in their relationship. It had started well enough: they met through a mutual friend—one of Caitlin's coworkers at Briarwood—and hit it off, so they started dating. Simple and normal. Caitlin allowed herself to get caught up in the relationship; she hadn't wanted anything serious at the time because of her devotion to her job, but Becca presented herself as easy-going and they had good chemistry. Caitlin threw caution to the wind and they moved in together after just two months of dating. At the time, Becca didn't live in Seabrooke, and her apartment was closer to Briarwood than Caitlin's parents' house, where she was unfortunately still living, so it made rational sense for them to shack up so quickly. At least that's what Caitlin told herself... and Lina...and her parents.

Fast forward to a year later when Becca proposed. Caitlin was surprised but happy. They hadn't talked much about marriage, but all of Becca's friends were either married or engaged, and Caitlin knew Becca wanted to be a part of that. Saying yes wasn't a hesitation or a struggle. Their relationship was fine—they got along, they had some similar interests, it was comfortable. They didn't argue much, and when they did, it seemed to blow over like nothing had happened. Having had a couple not-so-easy relationships prior to this one, Caitlin felt the complacency and predictability was a good thing.

Maybe it was Becca's strict adherence to no caffeine in her or around her. Maybe it was the wedding (which in planning and execution had been a study of What Else Can Go Wrong?). Maybe it was buying a house in Seabrooke. Maybe it was that the house they bought was a fixer-upper and neither woman was especially handy or motivated to do renovations. Maybe, just maybe, it was that the comfort and complacency Caitlin had felt throughout the first three years of their relationship wasn't as valid as she'd thought it was...nor was it the recipe for a lasting marriage.

Whatever the case, something went terribly wrong in the shadows of their relationship and Caitlin, wrapped up in her job and comfortable with complacency at home, didn't see it coming and barely noticed its arrival. Becca, however, welcomed the sudden downfall with open arms. It was her time to shine, and it seemed to Caitlin that Becca became a controlling, manipulative, irate wife overnight. Caitlin could do nothing right. She spent the last two years of their marriage trying and failing to please Becca. She planned trips and surprised Becca with spontaneous dates and gifts. She cancelled plans with Lina in order to stay home with Becca, only for Becca to change her mind at the last minute and go out with her friends. The cruel and accusatory side of Becca was new to Caitlin. She blamed Caitlin for being more involved in her work than in their relationship; she claimed Caitlin was in love with Lina; she accused Caitlin of being too attached to her family and relying on them for too much. Caitlin couldn't even unload the dishwasher without getting a snide comment about putting a spoon away incorrectly. It was impossible to pull Becca out of the darkness and anger she had toward Caitlin; it took Caitlin far too long to see that Becca already had a foot out of the marriage. By the time she realized that, she was signing the divorce papers.

Caitlin clenched her jaw as she pulled into Vanderbilt's faculty parking lot. The memories of her failed marriage brought her no solace, no happiness, no lingering what-if sensation. She had regrets, as many as likely any divorced person would have, but she also had a bitterness toward Becca that she couldn't shake. It was difficult not being able to pinpoint an exact moment or event that had caused the marriage to end, especially when Caitlin had tried so hard to keep them together. As Lina repeatedly told her, she and Becca simply were not meant to be, and Caitlin had to accept that.

* * *

Homeroom, something new to Caitlin's teaching repertoire, was a whirlwind. Twenty lively, summer-tanned bodies squirmed in their seats while Caitlin dispersed handouts and information. To their credit, the kids actually seemed to be listening, which was a far cry from Caitlin's experiences during her first teaching stint at River Valley. One girl was actually *taking notes*. And not a single cell phone was seen during the twelve minutes Caitlin spent being an information factory. She was starting to see just how different things here at Vanderbilt would be.

At the bell, which was a soothing set of chimes and not the ear-grating buzzing that Caitlin was used to, the students rose and quietly left the room. Caitlin stood for a moment taking in the calm atmosphere. Honeymoon period, she reminded herself. Give them a couple weeks and they'd be so talkative she wouldn't be able to hear herself think.

Caitlin wandered out of her classroom and stood by the doorway. Even in the hallway these kids were calm—sure, there were some banging lockers and a few enthusiastically loud greetings, but Vanderbilt's halls lacked the chaos that Caitlin had known at River Valley. They also lacked the strict enforcement of "acceptable pathways" that Briarwood relied on to keep kids safe and accounted for. This was a whole new environment and Caitlin was into it.

The open classroom door across the hall caught her attention. She wandered over and peeked inside, dually impressed and mortified by the military-precise organization of the room. Everything was neat and aligned; granted, school had been in session for only twenty minutes, so the teenagers hadn't had enough time to destroy anything yet. Caitlin took a tentative step inside the room. She was truly intrigued by the orderliness of this classroom.

The organization wasn't the only attention-grabbing facet of the room. As Caitlin's glance moved to the back of the classroom, her eyes settled on the most exquisite ass she had ever seen.

"My God," she mumbled, stepping fully into the room to admire this piece of art.

A woman was bent over in front of a filing cabinet, clearly looking for something in the bottom drawer. Caitlin would have offered to help, but she was too busy ogling the round, tight butt in a pair of made-for-her-body black dress pants. It really was impressive—both the ass and the organization of the room.

"Hey, I found the Scantron for the Civil War test." A man's voice in the doorway bumped Caitlin out of her reverie and into the awkward realization that she was standing, uninvited, in someone else's classroom.

The woman at the filing cabinet straightened up and turned around. Oh, shit. Not just anyone else's classroom: Mallory Walker's classroom. Caitlin recognized those icy features immediately, and they didn't melt a bit when Mallory looked at her.

"Thanks, Jeff."

Jeff took this as a dismissal and left without another word.

Caitlin cleared her throat, ready to introduce herself and apologize for showing up awkwardly and silently.

"I'm sorry, who are you?"

*Well she doesn't waste any time.*

"I'm Caitlin. Gregory. I'm, uh," she pointed toward the classroom door that Mallory couldn't see from her position, "Nicole Donovan's sub for the year."

Those dark eyes, more blue today than the black they'd radiated last week, held steady on Caitlin. Not a flicker of emotion rose out of Mallory.

"Right. Did you need something?"

Caitlin smiled. *Yes, I need you to turn around and bend over again so I can admire what is clearly your best feature.* She had a feeling that response would fall flat or Mallory would accuse her of sexual harassment.

"Oh, no. I was in the hall and noticed how organized your classroom is. Just wanted a closer look. It's impressive."

"Thanks."

Caitlin nodded slowly. Okay, this woman was a little more reserved than she'd anticipated. "Great! Good talk."

Finally: an emotion. Unfortunately for Caitlin, it was one of annoyance. It passed over Mallory's face quickly, and Caitlin wondered if maybe she was trying not to be as rude as Valerie had implied she was.

"Nice meeting you," Mallory finally said before turning her back to Caitlin. "You know where the door is."

A surprised and genuinely amused laugh burst from Caitlin's mouth. Mallory whipped around, a blush moving its way up her cheeks.

Caitlin, still laughing, held up a hand. "I'm sorry. You caught me off guard. That was pretty rude."

A fierce gleam shone deep and dark in Mallory's eyes. Coupled with her flushed cheeks, Mallory looked both angry and embarrassed, and Caitlin knew from Becca that this was a terrible combination of emotions. Now was not the time to be blunt or try to make nice.

"The door," Caitlin pointed and moved toward it. "Found it, using it. Have a great rest of your day, Mallory."

* * *

Three forty-five p.m. Caitlin groaned with happiness at the sight of her driveway. The first day of school could not have been longer, even with assemblies that took the place of two of her classes. Teenagers were *exhausting*; how had she managed to forget that?

Once she'd changed into shorts and a T-shirt, Caitlin grabbed a beer and collapsed onto a chair on her back porch.

"You're gonna break the chair if you keep falling into it like that."

"Jesus, Lina!" Caitlin sat up in alarm and glared through the slats to the neighboring porch. "A little warning next time, please."

"Excuse me, I was out here first. Maybe *you* should have given me warning that you were going to tornado yourself into your chair and disrupt my peaceful afternoon."

"Hmm, hold that thought." Caitlin yanked her phone out of her pocket. She felt Lina's curious stare on her. "Okay, looks like we need to hire a mason and they'll be able to build a nice brick wall between our porches."

Lina snorted. "Please. You'd knock that wall down in a week."

"Since you're out here disturbing what was supposed to be *my* peaceful decompression session, would you like to hear about my day?"

"I know you phrased that as a question, but you're not asking, are you?"

"Nope. Okay!" Caitlin launched into a retelling of her entire day, giving Lina far more information than she needed about students she barely knew. "There's this one kid in my first block class who's a dead ringer for your cousin Mark," she said to cap off her review.

"That poor kid."

"I know. Oh, and I sort of got caught checking out this history teacher's incredible ass."

At that, Lina jumped out of her chair and leaned around the slatted wall. "You did not."

Caitlin shrugged. "Guilty."

"Who caught you?"

"The owner of the amazing ass, naturally."

Lina threw her head back and laughed. "I knew you'd come around eventually. Like hell you're never dating again. Tell me more about this woman."

"Oh no. Absolutely not. I am not interested in dating, and I'm definitely not interested in dating her. She's uptight and rude."

"So she's your type."

Caitlin looked for something to throw. "Sounds more like your type, actually." She settled on a small pillow and chucked it at Lina, who deftly caught it.

"You know, you're eventually going to have to rejoin the world of dating, Cait. The solitary life doesn't work for you."

"Mmhmm, this coming from the woman who refuses to get involved with women except for when they're–"

"Don't go there." Lina shifted back behind the slatted wall and into her chair. "Tell me more about the woman with the phenomenal ass."

Caitlin exhaled forcefully. "I don't know, Lina. She's got this fortress around her. I don't even know if she's into women, but it doesn't matter because even after just one conversation, I can tell her walls are sky-high."

"She probably got burned in the past."

"Maybe. If she'd engage in an actual conversation with me, I could give you more information. I'm pretty sure she hates me, though, so don't hold your breath for updates."

"Doubtful on the hating front. She's got your attention, Cait. That means something."

Caitlin mulled that over. Though it had been in the works for a year, it had only been three months since her divorce became official. She wasn't in a rush to find someone to date, love, or marry. She shuddered at that thought: nope, marriage was so far off the table it wasn't even in the room.

"I know what you're thinking and no, it's not too soon."

"I genuinely hate that you can do that," Caitlin muttered. "And I'm not thinking, or saying, it's too soon. I know nothing about this woman other than she has a great ass and she's kind of hot in this dark, icy way."

"Like…a glacier in hell?"

"Why am I friends with you?" Caitlin shook her head and glared through the slats. She could see Lina was smiling and thoroughly enjoying herself.

"Because you'd be lost without me."

The thing was, she wasn't wrong about that.

# CHAPTER SIX

The sound of teenage voices filled the classroom, punctuated with flipping pages and fingers tapping on laptop keyboards. Four girls toward the back of the room were intently focused on their group's assignment, whereas a group of two girls and three boys at the front of the room was obviously not as focused. Caitlin overheard the words "party" and "so drunk" and quietly moved closer to that group.

Her proximity did the trick as the group members dropped their off-topic conversation and moved back to topical chatter about *The Crucible*. Caitlin turned toward the wall of windows before letting the smirk take over her face. These Vanderbilt students scared so easily—they were nothing like the unflappable and apathetic kids back at River Valley. Sure, there were a couple slackers in each of Caitlin's classes, but the overwhelming majority of students were producing great work and showed consistent respect toward their teachers. Here, Caitlin could use her Teacher Glare and it worked without a word. The best part, though, was that she rarely needed to whip out that refined and terrifying (it wasn't; she just liked to imagine it was) stare. Vanderbilt students actually seemed to *want* to learn.

That or they wanted the grade that came with learning. It was a toss-up.

"Okay everyone, let's hit pause so I can give you more background information." Caitlin waited till the room quieted and all twenty-three eleventh graders were focused on her. She yanked down the projector screen. "Quick review: how long had the Puritans been in the New World when the witchcraft hysteria began?"

Hailey McCoy, who had quickly made herself known as one of the stand-out students in the class, raised her hand. "About forty years, so, long enough for people to be settled and expanding."

"Great, Hailey, thank you. Forty years is a good chunk of time, right? Our Puritans weren't living in shacks and spending all their time defending their settlements. They had made cities, or villages—Salem being one of them—and they had created a religiously framed way of life."

Another hand shot up near the back. Grace Hernandez. "I still don't understand why everything is all about God in this unit."

Caitlin nodded and perched on the edge of an empty desk. "I know it seems weird because we're sitting here in a public school and we've been talking about God, God, God for three weeks now. But remember, the Puritans wanted religious reformation, so everything they're doing in the New World is going to be framed by that."

A movement outside the classroom door caught Caitlin's attention as she went on about the Puritans and religion. Mallory Walker stood outside the classroom, just barely in Caitlin's sightline. She was standing stock still and appeared to be listening to Caitlin's mini-lecture.

*Weird*, Caitlin thought, but she wasn't going to let Mallory distract her, not when she was in her teaching groove. She turned her attention back to her students.

"Now let's shift our historical lens to when Miller wrote the play. What was happening in America during that time?"

Several hands flew up, and Caitlin fielded answers about Joseph McCarthy and the Red Scare. Again, Caitlin was impressed by how much information they had retained from earlier in the week. When the responses started to die down, Caitlin pressed a key on her laptop and moved her presentation to the next slide.

"All excellent answers. Let's focus for a bit on Joseph McCarthy's political agenda." Caitlin launched into another mini-lecture as she pointed out the most salient factors of McCarthy's rise to infamy. "Keep in mind that not only did this guy start his rampage against supposed Communists in 1950, but he was also reelected to the Senate in 1952 and gained even more power."

Some of the students shook their heads and expressed disdain for this total asshole Joseph McCarthy. A couple kids had glazed-over expressions on their faces. Caitlin made a mental note to check in with them once she was done talking.

Grace raised her hand again. "I know McCarthy is behind the whole Red Scare thing…but isn't he also responsible for the Lavender Scare?"

Mumblings around the classroom. Caitlin felt a bead of sweat roll down her back. She had no problem talking about LGBTQ+ topics with students, and she was totally comfortable in her own gay skin, but being so new in a school like this… It felt like a risk to go there right now.

Caitlin cleared her throat to stall and get the rumblings to stop. She snuck a glance toward the hallway and noticed Mallory was still there, staring intently at the floor as she listened. Did she realize how obvious she was being? And didn't she have her own class to teach?

"McCarthy certainly played a role in the Lavender Scare, absolutely, Grace." Caitlin paused, wondering how far she should dig into this tenuous topic.

"He wasn't the one behind it," Hailey piped up. "Not really, I mean. Like, it was his accusations against members of the

LGBTQ+ community that got the ball rolling, but McCarthy didn't make the Lavender Scare a thing like he did with the Red Scare." Hailey ducked her head as though she'd just realized she'd taken over for her teacher. "Right, Ms. Gregory?"

"I couldn't have said it better myself. Thank you, Hailey. Okay! We have…" Caitlin checked the clock above the door and saw that Mallory was gone. "Forty-five minutes left in class." Caitlin rattled off more instructions for her students and watched them get back to work.

After third block released, Caitlin stood in the hallway outside her classroom and chatted with some of her students. This was her favorite part of the day: fourth block was her prep period, and it was the best way to slide into the end of the school day. As soon as that bell ending third block rang at twelve forty-eight, she felt all the stress of the day slip right off her shoulders.

Caitlin smiled to herself as her students departed. She'd been at Vanderbilt for almost four weeks, and while it wasn't seamless yet (was teaching *ever* seamless?), she felt comfortable and confident. That is, she felt confident until she looked across the hall and saw Mallory standing guard in her classroom doorway, openly eyeing Caitlin with a mystified look on her pretty face.

"Everything okay?" Caitlin asked as the hall emptied and Mallory continued to stare.

"Yes. Everything is fine."

"Cool. What's up with that look on your face, then?"

Mallory straightened up, which Caitlin didn't think possible since her posture always appeared to be ramrod straight, and crossed her arms across her chest. "I don't have a look on my face."

"Oh, but you do. You're looking at me like I've mortally offended you in some way."

The look slipped a bit. "You haven't." They stared at each other. Caitlin raised an eyebrow, waiting for Mallory to continue. "I, uh, didn't realize you knew so much about history."

Caitlin had no intention of making this easy for Mallory. She spun in a slow circle, pretending to look for information around her. "What gives you the idea I know about history?"

Mallory's face reddened. "I may have…overheard you teaching during second block."

"Wow. Was I that loud that you could hear me in your classroom? I'll have to tone it down. I'm sorry about that, Mallory."

"No, no. You weren't loud."

Caitlin leaned in closer to Mallory, kind of a hard thing to do with a hallway between them, but she was learning that this woman was a tough egg to crack and she didn't want to send her running. In fact, Caitlin thought, what she truly wanted was to get closer to Mallory—intellectually. And maybe physically. She wasn't sure about that quite yet.

"If I wasn't loud, then…"

"I stopped. Outside your room." Flustered was a good look on Mallory. "I'd just stepped out to grab…it's not important. Anyway, fine, yes, I stood outside your room and listened to you talk about McCarthy."

"Did I do okay?" Caitlin grinned, knowing she'd done perfectly fine.

Mallory cracked something that resembled half of a smile. "I was impressed."

"Impressed!" A smug but playful look took over Caitlin's face. "Go on, Ms. Walker."

"I was also surprised. I don't know any other English teachers who seem to know so much about something they're not required to teach."

"It may not be required but I've found that incorporating historical context helps develop the literature I teach. It gives necessary context that helps the kids better understand the material."

Mallory's eyes widened. She looked extra hot today in tailored navy pants and a simple white button-down that was tucked neatly into her pants. Her dark hair was pulled back and not a single strand escaped the low ponytail.

"Why do you look so shocked?" Caitlin asked.

"You're different than what I expected you'd be," Mallory stated plainly.

Caitlin liked that this woman spoke her mind—even if it was blunt. "You mean, I'm different from what you *assumed* I'd be, since I'm just a lame long-term sub?"

Mallory stuffed her hands in her pockets. "I don't know anything about you, Caitlin."

"Ah, but you do know my name." Caitlin turned to go back into her classroom. She had a feeling Mallory was going to ice up and bolt soon, and she wanted to have the upper hand by leaving first. "And that's a good enough start for me."

# CHAPTER SEVEN

A grunt sounded from Caitlin's left. She focused on a water stain on the wall in front of her and took a deeper exhale, trying like hell to ignore the sporadic grunts and groans next to her. Bending further into Warrior Two, Caitlin felt her hip muscles softly scream. It was a good scream, though—running made her muscles tight, and Caitlin didn't stretch as much as she should. This yoga workout was killing her and reviving her all at once.

Another throaty groan rose from the mat next to Caitlin. She risked a quick look to check on Valerie, who apparently was not enjoying this as much as Caitlin, even though it had been Valerie's coercing that had gotten her here.

Caitlin stifled a laugh, mostly because she didn't want to lose her balance. Valerie had given up on the warrior sequence and collapsed into Child's Pose on her bright pink yoga mat. The unfortunate sounds coming from her echoed throughout the small, warm room where one of the Vanderbilt gym teachers was leading a de-stressing yoga session.

Marcy, on Caitlin's right, was flowing through the poses like it was second nature. Caitlin hadn't expected Marcy to be so coordinated or flexible, but she was grateful that only one of her yoga friends was making a distracting array of sex noises.

"Now relax your body, one muscle at a time. Relax your neck, unclench your jaw. Come into Shavasana."

The gym teacher, whose name Caitlin could not remember, changed the energizing yoga music to a calm instrumental song to help ease everyone into a state of relaxation. Caitlin closed her eyes, allowing the music and her body's stillness to slow her racing heart. She inhaled deeply and did her best to be a yogi as she exhaled and envisioned her breath leaving her body as she emptied her mind of clutter. Thoughts continued to stubbornly bounce around her brain: she had to call her mom; it was trash night; there was a 5k she was thinking about signing up for and the deadline was approaching. Nope. The meditative yoga life was not for her.

Several minutes later, Namaste and all, the small group of staff began to chatter amongst themselves as they rolled up their mats and collected their belongings. Caitlin couldn't wait another second before confronting Valerie.

"That was the most interesting yoga session of my life," she remarked coolly. "I never knew someone could get so sexually inspired by the warrior sequence."

"That was nothing, Caitlin. You should hear what comes out of her when she's doing strength training," Marcy said.

Valerie grinned and shrugged as she not-so-gently hit Caitlin's leg with her rolled up mat. "What can I say? I get into my workouts."

Caitlin shook her head as she laughed. She hadn't expected Valerie and Marcy to be such good friends, especially given Marcy's reaction to Valerie coming late to the back to school faculty meeting. But the two of them, polar opposites as they were, had a bond that seemed like an older sister (Marcy) constantly trying to make her younger sister (obviously Valerie) more socially acceptable, but loving her in spite of all her faults. Caitlin was happy that they'd drawn her into their friendship; it made working at a new school much easier and more comfortable.

"So, Caitlin," Marcy began, "we haven't chatted lately. How's it going with the kids?"

"The kids are great. They're a far cry from what I remember at River Valley."

"Oh, I can imagine. My cousin's daughter teaches there and she tells the craziest stories!" Marcy shook her head. "It's unbelievable what she has to put up with."

"Teaching is not for the weak of heart," Valerie interjected. The three women left the room and began walking toward the exit closest to their cars. "How are the Puritans going?"

"Swimmingly. We're about finished with *The Crucible* and then I'm going to do a mini writing unit before starting The Age of Reason. Actually! I meant to tell you guys—I'm doing a unit collaboration with Mallory. We both have off fourth block so we're going to start meeting next week to plan out how to best incorporate the historical end with the literary end. I really think…" Caitlin trailed off, noticing the shocked looks on both Valerie and Marcy's faces. "What? What's wrong with you two?"

Valerie pressed her hand to her chest, then her mouth, as she started laughing hysterically. Marcy kept blinking as her mouth made weird shapes like a fish blowing bubbles. It looked like she was holding back laughter but Caitlin wasn't sure.

She crossed her arms, a difficult feat while holding a yoga mat and her school lanyard, keys and ID attached, with her messenger bag slung over her chest. "Out with it. What's your issue?"

Marcy recovered first; Valerie was turning an unusual shade of maroon through her laughter. "Nothing, honey. Nothing at all! It's just…Mallory! Wow. I didn't see that coming."

"Oh, I totally did," Valerie said, suddenly serious once more but still an alarming shade of magenta. "Caitlin's just the type who can handle that arrogant ass."

"Sure, she can be arrogant, but I'm still missing the point of your dramatic reactions."

"It's not you, Caitlin. Really. Mallory is…well, she's a tough cookie. Right, Valerie?" Marcy made a "help me" face that was so obvious Caitlin couldn't help but to chuckle.

"The toughest." Valerie nodded sincerely, then gave Caitlin a condescending but playful pat on the arm. "Mallory doesn't play well with others. It's well-known. We could list examples for you if you'd like."

Caitlin shook her head as she toed her yoga mat. "No thanks. I'll figure it out for myself."

"I think we're being too harsh, Valerie. Honey, Mallory is a good person. She *is*," Marcy reinforced as Valerie scoffed. "She just tends to keep to herself. I'm really surprised that she'd even want to collaborate with someone after what happened with Amy."

"Who's Amy?"

The two charming idiots in front of Caitlin stared at each other with comically wide eyes. Valerie pointed at Marcy, who shook her head vehemently. Marcy did something with her hands that looked like the sign of the cross gone horribly wrong. Valerie sighed loudly before turning to Caitlin.

"No one!" she exclaimed cheerily and motioned for everyone to move along.

"Marcy, tell me who Amy is." Caitlin knew the weaker link and had no issue with pressuring it till she got what she wanted.

"Oh…she's…well she was a teacher–"

"Enough!" Valerie yelled. "We are not gossip whores, Marcy Thomas!"

Marcy gasped. "We're not whores of any kind!"

"Eh, speak for yourself," Valerie said with a shrug. "Okay. Fine. I will tell you that Amy was a teacher here for a couple years. And I'll tell you that she and Mallory worked closely together. That's it. You'll have to ask Walker for the deets."

As Marcy pushed open the door, Caitlin—resolved to asking Mallory about this Amy thing instead of trying to pry information out of these two weirdos—patted the side of her messenger bag and groaned.

"I left my car keys in my desk drawer. You two go ahead."

"Are you mad at us?" Valerie asked, her bright blue eyes pleading and twinkling with mischief all at once.

"Infuriated, truly. I could not be more angry with you two strange humans."

"Good. Oh, I meant to tell you earlier—you should come to trivia tomorrow night! Drew and I need your brain, plus it's super fun."

"I have plans with my best friend, but maybe next time?"

Valerie pointed at Caitlin's chest as she backed out of the doorway. "Definitely next time."

Caitlin grinned as she trekked back to her classroom. She was lost in her thoughts, remembering the awkward and sweet moment when Mallory had approached her in the hallway and asked her to collaborate on a unit. It had seemed like Mallory was expecting to be turned down, and the way her face lit up when Caitlin excitedly agreed to work with her was priceless. It had, if Caitlin had to be honest, played repeatedly in her head since then. Something about seeing Mallory express a genuine emotion made Caitlin feel a stirring in her chest. The girl wasn't all icy darkness after all.

A familiar strain of music stopped Caitlin at the end of the hallway. Was that…"Shake it Off"? Caitlin hummed along as she walked the last stretch to her room at the end of the hall. One of the custodians was probably enjoying a Taylor Swift jam session while wiping down the whiteboards.

Or not. As Caitlin reached her door, she realized the music was coming, loudly, from Mallory's classroom. And it wasn't just Taylor's voice ranting about the players and haters. Oh, no. There was another female voice singing along, full volume: a little throaty, a little silly, and very sexy.

Caitlin crept toward Mallory's classroom door and slowly peeked inside. Sure enough, and surprisingly so, there was Mallory Walker: standing in the middle of the room, appearing to have been sorting copies on desks, belting out Taylor Swift while executing a full-blown coordinated dance routine. Caitlin was, as the kids say, *shook*.

She didn't want to interrupt this unbridled moment. Mallory looked so free and happy—*and* the woman could sing. The dancing was not exactly as great as the singing, but Caitlin could look past that. She stood silently in the doorway watching this arrogant, uptight woman completely lose her mind to Taylor Swift. It was breathtaking. No, Caitlin realized. *Mallory* was breathtaking. Wait. When had that happened?

Caitlin took a quick step backward to have a silent *what the fuck* moment but unfortunately, she didn't remember the recycling bin immediately behind her. She gasped and flung her arms out in a lame attempt to grab onto something, but there was nothing to break her beautifully uncoordinated fall over the recycling bin and onto the hallway floor. She splayed out, her classroom keys went flying, and her yoga mat gave her a nice jab in the ribs.

"Mother FUCKER," Caitlin yelled. Then she went still. The music had stopped. "Oh no. No no no no no." She scrambled to get to her feet, but her messenger bag was weighing her down and, in the most unathletic maneuver of her life, Caitlin pulled herself off the floor with her ass aimed directly at Mallory's door as she untangled her bag from her shoulders.

"Are you okay?"

Caitlin froze. "Yes. Absolutely. I'm great!"

"You look a bit stuck."

A couple wiggles and thrusts got the bag adjusted and Caitlin stood straight up before whirling around with a smile. "Nope! All good. I just–" She jerked her thumb down the hall. "Dropped my keys."

Mallory stepped into the hallway and looked toward the keys. She quirked an eyebrow at Caitlin. "Were you spying on me?"

"No! I wasn't. That's, yeah, that would be crazy. And I'm not. Crazy." Caitlin shut her eyes for a moment. Where was her cool, calm self? What was this woman doing to her? *Control yourself!* "You have a great voice, Walker."

To her credit, Mallory blushed the tiniest bit. "And you'd know that because you were spying on me."

"Not spying. I left my keys in my classroom."

Mallory pointed down the hall. "You mean those keys?"

"No, my car keys. I forgot to throw them in my bag before I went to yoga."

Caitlin watched as Mallory's eyes scanned her body, taking in the cropped leggings and slightly sweaty T-shirt. Her eyes lingered just long enough to give Caitlin a tumbling sensation in her belly. "You don't strike me as the yoga type."

"Well, as you once stated, you don't know anything about me," Caitlin said lightly, making sure she smiled with that gentle dig.

The corners of Mallory's mouth rose ever so slightly into something that was almost a smile. Caitlin pounced immediately. "I'm sorry, what is that? Are you smiling?"

"No. I flinched."

Caitlin cocked her head to the side and assessed Mallory. The tiny flinch-smile was gone. "Well, it was a pretty flinch. You should flinch more often."

Her mouth opened then closed immediately. Caitlin could almost see the wheels turning in that pretty head. "We'll start working on the unit on Monday," Mallory finally said.

"Monday it is."

Mallory turned away to return to her classroom and presumably Taylor Swift, and Caitlin wondered if another flinch-smile was working its way onto those gorgeous lips.

*What the actual fuck. Gorgeous lips?*

"Oh, and Caitlin? Don't compliment me."

Caitlin grinned at Mallory's retreating form. "Wouldn't dream of it, Walker."

# CHAPTER EIGHT

Ending the week with Lina was one of Caitlin's favorite ways to ring in the weekend. She was looking forward to having a relaxed Friday night with fried and greasy takeout and her best friend. Now that she had about a month at Vanderbilt under her belt, she was less stressed about planning and grading, but she wasn't fully adapted to her new routine yet. Running had fallen to the wayside as Caitlin struggled to get up early enough to get the miles in before work, and then came home from work feeling utterly exhausted. She'd snuck a couple two-mile jogs here and there, but this was the first day Caitlin was able to run a full three miles after work and it felt fantastic. Maybe she'd sign up for that Thanksgiving 5k after all.

Caitlin jogged slowly down her street before letting herself fall into a walk to cool down as she approached her driveway. Fall was coming in full swing in New Jersey and Caitlin was stoked about it. She was over summer—shouldn't all the heat and humidity and sunshiney beautiful days disappear as soon as school started? Some days it was downright cruel to gaze out her classroom windows and see the gorgeous day unfolding, out of reach and completely untouchable.

Lina's car wasn't in her driveway so out of curiosity, Caitlin peeked through the garage windows. Not there. Weird. Caitlin checked her watch. They were supposed to order dinner in a half hour. It wasn't like Lina to be late, nor was it like her not to communicate about it if she was running late.

Caitlin shook it off and went inside, figuring Lina would call or text when she could. She did sometimes get stuck at work. But when Caitlin got out of the shower and threw on sweatpants and a worn-in T-shirt, she checked her phone and saw that Lina was still MIA.

A call went unanswered, so Caitlin followed up with a text. While waiting for a response, she busied herself with cleaning up her bedroom. She'd developed a terrible habit of throwing her worn outfits onto an armchair in the corner of her room instead of simply putting dirty clothes in the hamper and hanging up the clothing that could go another wear or two before needing to be washed. This was a new habit; married life with Becca had demanded that Caitlin be impeccably neat all the time, in all areas of her life. Being on her own again gave Caitlin the unfortunate freedom of being a little sloppy.

By the time Caitlin had straightened up her room and moved a load of laundry from the washing machine to the dryer, an hour had passed. Still no word from Lina. Now Caitlin was getting worried. There was only one other time Lina had pulled this disappearing act and if that was the case again...suffice it to say that Caitlin was going to have words with her.

Finally, roughly three minutes before Caitlin was going to call the police to file a missing person report, Lina called.

"Where are you?"

"Well hello to you too."

"Lina, what the fuck? You were supposed to come over almost two hours ago! Are you even home?" Caitlin peered out at their connected driveways. Still empty.

"So...no. I'm not." There was muffled conversation in the background. "I'm really sorry and I swear I'll make it up to you, but I can't hang out tonight."

"Okay fine, but what's with the disappearing act?"

A long pause came from the other end of the phone. Lina didn't even need to respond; Caitlin knew immediately what was going on.

"Lina."

"It's not what you think."

"I think it is what I think, and you have a lot of explaining to do tomorrow." Caitlin sighed. She knew this story, and the ending never changed. "You better be home tomorrow."

"I will be. Promise. Don't miss me too much tonight."

"Wouldn't dream of it."

Caitlin dropped her head into her hands after she'd hung up. This wasn't going to end well—it never did—and she knew her role was to be the supportive friend. Lina was going to do what she wanted to do, and Caitlin would be there for her. For now, though, sitting at home alone on a Friday night didn't sound so enticing. Caitlin shot a quick text to Valerie, then went upstairs to change into jeans. She grabbed a hoodie on her way out of her room.

Her phone pinged with the name of the bar and a lot of excited emojis. Trivia night didn't know what was coming.

Ollie's, the one-step-above dive bar that Valerie and Drew frequented, was halfway between Caitlin's house and Vanderbilt. It was also crowded and loud, which Caitlin appreciated; she was ready to disappear into a crowd and simply have fun.

It didn't surprise her that Valerie was friends with Drew, the guy Caitlin knew from college. Drew had the looks of a totally average middle-aged man with a slightly receding hairline, which he was and had, but his personality was off the charts with dark humor and a level of sarcasm not recommended by the FDA. When Caitlin arrived, she found the two of them several drinks in at a high-top table not far from the booth where the trivia people were setting up.

Valerie cheered when she saw Caitlin approaching their table. "I knew you couldn't stay away!"

Caitlin accepted an exuberant high-five from Drew as she sat down. "I am prepared to get jolly at Ollie's."

Drew winced. "Someone's sense of humor hasn't evolved since college."

"Never! Gotta keep it real and lame, you know?"

"Speaking of lame…Drew, tell her what you wanted our team name to be."

Drew spread his hands open as if proffering an offering. "Two Queers and a Beer."

Caitlin glanced from Valerie, who was shaking her head with an exasperated eye roll, to Drew, who was grinning. "I know she's not queer. When did you hop the fence, Drew?"

"Oh, I'm not gay."

"He liked the rhyming," Valerie explained. "Like I said: lame."

"You two are the English teachers here," Drew said. "You're made of puns and wordplay. You have until I get back with drinks to come up with something better, or else Two Queers and a Beer it is."

Caitlin sat back and looked around the bar as she mentally scrolled through her always-ready list of puns. (Drew wasn't wrong about that.) By the time he returned, she had three options for them.

"Number one: Make America Gay Again. Number two: Victorious Secret. Number three: Save a Tree, Eat a Beaver."

"Three!" Drew and Valerie exclaimed together.

"I love having my beaver eaten," Valerie added with a contented sigh.

"Please don't ever say that again." Caitlin shuddered dramatically.

And so Save a Tree, Eat a Beaver excitedly entered the trivia contest. While they waited for the game to begin, Caitlin sipped a standard dive-bar vodka tonic and listened to Drew and Valerie gossip about work, adding her input when she knew the people being discussed. When their conversation moved toward drama from the past, Caitlin shifted her attention to the rest of the bar. Something was nagging at her and she had a feeling someone was… *Oh, wonderful.*

Yet another ex-wife sighting when Caitlin was at a place where she figured Becca wouldn't be. Caitlin was truly perplexed; Becca had *never* wanted to go out when they were together. Apparently some things *had* changed.

Yes, there was Becca, nestled into a booth with three other women. Caitlin could only see one of them clearly, and she didn't look familiar. She was cute though, and Caitlin wondered if Becca was dating her. As she continued openly staring at the group from across the room, the cute woman leaned into the woman next to her for a kiss. Well, there went that idea.

"Caitlin, focus. We need your brains." Valerie snapped her fingers in Caitlin's face. "Who are you checking out?"

"No one. I thought I saw someone I knew but it wasn't her."

Valerie started to say something but was drowned out by Jimmy, the trivia master, announcing the beginning of the event. As he moved through the list of team names, loud cheers could be heard bursting from each group. Save a Tree, Eat a Beaver got some decent laughs, maybe because Valerie got up and did a seductive hip shimmy at their introduction. Caitlin glanced over at Becca's table and found Becca staring directly at her. Well, so much for fading into the background.

"Bed Bath and Beyoncé!" More cheers, and since she was trapped in that unpleasant stare with Becca, Caitlin saw the woman sitting next to her lean forward and high-five the cute woman across the table as their team was introduced.

Caitlin's heart flipped over on itself. No way. *No way*.

"Holy shit, is that Walker?" Valerie exclaimed.

Caitlin whirled back around in her seat and put her back to Becca's table. She took a calm sip of her drink and managed not to chug it.

"Wild! I had no idea she had friends." Drew and Valerie dissolved into laughter. "I also figured she lived at school, so this sighting is truly unprecedented," Drew continued.

Caitlin fought the urge to jump to Mallory's defense, focusing instead on the ice cubes and near emptiness of her glass.

Valerie caught her silence and raised an eyebrow. "Don't be too hard on her, Drew. Our Caitlin here has fallen under Ms. Walker's spell."

Drew studied Caitlin. Before he could respond, Caitlin jumped in.

"I'm not under anyone's spell. But she's not as horrible as everyone makes her out to be." Caitlin cringed at her overly defensive tone.

Valerie and Drew exchanged a look.

"Oookaaayyy," Drew said slowly. Valerie must have kicked him under the table because he jumped up to get another round of drinks.

Caitlin risked another look over at the booth. She wasn't sure what she'd been expecting but she wasn't surprised to see Becca had snaked her arm around Mallory's shoulders and was pressing into her in a way that suggested they were definitely more than friends. Becca had also shifted her body so that her back was facing Caitlin. A mixture of relief and anger, touched with a whisper of another emotion, rose up inside of her. Valerie followed Caitlin's stare before gently knocking the table in front of her and bringing Caitlin back.

"You know I'm just messing with you, right?"

"Yeah. I just don't understand why everyone hates her so much."

Valerie looked over at Mallory again before responding. "She's a great teacher. I'll be the first to admit that, Caitlin. It's a personality issue: she's a cocky snob. Sometimes she's a flat-out bitch. Depends on the day."

"Has it ever occurred to you that what you perceive as arrogance or bitchiness is simply someone keeping to herself?"

"Honestly? No. But I don't want to tell you how to feel about her. You'll figure it out for yourself. And maybe you'll prove me wrong, who knows."

The two women fell into silence as Drew returned, bursting with a story about an incredibly drunk woman he'd encountered at the bar. While he rambled on, Valerie and Caitlin exchanged a smile, wordlessly agreeing to disagree about their perceptions of Mallory Walker.

\* \* \*

The smell of bacon roused Caitlin from her sleep. She rolled over and saw that it was almost nine a.m. Having gotten home close to two and being kept awake until almost four by her repetitive, rolling thoughts, Caitlin was feeling less than refreshed, but the bacon told her someone was downstairs with an apology.

Sure enough, when Caitlin walked into her living room, she found Lina reclined on the sofa, Pepper on her lap. Lina was giving Pepper a good head scratch and sweetly telling her how beautiful she was.

"Buttering up my cat so I'll forgive you for ditching me? Nice try, Sergeant Ragelis."

Lina put her face close to Pepper's. "That's right, my little spicy baby, your mean mommy is here. She's so rude to me. You should pee on her pillow."

"Pepper, don't you dare listen to your Aunt Lina." Caitlin peered into the oven: oh yeah, that was bacon. She inhaled deeply. "Is this Forgive Me Bacon?"

"The one and only," Lina said. She gently moved Pepper from her lap onto a sofa cushion and joined Caitlin in the kitchen. "It also comes with a side of I'm an Asshole Eggs and even some Don't Be Pissed at Me Toast."

Caitlin sat at the island and gathered her hair into a lopsided bun. "All of the above, please, and heavy on the bacon." She leaned her arms on the counter and rested her chin on her arms as she watched Lina move around the kitchen. Forgiveness Brunch was a rare but wonderful thing.

"Rough night?" Lina asked casually.

"No. I had a great night, actually. Just didn't sleep well."

"Because you missed me?"

"Don't say shit like that unless you're ready for me to twenty-question you, Lina."

Lina raised her hands in submission. "I'm sorry you didn't sleep well."

"Yeah, me too." She paused. "I saw Becca again."

"Saw her? As in you ran into her, or you deliberately met up with her?"

"Obviously it was an accident. You know I haven't spoken to her in months."

"Just making sure. So where was the scene of the crime this time?"

Caitlin filled Lina in on her evening at Ollie's and the shock of not only seeing Becca, but also the irritating reality of her arm around Mallory.

Lina slid a full plate of hot food in front of Caitlin before sitting down next to her with her own plate. "Mallory, huh."

"Mallory," Caitlin nodded.

They ate in silence for a while. Then, Lina piped up with "But did Save a Tree, Eat a Beaver win?"

"Third place."

"An admirable achievement." Lina clinked her fork with Caitlin's. "Did you know Mallory was gay?"

A piece of bacon lodged in Caitlin's throat. She flushed, unsure if it was from the near-miss of choking or the subject of Mallory's sexuality. "Not officially. She certainly hasn't said anything to me about it."

"All of your conversations have been about school, right?"

"Yeah. She's super closed off. Then again, we haven't exactly had an opportunity to talk about anything but school."

"Maybe this unit planning situation will open that door," Lina said.

"It might." Caitlin exhaled slowly. "It also doesn't matter, since she's clearly involved with Becca."

Lina began cleaning up—another beautiful part of Forgiveness Brunch. She shot Caitlin an are-you-serious look. "I don't know Mallory, obviously, and you don't truly know her yet either. But we both know Becca."

"I know what you're saying." Those personalities, at least in regard to what Caitlin knew about Mallory so far, were so not a match. But stranger things had happened in the lesbian dating world.

"Are you ready to admit that you're into her, Cait?"

"How can I be into someone that I barely know?"

"Don't be an idiot. You're attracted to her and you like her smart brain. The arrogance turns you on because you see it as a challenge. You're into her."

Caitlin glared at Lina. "Fine but we're not talking about this anymore."

"Message received."

"What we *do* need to talk about is where you were last night."

Lina's body went still for a moment. Then she started washing dishes with more gusto than was necessary, a weak attempt at creating noise so Caitlin would shut up.

"You can't avoid this conversation, Lina," Caitlin yelled above the noise.

"I absolutely can," Lina yelled back.

"Just admit you were with Barrows and I'll let it go."

Lina stopped clanging in the sink and turned to face Caitlin. Pepper wound her robust self through Lina's legs. "Yes."

Caitlin cocked her head to the side and fixed a stern look on her face. "That's it? 'Yes'?"

"You said you'd let it go if I admitted it, so I did. Now let it go."

"Lina…"

"I told you yesterday, it's not what you think." They stared each other down. Caitlin knew Lina would break; for as much as she'd always wanted to keep this situation to herself, she'd confided everything in Caitlin after the original shit show went down. Lina hadn't had a choice at that point. Even she had recognized she needed her best friend to help her wade through the mess of Lieutenant Candice Barrows.

"I was helping her move." With that, Lina turned around and thrust her hands back into the dishwater.

"Okay…"

"That's it, Caitlin. No more."

Naturally, Caitlin wanted more. This Lina-Candice situation was deeply problematic, but it was also a soap opera Caitlin could not get enough of.

"Li, you know I worry about you."

"And there's no need for that. What you should be worrying about is how you're going to steal Mallory away from Becca."

Caitlin pushed herself off her stool and bent down to pick up her purring feline. She nuzzled Pepper's grey and black fur. "There will be no stealing. I have all I need right here: my best friend acting like an asshole so I get Forgiveness Brunch, and my perfect chubby cat." Caitlin covered Pepper's head in loud smooches. "You know you're my beautiful chunky beast, right, Pepper?"

Pepper meowed loudly in response. Yeah, she knew.

# CHAPTER NINE

Caitlin was nervous. A stupid wasted emotion, really, but at the bell signaling the end of third block, she felt the anxious energy pulse through her body. Part of her was looking forward to sitting down with Mallory and getting some planning done, but another part of her was fixated on the Becca element and how that might play out in their interactions. Then again, Becca didn't know Caitlin was at Vanderbilt, so she would have no reason whatsoever to even mention Caitlin's name to Mallory.

Right. Because no lesbians ever talk about their exes when they start dating someone new.

Caitlin paused at her classroom door and took a moment to tell herself to chill out. Collaborating with Mallory wasn't a big deal; she'd had plenty of practice working closely with other teachers over the years, and why should this be any different? Because Mallory was arrogant? Because she was hot?

"You can handle arrogance, and you can certainly handle being around someone you're attracted to," Caitlin told herself. She smoothed the front of her half-tucked-in chambray button-down and glanced at her olive green high-waisted pants to check for wrinkles or pen stains. A quick glance at her reflection in the window showed that her hair was mostly tucked into a loose braid. All clear.

"Just don't make an ass out of yourself," she mumbled before closing the door behind her and walking across the hall to Mallory's open door.

*No Taylor Swift today*, she noted as she knocked gently on the doorframe. It was quiet and Mallory was focused intently on her laptop. She glanced over as Caitlin entered and gestured toward the desk in front of hers.

"Have a seat. I need to send an email, then I'm all yours."

Caitlin's body betrayed her and lit up at that statement. She had to get a handle on this weird little crush ASAP.

She cleared her throat and pulled out her planning binder along with her laptop, then set up a little makeshift workspace as she waited for Mallory to finish pounding on her laptop. The woman did not have a light touch, that much was for sure. That, or the email was fueling an angry beast inside her. Either way, Caitlin was concerned for Mallory's laptop. She watched in awe, waiting for a key to fly off.

"Okay, that's done." Mallory shifted in her chair and rested her hand on a thick pile of papers. "Where shall we start?"

"At the very beginning? A very good place to start?"

Mallory narrowed her eyes at Caitlin, who was grinning like a fool. "Did you…was that…"

"Sometimes I randomly quote musicals. Nervous habit."

"You're nervous?"

*Shit.* "No, I don't know why I said that. Mostly I just like musicals and quoting them out of context, no matter how I'm feeling." She cringed internally, not wanting Mallory to see her embarrassment.

*Well, Caitlin, so much for not making an ass out of yourself.*

Mallory nodded slowly. "I see. I guess we could, as you said, start at the very beginning of the Age of Enlightenment."

"Reason."

A quick but heavy sigh escaped from Mallory's lips. "Are you always like this?"

"Like what?"

"*This*. Quoting musicals instead of giving a straight answer, needing to use your own terminology for something that has multiple accepted titles, being smiley and cute like you don't have a single care in the world."

Caitlin watched as Mallory's face went white. If it weren't for that little slip of the tongue, Caitlin would have thought Mallory actually hated her—or, at the very least, didn't like her quirkiness.

She weighed her options before responding, taking her time, as Mallory had gone stone cold silent and wouldn't look Caitlin in the eye. She was practically squirming with discomfort. Caitlin didn't want her to retreat so she treaded carefully, avoiding what she really wanted to say.

"Unfortunately for you, yes. I am always like this. It's who I am." *Don't mention the cute part. Don't make her run.* Both the thought and the urge looped through Caitlin's head.

"That came out wrong."

"She speaks!" Caitlin smiled and reached out to pat Mallory's arm. "I know I'm weird, and honestly, I am nervous."

Mallory's sightline was still focused on Caitlin's binder, refusing to move to her face. "Why would you be nervous?"

"You're a little intimidating, Mallory Walker. I'm sure you hear that a lot," Caitlin added quickly, seeing the tension stripe across Mallory's face. "But I don't mean it in a negative way. It's more like…I want to impress you."

"You don't need to do that," Mallory said earnestly and finally met Caitlin's eyes. She then gasped out loud and pointed at Caitlin's face. "Your eye!"

Oh God. It had to be an eye booger. Caitlin swore she'd checked before she came over here, but she must have missed one. She swiped furiously at her eyes. Her fingers came back clean.

"Are they always like that?" Mallory continued, still pointing.

*Oh right.* How many times had Mallory looked at her by now? Apparently she wasn't very observant. Or maybe she'd never looked this closely until now.

"Yes. They are. It's called heterochromia. Sectoral heterochromia, to be exact." Caitlin gestured toward her right eye. "This one is perfectly green, whereas this one," she pointed to her left eye, "has that delightful brown splatter in its green ring."

"Wild," Mallory said softly. She continued to stare unabashedly, moving from one eye to the other.

"It's the only hetero thing about me," Caitlin added gleefully.

And there it was! The flinch-smile. "Was that a joke?"

"It was! Well, the kind of joke that's true but still funny."

"Isn't that the point of a joke?"

Caitlin pressed her hand to her heart. "She *does* understand humor," she whispered reverently.

"Anyway," Mallory said pointedly as she pushed a folder toward Caitlin. "We need to get started on this unit."

The two worked amicably, sharing ideas and identifying the most important elements of the time period in reference to both history and literature. Caitlin could see that Mallory was surprised when she rattled off a list of historical events from the eighteenth century that influenced some of the literature she taught. When Mallory suggested they create a multigenre final project that would have their two honors-level classes working together, Caitlin was the one surprised. It meant they'd be coteaching for a couple weeks. Their styles were so different, but if Mallory was willing to try it, Caitlin was game.

Caitlin was skimming through her notes on Thomas Paine—she'd just geeked out big time gushing to Mallory about how much she loved his work—when Mallory, from the back of the room at her filing cabinet, said, "So did you have fun on Friday night?"

Caitlin whipped around in her seat to find that Mallory had her back to her. *Convenient.* "I didn't realize that you saw me."

"You were hard to miss."

Warmth tentatively spread over Caitlin's cheeks. *Did she really just say that?*

Before Caitlin could come up with a witty response, Mallory continued, "I mean, Valerie's got the kind of presence that doesn't go unnoticed."

Right. Valerie. This wasn't about seeing Caitlin at all.

"You looked like you were having a good time." Caitlin threw that little dig out, curious to see if Mallory would mention Becca.

"It was all right."

"Your friends were less obnoxious than mine, of course," she continued, cautiously poking the bear.

"True."

Caitlin sighed. She didn't want to keep poking and push Mallory away, nor did she truly want to know about the context of her relationship with Becca, whatever it may be. And Mallory obviously wasn't interested in sharing anything about her life with Caitlin.

Glancing at the clock, Caitlin realized their prep period was almost over. "I think we got enough done for today," she said, starting to pack up her things.

"Caitlin?"

She jumped a bit. Mallory had crossed the room and was standing directly behind her. Caitlin turned and draped her arm across the back of her chair. "Yes?"

Mallory fidgeted, tucking an invisible strand of hair behind her ear. Again, Caitlin was struck by how pretty she was. Being this close allowed her to see the light dusting of freckles that spread across Mallory's nose and cheekbones. Her midnight blue eyes flickered to meet Caitlin's and the blue in them outshone the darker hues for the first time.

"I don't usually do this," Mallory said abruptly, gesturing to the space between them. Caitlin's heart skipped. "I mean, I don't usually work with people."

And then her heart deflated a bit. "You don't work with people, or people don't want to work with you?"

Mallory's eyes widened, then a genuine smile poked through her mask. "Wow, you really don't mince words, huh."

"No. I didn't mean for that to be harsh, but–"

"It's okay," Mallory said, resting her hand on Caitlin's forearm. They both looked down at the touch. Mallory yanked her hand back like she was a burning match and Caitlin was a can of hairspray. "I understand what you mean. And it's probably true."

"Well, for what it's worth, Walker, you don't scare me."

She quirked an eyebrow at Caitlin. "Is that so?"

"Truly. But what *does* scare me is not being prepared for this unit, so…same time, same place tomorrow?"

"It's a date. No. Not a date. It's a meeting. A planning meeting."

Caitlin was unable to hide her grin as she watched Mallory get extremely flustered and walk away to a safe distance. Seeing that Mallory actually did have real human feelings made Caitlin inordinately happy. This could only get better.

# CHAPTER TEN

*Better indeed*, Caitlin thought as she scrolled through her phone on Saturday. On Tuesday, Mallory had casually suggested they exchange phone numbers "in case we get any great ideas when we're not at school." Caitlin, the picture of coolness, had agreed and tapped her number into Mallory's phone, then sent herself a text from Mallory's number. She'd been tempted to open that text thread with Becca's name at the top, but seeing the simple "Hi" in Mallory's messaging app had been enough to remind Caitlin to mind her own business. She had, however, taken it as a good sign that Becca's last name wasn't included in the text. Maybe they weren't serious.

Caitlin shook her head and slipped her phone into her back pocket. She grabbed the neon orange frisbee on the grass in front of her and whistled loudly. Rigby, the family golden retriever, bounded over from the side yard and waited, panting, for Caitlin to lob the frisbee.

"You're still the only person who can get him to actually come. That dog is deaf to my whistles."

Shielding her eyes from the sun, Caitlin looked over at the deck where her father stood, elbows resting on the railing as he watched Rigby run after the fallen frisbee. Rigby wasn't the best frisbee player as far as catching went, but he had the retrieving part down pat.

"Maybe that's because he's tired of you shipping him off to Miles every time you and Mom go on vacation."

Paul Gregory laughed and shrugged. "Guilty. It's good to see you, kiddo."

"You too, Dad. But let's be real. I'm only here for the home-cooked meal."

"I figured. Your brother and his girlfriend should be here shortly. You want a drink?"

Caitlin took the slobbery frisbee from Rigby and tossed it to a different part of the large yard. "Did you say *girlfriend*? That can't be!"

"It is, so get your jokes out now. He seems to be serious about this one."

Caitlin snorted. Miles was not known for long term relationships; he was twenty-seven, eight years younger than Caitlin, and still existing like he had in college except for the part where he went to his job as a dental assistant instead of classes. After dating three-quarters of his classmates, he'd dated a handful of his patients, which Caitlin found utterly disgusting. Why in the world would anyone sleep with someone who had dug into their mouth with metal tools and floss? Gross. Then again, at least Miles knew the mouth he was kissing had been professionally cleaned recently.

"Please tell me it's not another girl he picked up after convincing her to try the peppermint-flavored fluoride."

Paul turned and looked inside the sliding doors before responding. "They're here. Be nice, Caitlin."

While her father went inside to greet Miles and his fluoride flavor of the week, Caitlin resumed throwing the frisbee for Rigby. He was bound to catch it eventually, she told herself, even though she knew this dog had never caught a frisbee in his four years of spoiled life.

A buzzing from her back pocket drew Caitlin's attention away from Rigby, who was sniffing the grass near the discarded frisbee. Mallory had texted. Caitlin ignored her body's burst of excitement.

*Hey. I emailed you some additional ideas for the final project. Let's try to finalize the options on Monday. Hope you're having a good weekend.*

There hadn't been many, but not a single text over the past week had been anything other than work talk. Caitlin so badly wanted to break through this woman's work-only texts, but she was trying to play by Mallory's rules. For a while longer, anyway. Becca's face appeared in Caitlin's head. Or forever, she supposed.

*Sounds good! I'm having dinner with my family tonight but I'll take a look tomorrow. What are you up to this weekend?*

Take that, Business Only Mallory. The response came much faster than Caitlin had expected.

*Not much. Enjoy.*

Those excited feelings bottomed out as soon as Caitlin read the text. She read back through the thread, searching for the bomb that had blown Mallory away. There was nothing, of course. Caitlin shoved her phone into her pocket and whistled for Rigby to come. No use in trying to navigate that dead-end conversation. She might as well go meet Miles's new lady friend.

"Mom, this is so good," Caitlin said before shoving more of the homemade steak sandwich into her mouth.

"Thanks, sweetheart. I remembered this is one of your favorites." Leslie Gregory smiled across the table at her daughter. The two looked uncannily similar except for the strands of gray lacing through her mom's dark brown hair, and of course her eyes were completely green. Leslie was glowing with a fresh tan from their recent trip to St. John. Retired life was treating Caitlin's parents very well.

"So, Miles, tell me where you and...Jenna, was it?" The young woman nodded. "Where did you two meet?" Caitlin wiggled her eyebrows at her younger brother, fully expecting this was yet another woman he'd picked up after picking the grime out of her otherwise perfect teeth.

"It's a funny story," Jenna began, gazing sweetly at Miles. "I had recently broken up with someone and I went out with some of my girlfriends. This guy started talking to us, buying us drinks, really working us." She laughed self-consciously. "It was kind of crazy. Anyway, he gave me his number and I called him the next day. I was at brunch with my friends and they made me do it. That's not normally something I'd do!"

Miles wrapped his arm around Jenna. "She's definitely not the type to take charge."

"So she's your type." Caitlin grinned and winked at Jenna.

"I guess I'm just old-fashioned. I wait for the guy to make the move."

"I think that's sweet, Jenna. Men need to be reminded to be chivalrous!" Leslie blew a kiss to her husband, who was focused on his dinner and oblivious to the tossed kiss.

"So Miles was the pushy guy at the bar? Sounds about right," Caitlin mused.

"Oh! No, he wasn't. That guy gave me a wrong number. Or a fake number, I guess. When I called, your brother answered. He was so confused!"

Miles grinned in that self-assured manner that he'd had since he a kid. "I had no idea what she was talking about, but she was so embarrassed and so sweet. I asked her if she'd like to meet me for coffee when she was done with brunch so I could apologize on behalf of that asshole from the bar. She agreed and here we are."

Leslie ooh-ed and ahh-ed over this darling meet-cute. Paul nodded approvingly at Miles, proud of his chivalry or whatever.

Caitlin folded her hands on her lap. "Seems like a unique beginning to what's sure to be a lasting relationship!"

A glare came from Miles. "It's not like you're an expert on lasting relationships, big sis."

"Miles," Leslie said, warning in her voice.

"It's fine, Mom. He's got a point."

Jenna looked questioningly between her boyfriend and Caitlin. "Are you two always like this?"

"We are!" Caitlin said happily. "He's still pissed at me for dressing him up like a girl when he was a toddler, so he gets his digs in wherever he can now that we're mature adults."

"My sister married someone we all hated and seemed shocked when she got divorced and we were all thrilled," Miles explained calmly as he helped himself to another steak sandwich.

Beads of sweat popped up under Caitlin's arms. "That was a bit too far, Miles."

"Kids, come on," Paul said soothingly. "We didn't hate Becca, honey."

"Not at all! She was…she was a really lovely young woman." Leslie's skin flushed pink, a telltale sign she was lying through her teeth.

It was no secret that Caitlin's family hadn't been Becca's biggest fans. They'd always been supportive of the relationship but in a reserved way. Leslie and Paul made it clear that Becca was always welcome at family events, but there was an underlying stiffness when they interacted with her. If Caitlin didn't know that her parents were completely accepting of her sexuality, she would have assumed that was the issue. But they'd never taken issue with any of her previous girlfriends. Becca stuck out like a wilting rose with all the thorns attached.

Caitlin looked directly at Jenna, doing her best to ignore her parents and brother as they bickered about Becca and which child was currently out of line with their dinnertime behaviors. "You know how sometimes you're with someone for a long time? And you stop seeing the things about them that are so obvious to other people?"

Jenna nodded slowly. "Sounds a lot like my last relationship. Once we broke up, all of my friends could not stop talking about how much they hated him." She shrugged. "I never saw it."

"Exactly." Caitlin took a cool sip of her iced tea. "No one at this table had the balls to tell me what I couldn't see, even when I told them I was marrying her. But the truth is—even if they had told me, I would have married her anyway."

"Because you had to see it for yourself." Jenna smiled. "And you did."

"Hence the divorce."

Jenna raised her glass to Caitlin and they clinked. "I know we just met and I barely know you, Caitlin, but I can already tell you're better off without her."

Caitlin yawned and stretched her arms over her head. It was nearing eleven and she had watched two episodes of *Mindhunter* after coming home from her parents' house. She knew she should go to bed, especially since she wanted to get four miles in the next morning. She'd told her mom about the Thanksgiving 5k she was considering and both Miles and Jenna had jumped at the chance to join her. Now that it was official, *and* her annoying little brother was doing it too, Caitlin was determined to kill her first 5k (and beat her brother in the process).

Just as she pressed play on the next episode, unable to hit pause on Holden's current drama with some very angry mothers of missing children, her phone buzzed. Probably Lina, or maybe Valerie was sending drunk texts from wherever she and Drew were out looking for love. Caitlin glanced at her phone and sat up straight.

Mallory? At this time of night?

*How was your family dinner?*

Caitlin stared at her phone. This was unexpected, to say the least. She had to tread carefully. After starting eight different responses, she pressed send with: *Good, good. I hope you had a good night.*

There. That was Mallory's rule, right? Respond and shut down. Caitlin pressed play to get back to *Mindhunter*, assuming there was nothing for Mallory to respond to, but–

*It was okay. I had to have a hard conversation with someone but I think it went well.*

Forget *Mindhunter*; Mallory was maybe sort of opening up! Caitlin resisted the urge to cheer.

*Yikes…that can be tough. Are you okay?* Caitlin hit send before she could overthink this slight pushing of the boundary that was so firm between them.

A couple minutes went by with no response. When five minutes turned to ten, Caitlin turned her focus back to Holden and the missing children. She had almost gotten fully absorbed back into the show when her phone buzzed again.

*I am. It's hard when you know what you're doing is right, but someone else can't see that yet. Thanks for asking. Goodnight, Caitlin.*

After responding immediately with *Night, Mallory*, she read the text over and over, searching for the context that was sitting right below the surface of the words. It sounded like a break-up reference, but Caitlin didn't want to assume that, especially since, well, *Becca*. Maybe it was a family issue; maybe Caitlin saying she was with her family allowed Mallory to make a connection and decide to send a vague text alluding to an issue with a family member… *Stop.*

She huffed and tossed her phone further down the sofa. Pepper jumped at the thud then nuzzled deeper into Caitlin's side. Mallory was an enticing mystery, but Caitlin paused her to turn her focus back to the more accessible mystery of Atlanta's missing children.

# CHAPTER ELEVEN

Caitlin hopped from foot to foot, trying to expel her nervous energy before the end of third block. Her students were working intently and didn't seem to need much from her, which under normal circumstances was a dream come true. Today, however, Caitlin needed the distraction of kids needing her attention.

Saturday night's communication had made Caitlin sense that Mallory needed someone to talk to. She'd taken a little risk and texted a simple check-in on Sunday morning. Mallory had responded right away and they'd gone back and forth a few times—no work talk, but nothing of incredible substance either. Caitlin still didn't know anything more about that difficult conversation Mallory had with someone, and perhaps it wasn't her business—were she and Mallory even friends? Caitlin thought so, but with Mallory Walker and her towering, icy walls, she couldn't be sure. *Oh God. She's Elsa.* Caitlin snorted at her private joke, hoping her students were too involved in their work to notice.

She glanced at the clock. In fifteen mere minutes, she would walk into Mallory's classroom and they'd wrap up their unit planning. They hadn't seen each other yet today, and Caitlin's nerves jangled at the thought of Mallory acting like nothing had changed between them. It was only eleven texts back and forth, but something in that exchange had shifted their relationship. While Caitlin felt and welcomed the shift, she wasn't sure what was happening on Mallory's end. In some ways, she felt like she never would know what was going on inside that pretty head.

"Ms. Gregory?" Grace's hand was waving in the air and the look on her face suggested she'd been trying to get Caitlin's attention for some time.

Yanking herself out of her Mallory reverie, Caitlin hustled to the back of the room to assist Grace and her partner with their task. They were stuck on creating an original thesis using the gender/feminist critical lens for *The Crucible*. Caitlin suggested they look closer at the contrast between Abigail's behavior and that of the older, married women in the play.

Once Grace and her partner were off and running with a new idea, Caitlin checked in with the other small groups. Her attention was snagged by a topical discussion taking place in Hailey's group. Hailey had chosen, as Caitlin noticed she often did, to work with a couple popular and predictably cocky, lazy male classmates. Not even two full months of school had passed but it was obvious to Caitlin that the boys picked Hailey because she did ninety percent of the work and they could coast through the remaining ten percent. Plus, Hailey was an extremely pretty, athletic young woman. The entire situation was so high school that Caitlin found it both funny and depressing.

Currently, the group was working with the psychoanalytic lens and two of the boys were only interested in pointing out phallic symbols within Miller's text. Hailey was visibly frustrated; Caitlin wondered why she didn't break free from these little jerks and find an equally nice and intelligent student to work with.

"We have to use Proctor's machete as an example. It's so phallic." This came from Brice Bradford, perhaps the most stereotypically privileged sixteen-year-old Caitlin had ever encountered.

"It's not a machete, dickhead. It's a scythe."

"Language," Caitlin said quietly but sternly from her place behind the offending speaker's chair.

Blaine Hughes whipped his head around. He didn't seem embarrassed, but he didn't meet Caitlin's eyes before he turned back around to slump lower in his seat.

"Inappropriate language aside, Blaine's right. John Proctor uses a scythe, but you'll have to come up with a strong and creative argument to claim it as a phallic symbol."

"I told you," Hailey scoffed. Her honey blond hair was hanging in her face, almost curtaining her away from the offending boys in her group.

Caitlin shot a look over at Devon Shire, the remaining, and silent, member of the group. He was a foot taller than most of the kids in the class, and in a school like Vanderbilt, his dark skin stuck out in the sea of mostly white students. Devon hung out with Blaine and Brice in class but didn't seem to actually like them. Hailey, on the other hand, was the subject of some speculation. She was the type of girl one would assume would date someone like Blaine or Brice, but rumor was she'd ditched her date—a Brice-type senior—at the doors and spent the rest of Homecoming dancing with Devon. Through the faculty gossip train, Caitlin was realizing, unfortunately, that Vanderbilt wasn't very progressive.

"It might be a good idea to read over your psychoanalytic notes. Phallic symbols aren't the only means for analysis," Caitlin pointed out.

Brice snickered. He avoided eye contact with Caitlin but made an obvious leering face at Blaine. Hailey looked extremely uncomfortable and busied herself with shuffling through her notes. Devon remained impassive, absently flipping pages of the text.

"Something wrong, Brice?" Caitlin felt the hairs on the back of her neck raising, readying for protection. She instantly regretted addressing Brice's rude snicker. Nothing good could come of that kind of noise coming out of a kid like that.

"What if we want to focus on phallic symbols?" he asked, so nonchalant in his tone.

"I'm not saying you can't involve them in your overall project, but I do recommend that you revisit your notes and look for other elements of the lens."

Brice mumbled something Caitlin didn't catch but Blaine did and started laughing. *Ignore it*, commanded the reasonable teacher's voice inside of Caitlin. *Walk away*.

Caitlin watched as Hailey took on a look of mortification. She looked up at Caitlin with apology in her eyes. Well, now Caitlin *had* to know what the little entitled asshole had said.

"Sorry, Brice, I didn't catch that," Caitlin said calmly.

He tapped his pencil against the desk. "Nothing."

"He said 'of course the lesbian doesn't want to talk about dick,'" Devon said, voice silver-cool, his placid gaze leveled directly at Brice.

"Fuck you!" Brice yelped. His face had turned nearly as red as the vibrant shade of his hair.

"Dude, what the fuck, Devon!" Blaine exclaimed.

"Okay, first of all, calm down with all the fucks." Caitlin paused. She willed her eyes not to widen as much as she felt they were expanding. She'd just said fuck. In a classroom. To students. While teaching.

Hailey, who had momentarily buried her face in her hands, peeked out at Caitlin. "Holy shit," she whispered.

The rest of the room had gone silent. Caitlin took a deep breath and closed her eyes. She had a couple options for how to proceed, but nothing felt right. Was it possible to press a button and eject all of these kids into another classroom filled with candy and puppies? Could she somehow eternal sunshine them real quick before the bell rang?

Nope. She had to face it. *All* of it.

"That wasn't very professional of me, and I'm sorry about that. I hope no one was offended by me using the word you," she looked pointedly at Brice and Blaine, "were using so freely. I know you hear it and say it all day long in these hallways, but you shouldn't hear it from a teacher."

"You're human," a voice said from the back of the room. A blessed voice. The voice of an angel, Grace Hernandez. Hailey smiled and nodded, having recovered from her shock and mortification.

"True." Caitlin shrugged and left Brice's group so she could sit on the stool in front of the classroom. "And–"

"And Brice is an asshole."

Caitlin waited for the collective gasp after this truthful bomb from Devon. None came. Instead, more smiles and nods, a couple laughs. Great, the entire class (rightfully) couldn't stand that little prick. But that little prick had feelings and a life—including parents—outside this classroom. Caitlin knew she'd have a parent email in her inbox within the next half hour if she didn't nip this in the bud.

"Devon, please stay after class." Before the class could begin whispering, Caitlin added "Blaine and Brice, you stay, too."

She opened her mouth, determined to address the lesbian comment but really not sure how to begin, but was cut off by chimes as the bell rang. How convenient. The kids scattered like ants and within moments only the three boys remained.

Caitlin glared at them, using her best adaptation of Angry but Compassionate Teacher. "Well, boys. We've got some talking to do."

Ten minutes later, Caitlin walked into Mallory's classroom. She was frustrated and annoyed, but pretty sure she'd gotten her point across to all three of those boys. They'd all apologized, much of their bravado gone without the audience of their classmates. Brice, however, held onto his arrogance like a shield. Caitlin was left feeling unsettled about him.

"Rough day?"

Caitlin dropped into the chair and looked up at Mallory. Her lingering irritation floated off into the poorly circulated air as she took in Mallory's striking beauty. Her short, dark hair was pulled back neatly into a ponytail, as always. Navy pants hugged her toned legs, topped off with a grey V-neck sweater. It was the most casual outfit Caitlin had seen Mallory in at work. She was adorably sexy.

Despite their interactions and growing friendship, Caitlin still wanted to impress Mallory. Like hell was she going to open up about what had just gone down in her classroom. "Nah, it's just Monday. You know how Mondays are," she rambled, pulling a folder out of her bag. "I'm ready for the day to be over."

The look on Mallory's face suggested she didn't believe a word that Caitlin had said, but she let it go. They dove back into planning their unit. Differences in teaching styles aside, they worked remarkably well together and had developed their unit much faster than either had anticipated. Now they were at the point of working out some kinks and adding final touches. Then, all that was left was to finalize the options for the final project.

"I liked the ideas you emailed over the weekend," Caitlin said as she finished adjusting the math on a rubric. "I'm all about giving them lots of options."

"I don't think we should give too many options. That could get overwhelming. Maybe four?"

"Six?"

Mallory shook her head, but Caitlin saw the edge of a flinch-smile on her lips. "Did you say six so we could compromise at five?"

"No…I actually want to use six options."

"Meaning you don't want to compromise? Interesting, Ms. Gregory."

A shiver went up Caitlin's spine. She bit her lip, liking Mallory's new flirty tone. "I'm all about compromise in some areas."

Mallory's eyes darkened as she leveled her gaze on Caitlin. Her eyes flickered down to Caitlin's bitten lower lip. "I think–"

A knock on the door crashed through their moment. They both turned their heads to identify the intruder. Grace Hernandez stood in the doorway, weighed down by an overloaded backpack. She waved awkwardly.

"Grace, hi, come on in." Mallory snapped back into teacher mode with impressive speed. Meanwhile, Caitlin felt the need to fan herself but tried her best to put on her game face as Grace approached.

"I'm sorry, I didn't mean to interrupt."

"No worries, Grace," Caitlin said with a smile. *Please don't mention what happened in class. Please don't say a word. For the love of God, please don't tell Mallory I said fuck in front of your entire class.*

"You said you would look over my National Honors Society application." Grace handed Mallory a thick folder. "I think I have everything in here."

"Sure looks like it. I'll check it out and have it ready for you tomorrow."

"Thank you so much, Ms. Walker. I really appreciate it. See you tomorrow." With a wave, Grace turned to leave. Caitlin took a relieved breath.

"Ms. Gregory?"

*Oh no.* Grace was lingering in the doorway, concern etched over her features. "Yes, Grace?"

"I, um, I just wanted to say I'm sorry for what happened in class. What he said was really stupid and out of line." She paused, her coffee-colored eyes nervously searching the room before they locked with Caitlin's. "I think it's cool that...you know. If you are. My aunt is and she's awesome and I always wanted a gay teacher because of how cool my aunt is, and wow I'm rambling so I'm gonna go. 'K bye!'"

Hurricane Grace left, and in her wake sat one shocked teacher and one curiously confused teacher with a side order of shock.

After a silence that spanned for far too long, Mallory cleared her throat. "So something *did* happen in third block."

A little piece of hope popped and deflated inside of Caitlin. Couldn't Mallory see that now was the time to do the friend thing, not the colleague thing?

"Yep. One of my darling students outed me." Caitlin sat up straighter in her chair. Fine. Colleagues could chat about these things.

"Oh. Oh, shit. Are you okay?"

Caitlin risked a look at Mallory. She was happily surprised to see that her colleague facade had dropped away. In fact, Mallory had never looked at Caitlin like this before. Gone was the icy protection; it was replaced by warmth and compassion.

The transition only made Mallory more beautiful, and Caitlin's heart pound even harder.

"I think so. I don't hide who I am but it's never fun to have a student try to use it against you."

"Who was it?" There was thunder in Mallory's voice, making it more of a command than a question.

"Mallory, it's not a big deal. I handled it."

"I want to know who it was."

"And I'm not going to tell you because I took care of it." Caitlin's voice went steely, pushing her point as far as she could. She didn't need Mallory to protect her from Brice Bradford. But she could admit she liked that Mallory wanted to protect her.

They held each other's gazes for several beats, neither backing down. Caitlin's emotions started stirring again at the flickers of fire dancing in Mallory's blue-black eyes. Her lashes were so thick and a small oval birthmark dotted the space between her eyelid and her eyebrow. Caitlin suppressed a rising urge to press her lips against that spot.

"I believe you," Mallory said quietly. She looked away from Caitlin, slicing right through the thickening tension. "Let's figure out these project options."

"Right," Caitlin breathed. "The project options."

# CHAPTER TWELVE

"Dress down Friday, I love you." Caitlin pulled on a new pair of jeans—thank you, post-divorce running—and admired herself in the mirror, giving her ass a quick slap. "Yeah, you look good. And she's gonna notice."

A Taylor Swift song came on the Pop Hits station and an image of Mallory came to Caitlin's mind. Today was the first day they were coteaching two of their classes and Caitlin was a mix of nervous and excited. Their personalities were so different, and Caitlin knew that their teaching styles reflected that. She wasn't sure how that would play out with both of them teaching in one room. Would they step on each other's toes? Or would their natural chemistry shine through? Their unit was solid and they both felt confident about it; the only catch was their ability to execute it to a group of more than forty students.

"Sorry Taylor, but we'll have to pick this up later." Caitlin paused the song and grabbed her phone before heading downstairs. Pepper trotted after her, serenading Caitlin with a beautiful chorus of "feed me now" meows. Caitlin obliged her, giving her a good head scratch after filling her bowl.

"Don't miss me too much, my voluptuous princess. Get some good naps today while mama works hard to keep a roof over your head and meat crackers in your bowl."

Pepper chomped noisily on her meat crackers, a fitting goodbye.

Strolling into Vanderbilt at seven a.m. was starting to feel like a routine Caitlin could get used to. The overall vibe of the school was more intense than other places she'd worked; the students were more focused on achievement but also more entitled, so it was a challenging mix. Regardless, Caitlin found that she liked the energy that coursed through the hallways. It kept her motivated, if a little anxious about her performance.

Caitlin poked her head into room 871, unsure of what she'd find. She was tempted to storm into the room with all the noise she could make but didn't feel like being that much of an asshole this early in the day.

"Good to see you're alive," she said a bit louder than her normal voice as she walked into the room. She placed a large coffee on the desk in front of Valerie, who looked like a mixture of death and elation.

"You're an angel." Valerie took a long sip of coffee. "I'm not entirely sure how I got here but, well, here we are. Ready to teach the youth of America!"

"Judging from your texts and the way they abruptly stopped after you sent, and I quote, 'OMG he has clean sheets on his bed,' I'm guessing you had a good night."

Valerie checked to make sure they were alone, then raised her hand for a high five. "Your girl got laid!"

"Please tell me it wasn't Drew."

"God, no. I don't fuck my friends." Valerie cocked her head to the side and appraised Caitlin. "Isn't that a lesbian thing? Fucking your friends?"

"It's way too early in the day to address that stereotype." Caitlin rapped her knuckles on the desk. "Speaking of lesbians, however…"

"Oh yes, go on. I love a good lesbian story."

Caitlin lowered her voice. "How the hell do I address being gay with these kids?"

Valerie nodded sagely. "Yes, you've come to the right place for this piece of advice." She paused, clearly for dramatic effect, and widened her eyes. "You don't."

"That doesn't work for me."

"Being open doesn't work for them."

Caitlin sighed. The Brice issue was weighing on her even though it was settled. She'd spoken with Marcy the day after it happened, and after giving her all the details, including the fuck-word moment, Marcy had simply said, "Well, these things happen." She'd assured Caitlin that she'd support her if anything came of it, but the week had crawled to Friday without any bigger issue presenting itself. For his part, Brice had been quieter in class and silently respectful toward Caitlin. Maybe her firm chat with him on Monday had done its work after all.

Hiding herself, though? Keeping herself tucked into the tightly organized closet here at Vanderbilt? That matter wasn't settled.

"I mean, we don't even have a GSA," Valerie said as an afterthought. "Don't get me wrong, I'm sure there are little gay kiddos walking these halls, but no one talks about it."

"Would that be a bigger scandal than a white girl dating a black boy?"

Valerie nodded slowly. "So you've reached the point where you realize Vanderbilt is actually a fictitious school set in 1950s Alabama."

"I gotta tell ya, I wasn't expecting this. And it makes me feel…dirty."

"I realize I'm possibly still a bit drunk, but you lost me there, teach."

Caitlin picked at a loose thread on the cuff of her Vanderbilt sweatshirt. "I've spent too much time living my life proudly to stuff myself back into the closet just to keep a bunch of teenagers happy. It feels wrong."

"You and I both know we're not talking about the kids, Caitlin. The kids aren't the problem."

"I know. Doesn't make it any easier to play the role of Closeted Teacher. Besides, I've been outed." Caitlin stood up from where she'd been perched on the corner of Valerie's messy desk. "What's that saying? The only way out is in?"

"Uh, no. Don't you teach English? That's fucking Frost, dude, and it's 'the best way out is always through.'"

"Mmm, yeah, I was never a fan of Frost." Caitlin paused and turned from the doorway to look back at Valerie. "So if I'm outed, now I go through? What the fuck does that even mean?"

"Honestly, how did you even graduate from college? Get out of here."

* * *

The classroom buzzed with a new energy—the kind that came from two classes of Honors students being smashed together into one room. Because of Vanderbilt's teaming of Honors and AP classes, Mallory and Caitlin shared the same Honors students. Mallory's block two class was Caitlin's block three class, and vice versa. Combined, the two women were facing forty-four students who were mostly thrilled to be in a room with friends who weren't usually in their classes.

Seeing Mallory in this position was new. The icy mask was up and in full force, but Caitlin noticed a nervous edge to her overall energy and posture. She'd overheard the students talking about Mallory's class every so often, and while they never said anything outright negative, Caitlin had gotten the clear vibe that Mallory wasn't exactly a favorite teacher around Vanderbilt. She was tough and she was strict. What she seemed to be missing was the human, compassionate element that Caitlin happened to have an abundance of.

Since they'd decided to meet in Mallory's room, Caitlin was waiting for Mallory to get the kids' attention. But Mallory seemed unusually flustered; she was rocking back and forth slightly on her heels, glancing rapidly around the room. The wheels were turning so fast in her brain that smoke was sure to puff from her ears any moment.

"Hey," Caitlin said, nudging Mallory. Mallory looked at her with pure anxiety shining in her eyes. "What's up? You good?"

"Of course. Yes." She took a deep breath. "It's a lot of kids."

"Yeah, but you know them all, remember? It's just two," Caitlin clapped her hands together, "smashed into one."

"I know. I guess I didn't think about how loud it would be."

That made sense—Mallory's classroom was typically very quiet, whereas Caitlin's cultivated a lot of noise. To each her own; neither was right, per se, but old school teachers demanded silence to ensure that students were paying attention and learning. Caitlin preferred a classroom filled with the sounds of students learning.

Realizing that Mallory was too flustered to get the attention of the room full of teenagers, Caitlin pressed her thumb and forefinger together before slipping them into her mouth. Out came one of her famous ear-piercing whistles. The room went instantly silent.

Out of the corner of her eye Caitlin saw Mallory gaping at her, but her whistling lesson would have to wait.

"Hey everyone! I know this is weird and new, having everyone together like this, but Ms. Walker and I are really excited to have this opportunity to work together with you all." Out of the corner of her eye, Caitlin noticed Mallory's posture changing, her confidence returning. "I know it's crowded in here now, but we won't always all be together like this, so don't stress about that. Today we're going to introduce you to the unit as well as most of the elements that we'll be using over the course of the unit."

"This unit is the Age of Enlightenment, also referred to as the Age of Reason." Mallory came to life, even throwing a small flinch-smile in Caitlin's direction. It was more flinch than smile, but Caitlin happily accepted it. "In Ms. Gregory's class, you've paved the way with the Puritans coming to America. Now, we'll watch as the New World expands. What happens when a population grows and a culture expands?"

Several hands popped up. Caitlin and Mallory exchanged a quick look as Caitlin turned on the projector and cued up the intro video. Caitlin felt the relief radiating off of Mallory as she addressed the students with raised hands.

Several minutes later, the class was mostly engaged with the intro video. Caitlin and Mallory stood at the back of the room, Mallory with her arms crossed tightly across her chest, Caitlin relaxed and leaning with one foot pressing against the wall.

"You need to calm down," Caitlin whispered, her tone playful.

"Are you recommending a Taylor Swift song, or telling me how to feel?"

"Yes."

Mallory smiled. And there it was: a genuine, full-face smile that lit up her entire damn beautiful face. That smile could melt a glacier. Caitlin's lips rose in response, completely out of her control.

"I've never done this before. I don't know how it comes so easily for you."

"It doesn't. Or it does, I don't know. I just do it."

"Yeah, well, you do it well."

"Why thank you, Ms. Walker. I appreciate you noticing that I'm not a hack teacher after all."

Mallory looked at Caitlin, the smile gone and replaced by a serious but warm look. "I never thought you were a hack. I just didn't know you." Her gaze steadied on Caitlin, full of a new curious heat.

"Do you feel like you know me now?"

A chorus of giggles rose from the students, an appropriate response to the video introducing Benjamin Franklin and some of his quirks. Caitlin waited for her moment with Mallory to vanish with the giggles, but Mallory's gaze didn't waver.

"I'm getting there. But I think I'd like to know more."

"I think that can be arranged." Caitlin was relieved her voice didn't betray the pulsing sensations flooding her body. It was ridiculous, the effect this woman had on her.

"I'd like that."

And then their moment was fully disrupted by the video ending and the voices of their students rising into the air.

Mallory shifted gears immediately—a feat that would never cease to impress and annoy Caitlin—and marched to the front of the room to give instructions for the first task.

Once the kids were settled down once more, Caitlin circulated the room, checking in and keeping tabs on the amount of work that was being done vs. the amount of gossiping taking place. Unsurprisingly, she was more lenient about the gossiping than Mallory was; Mallory was practically shushing small groups who were even vaguely off-topic. At one point, Caitlin managed to catch her eye from across the room and mouthed, "You need to calm down." Mallory glared at her, but it wasn't a glare filled with wrath. It was almost playful, and Caitlin's heart did an anticipatory dance of excitement.

"Coach? Can you come help us?"

Caitlin looked around the room, utterly confused. She recognized Hailey's voice but was fairly certain she and Mallory were the only adults in the room, and last she'd checked, neither of them did coaching of any sort.

Apparently Caitlin had missed a memo. She watched as Mallory squatted down next to Hailey's desk and pointed at the handout Hailey was highlighting. Coach? This was a new and mysterious title for Ms. Walker.

Also new, Caitlin noted as she circled back near Brice's group, was that Hailey had finally ditched her two ignorant partners and was working with Devon and three girls from Caitlin's block two class. Devon's entire demeanor was different; he was engaged and actively participating with his group members. It never ceased to amaze Caitlin how different teenagers could be when their environment changed even the slightest bit.

Block two swept into block three, and much to Caitlin and Mallory's surprise, the kids continued working. The two women had been worried that 180 minutes together would be too much, and they'd built in contingency plans in case something backfired and the classes needed to be separated. But so far, their experiment was working beautifully.

When their lunch period arrived, Caitlin lingered at the door after the kids had bolted for the cafeteria. After their thirty-minute lunch, only another thirty minutes remained in the class period. It had gone much faster than Caitlin had anticipated, and she was feeling a mixture of relief and disappointment about that.

"This is…going really well," Mallory said, sitting at her desk. She looked bewildered.

"It is. I love seeing the kids get to work with people they're not usually able to work with. I think it's going to be good for them."

"I agree. We might actually pull this off, Ms. Gregory."

Caitlin grinned. "I do believe you're correct, Ms. Walker. Oh sorry, I mean *Coach* Walker." Caitlin raised an eyebrow in question.

"Oh, that. It's not a big deal." A delicate flush spread across Mallory's cheeks. She fidgeted with a pen. "I'm the assistant coach. Basketball."

"That is a big deal! I had no idea."

"No, I guess it's not something I advertise." Mallory lifted her hands up in a shrug. "Like I said, it's not a big deal."

"I think it's awesome, Mallory. I also never would have guessed that you were a basketball coach, but maybe I should have, considering those long, strong legs of yours." Caitlin resisted the urge to facepalm herself. That was too far. Definitely too far.

Mallory glanced down at her legs, then looked back up at Caitlin. No flinch-smile this time; instead, a sly smirk shaped Mallory's entire face. "Long, strong legs, hmm? You've noticed?"

"I may have glanced at them once or twice. No big deal, as you've said." Glanced, thought about them wrapped around her torso, or naked and intertwined with her own legs. No big deal, indeed.

"Not at all." Mallory cleared her throat. "I'm starving."

"Me too," Caitlin said. She was extremely turned on, but 'starving' worked, too.

Mallory gestured toward the door. "I'm going to go get my lunch now."

"Oh, God. Right. I'm sorry. I'm holding you hostage in your own classroom." Caitlin backed into the hallway and Mallory followed her, closing the door behind them.

They paused there in the empty hallway, curious looks passing between them. Caitlin made a move toward her classroom, but Mallory grabbed her wrist, stopping her in her tracks.

"Would you want to grab coffee after work? To…to celebrate a great first day? And maybe go over some things for next week, just double check and whatnot."

Watching Mallory's confidence dip into shyness had a strong effect on Caitlin. She could barely restrain herself from wrapping her arms around Mallory's body.

"That sounds like an excellent idea," Caitlin said. "Want to meet at that cafe down the street? Or somewhere else? I live in Seabrooke, so I'm open to ideas."

"The place down the street would be great. They have the best tea selection."

"You invite me for coffee, but you drink tea? That's shady business, Walker."

Mallory smiled. The real smiles were setting Caitlin's world on fire. Though admittedly, she also liked the flinch-smiles. "I happen to like them both. Now let me go eat my lunch."

Caitlin stood back and watched Mallory walk down the hall. She suddenly couldn't wait for the school day to end.

# CHAPTER THIRTEEN

Caitlin pulled her sleeves over her hands as she bent against the wind, trying to make it into Beanie's before she got swept away. The New Jersey weather had made a sudden and unwelcome change. Even though November was just a couple weeks away, Caitlin wasn't ready to let go of the unseasonably warm and sunny weather that had dominated October so far. Sometimes it *snowed* in November. She shuddered at the thought. Nope. Not ready for that.

The cafe was warm and brightly lit, not crowded at all. Caitlin took a quick glance around but didn't see Mallory. She wasn't surprised; even though it was Friday, Mallory never seemed to leave school immediately at the bell like virtually every other teacher in the building.

After ordering a peppermint vanilla tea, Caitlin sat down at a table near the back of the cafe, warming her hands around the well-loved mug. She'd been a bit apprehensive about the proximity of Beanie's to Vanderbilt; it wouldn't have surprised her to see students stopping in for an afternoon caffeine jolt, and Caitlin really didn't want to deal with that. She had a hunch Mallory wouldn't like it either, but since Mallory had been on board with Beanie's, she must have known that this wasn't a popular place for their students to hang out.

The door opened and Caitlin looked up to see Mallory standing in the doorway, a frustrated look on her face as she smoothed down her already smooth hair. The woman couldn't have ponytail flyaways even if she tried. Caitlin's face warmed as she took Mallory in. In a move that had truly shocked Caitlin earlier that day, Mallory had departed from her rigorous formal outfits and was also wearing jeans today. She'd paired them with a quarter-zip sweatshirt embroidered with Vanderbilt's logo, completing a casual look that made her seem way more approachable.

Mallory lingered in the doorway as she pulled off her sensible black jacket. Only then did she search the small cafe for Caitlin. When their eyes met, Caitlin immediately smiled. Maybe that apprehension wasn't about potentially running into students. Maybe it was the reality of being near Mallory outside of school for the first time.

"Hey, sorry I'm a little late. I had to make some copies for Monday." Mallory draped her jacket over the back of the chair across from Caitlin. "What kind of tea did you get?"

"Peppermint vanilla. Ten out of ten, would recommend."

Mallory wrinkled her nose. "Peppermint anything makes me think of stomach viruses. Don't ask," she added quickly. "Be right back."

While she waited for Mallory to return, Caitlin scrolled through her phone. Lina had sent a couple texts throughout the day, which she didn't normally do since she knew Caitlin was working. Something was definitely going on with her. Caitlin tapped out a quick response, suggesting they hang out tomorrow; it was time to address the elephant in the room.

"Everything okay?"

Caitlin slid her phone into her bag. "Definitely. Why do you ask?"

"You have this look on your face and I can't tell what it means." Mallory kept her eyes steady on Caitlin as she lifted her mug to her mouth and blew gently on the hot water. "But you look mad."

"Not mad. But I am frustrated." She paused, running her thumb over the handle of her mug. "My best friend is dealing with something and she won't talk to me about it. It's tough when I can see her struggling but have to pretend that I don't."

"I'm surprised that you're pretending instead of addressing the issue. You've always been so straightforward with me."

Caitlin laughed. "Excellent point, Walker. I will address it with Lina. I've been waiting for the right moment, but it seems like I have to create that moment."

"Lina," Mallory said slowly. "That's your best friend?"

"Yep! We've been tight since high school."

"Wow. That's impressive. I'm not friends with anyone I went to high school with."

"Don't take this the wrong way, but I'm not surprised about that."

Mallory nodded. "You probably think I'm too much of a bitch for anyone to stay friends with."

"No, actually, it was more in reference to your secret love for Taylor Swift. I can imagine that was confusing to people since it clashes with your no-fun exterior personality."

"See? Straightforward."

Caitlin laughed. "You know I'm kidding, right?"

"Yes, but I'm not sure which part is the joke," Mallory said, smirking.

*Tread carefully*, Caitlin reminded herself. She could admit that she really liked Mallory and wanted to know (a lot) more of her. But she was still worried about saying the wrong thing and sending Mallory fleeing.

"I think you like T. Swift because she appeals to the actual fun personality that lives deep inside of you. Not many people get to see it, but I believe it's there."

Mallory's eyes glistened for a moment, but she stayed rooted in her seat. The glistening vanished as she said "Taylor Swift is my happy place. I've loved her music since she started her career and watching her evolve has been astounding. In some ways, I feel like I've grown up with her, which is ridiculous because I could probably be her mother."

"Whoa. Wait. Are you some kind of witch? How old are we talking, Walker?"

"Clearly no one ever told you that you should never ask a lady her age."

"Spill it. Now."

Mallory sighed and leaned back in her chair, crossing her arms. A fiery little glare shot over at Caitlin. "Thirty-nine and I swear if you make a single joke about me turning forty, I will get up and leave immediately."

"No jokes, just a really awkward realization that you would have been a nine-year-old with a newborn if you were Taylor's mother."

"Okay fine, but I *feel* old enough to be her mother."

"Well I can assure you that you do not look old enough to even be her older sister." Caitlin resisted the urge to wink.

"What did I tell you about complimenting me?" A playfully stern look, something only Mallory could pull off, danced across her face.

"My deepest apologies." Caitlin grinned, trying with all her might to ignore her impulse to leap across the table and kiss this ridiculous, frustrating, funny, gorgeous woman. "I promise I'll never do it again."

"No. I don't want you to make that promise."

The playful look was gone, and the moment shifted quickly. Caitlin warred internally, flipping back and forth between making another joke and bringing her own sincerity to the table.

"Then I promise I won't compliment you until you tell me you'd like me to compliment you. Does that work?"

*Slightly Joking Sincerity: A Memoir* by Caitlin Gregory.

Mallory exhaled heavily and leaned forward in her chair, planting her elbows on the table. She looked cautiously but deeply at Caitlin. "You've given me this incredible and annoying gift of being blunt with me. I think I need to repay you."

Caitlin's stomach turned uncomfortably. This didn't sound good.

Those bottomless blue-black eyes locked into Caitlin's bright green eyes. Mallory was still and quiet and Caitlin knew she was weighing her words before she let them out.

"It's obvious that you care about your students and they speak highly of you, so I know you're a good teacher, and I respect that. I like that. I know we're still getting to know each other, but from what I do know, I like you. You're funny and annoying, but mostly funny. You're really smart—honestly, smarter than I'd foolishly assumed you were. In my defense, long term substitutes aren't known for being…well, for being like you."

"I get that." Caitlin bit her lip, hoping Mallory would go back to listing all the things she liked about her. Caitlin was more than ready to hear more of that.

"A couple years ago, I got into a relationship with a woman who taught at Vanderbilt." Mallory shut her eyes briefly, clearly struggling with how to proceed.

"Mallory," Caitlin whispered. "Are you saying you're a… lesbian?"

"Can you be serious for one minute? Please?"

"Yes. Of course." Caitlin tucked a few wayward strands of hair behind her ears and straightened her posture. *Pause the jokes, idiot.*

Mallory avoided eye contact, looking instead out the window at the passing traffic. "Amy and I met at school and got into a relationship. Too quickly, probably, but you know how that goes. She struggled a lot with managing her classroom and I felt like I had to constantly defend her, stand up for her, step in on her behalf…I was way out of line. She wasn't a bad teacher, she was simply inexperienced. I think—no, I know I made it a lot worse for her." Mallory shook her head and brought her eyes back to Caitlin. There was genuine remorse on her face. "When we broke up, we had to work together for seven months before the school year ended. Then she got a job elsewhere and that was that."

Caitlin let the story sit between them, making sure Mallory was finished before she spoke. "That sounds like a difficult experience for you," she said quietly.

"On multiple levels, yes. It's also one of the reasons I keep people at an arm's length at school." She laughed bitterly. "The problem is, that makes people think I'm a cold-hearted bitch because I don't want to hang out, go to happy hour, have sleepovers, whatever."

Caitlin laughed, thankful that Mallory was coming back from her angsty place. "Sleepovers? I haven't gotten any emails about those. Damn. Who's in charge of that?"

"Pretty sure Valerie's the point person for sleepovers."

"Listen, Walker, if you and I are going to be friends, I'm gonna need you to respect the fact that Valerie is my friend."

Mallory looked up from her mug, clearly surprised to hear such a firm tone coming from Caitlin. "That was a joke."

"A joke threaded with a dig," Caitlin pointed out.

"She's not nice to me."

"Whining, Mallory, is *not* a good look on you." Caitlin paired this with a broad smile and a teasing tone. She actually didn't mind the whining. It was kind of cute on someone who presented herself as so unaffected.

The two fell into a mostly comfortable silence, each processing thoughts and realizations. Caitlin wasn't exactly sure what she was supposed to take away from Mallory's little speech about Amy and the more she rolled it through her head, the more confused she became.

"So when you–"

"You said we're–"

They smiled at each other, the previous awkwardness dissipating. "Go ahead," Mallory said before taking a sip of her lemony-scented tea.

"When you said you like me, you meant that in, like, a friends way?"

Mallory stared at Caitlin. Her eyes had gone almost completely black. "I meant that I like you. I don't think I completely know what that means yet."

Caitlin's breath hitched in her chest. "So it could be a like that means more than friends."

A heavy silence nudged its way onto the table, glancing back and forth between the two.

Mallory broke the moment, as Caitlin suspected she would. "I would be lying if I said I wasn't attracted to you," she said, each word dropping slowly and with purpose.

"That is a very mutual feeling," Caitlin responded, her words rushing out faster than Mallory's had.

The tense silence oozed further onto the table. It tapped its fingers impatiently, waiting for one of them to make a move.

"I think it would be a good idea for us to be friends and continue to get to know each other." Mallory almost looked pained to say it, but there it was. Simultaneously, the beckoning silence slid off the table, wholly unsatisfied.

Caitlin nodded, her heart rate slowing. After hearing about Amy, even though Caitlin didn't see how she was anything like her, she could understand that it was best for them to focus on being friends. She didn't like that very much, but if it was how she got to have Mallory Walker in her life, then so be it…for now.

"I am totally on board with that. You can start by telling me how you came to be the assistant basketball coach."

Mallory's relief at the subject change was tangible. Her swirling emotions—far more than Caitlin had previously seen from her—only made Caitlin want to draw her closer, though, which was going to be troublesome for this whole "friends" thing.

"I played in high school and college. Don't get excited—I wasn't that great. I was good enough to get a scholarship, which shocked me, and I had it on my resume." She snapped her fingers. "Vanderbilt needed a coach. Right place, right time."

"Let me get this straight. You're saying they hired you for your coaching abilities, not for your teaching prowess? I'm stunned. Truly shocked, Walker."

"You do realize that I had to create and execute a lesson during the interview process, right?"

"You do realize that I taught at River Valley for four years, right?"

"Actually, I did not know that." Mallory pointed at Caitlin. "See? I have a lot of learning to do."

"Lucky for you, I'm a good teacher."

Mallory opened her mouth, surely armed with a friends-appropriate response, and then closed it just as quickly. A blush spread across her lightly freckled cheeks. Caitlin decided to apologize for crossing the line (already! It had been only minutes!), but before she could, Mallory's phone vibrated on the table. A most excellent interruption.

The look on Mallory's face changed instantly as she looked down at her phone. Gone was the teasing warmth and edges of openness. She zipped up her features at warp speed.

"I have to go."

"Oh. Sure." Caitlin stood and carried their mugs back to the counter. Mallory was already up and yanking on her jacket. Caitlin followed her, noting that Mallory gallantly held the door open for her and secretly liking it in a more-than-friends way.

It certainly hadn't gotten any warmer, and the sun had dipped behind a thick cloud cover. Caitlin shivered in her sweatshirt. She wasn't sure if it was from the cold or a combination of that and Mallory walking so closely next to her. The four or so inches Mallory and her long legs had on Caitlin helped protect her from the wind. It was the proximity of this challenging and beautiful woman that was giving Caitlin more warmth than her height's protection, however.

"I'm sorry. I didn't mean to end this so abruptly." Mallory paused beside her car and looked at Caitlin, a soft plea in her eyes. "I like talking with you, Caitlin. And I'm serious when I say that I want to get to know more of you."

"Even though I'm annoying?" Caitlin winked.

"Your ability to annoy me is one of my favorite things about you."

"Mallory Walker, that is the sweetest thing you will probably ever say to me."

Emotions shifted over Mallory's face, each one dive-bombing into the next so quickly that Caitlin couldn't nail a single one down.

"I don't think that's true, Caitlin."

Mallory took a step toward Caitlin as Caitlin leaned in to toss a light-hearted friendly punch (she was trying! Really!) to Mallory's shoulder. Caitlin's balled-up hand collided with

Mallory's collar bone. Wordlessly, Mallory wrapped her hand around Caitlin's fist and gently pulled her closer. Mallory's pulse beat hard enough for Caitlin to feel it through her knuckles.

They stood there, staring at each other, deaf to the traffic and life rushing nearby. It took every bit of willpower Caitlin had not to kiss Mallory. But she knew she couldn't; this was not her move to make. That much had been made clear to her today.

Mallory's head ducked down, her eyes searching Caitlin's. Against her will, Caitlin licked her lips. She'd replay this moment for the entire weekend, wondering if it was the move that made everything fall apart.

Just as quickly as she'd ensnared Caitlin's fist in her hand, Mallory dropped it and took two steps backward. Caitlin stood statue-still. *Please don't run.*

"I'm seeing someone," Mallory blurted. She spun on her heel, got into her car, and drove away without another word, without another look.

Caitlin watched Mallory drive away. She suddenly felt sick and strangely empty, as though Mallory had taken a piece of her away.

# CHAPTER FOURTEEN

"For the record, this was not what I meant when I said we needed to spend quality time together."

Lina threw a towel at Caitlin and motioned for her to sit down on the weight bench. "Yeah well, this is what I need to do today, and you said you wanted to tone up. You'll thank me later."

"I highly doubt that," Caitlin muttered under her breath. She sighed as she picked up a five-pound weight and began doing a move Lina called Around the World. She promised Caitlin that it would firm up her triceps, but Caitlin had a hunch she'd have to do it more than just today for that to happen and, well…she'd see about that.

The ambience at Lina's gym was not for the faint of heart. This was a gym that used to be an auto repair garage and it still smelled like it. It also carried the odor of stale sweat and someone was definitely wearing too much Axe. Lina swore she only came here because it was close to home and it was privately owned by a couple guys she'd served with in Syria. She paid next to nothing to use the facility, which, in its defense, was nicely appointed for being such a dive.

As Caitlin rounded the world for another set, she watched Lina jump rope. It wasn't fair how physically fit Lina was. It was kind of insane, to be honest. But she'd always been in good shape; she'd had a six-pack when she was seven thanks to a couple years of gymnastics that she would deny if Caitlin ever brought it up in front of anyone. In high school, Lina had dominated several sports: field hockey in the fall, track and field—she was a thrower—in the spring, and basketball in the winter.

Basketball. Hmm. It was a long shot, but…

"Hey, Li? Remember how you played basketball in high school?"

"Uh, yeah. Why wouldn't I?"

"Do you remember playing against Mallory Walker?"

Lina dropped her jump rope on the floor and rolled her eyes at Caitlin. "No. Don't be weird." She crouched down and pushed some weights around, searching for her favorite ten pounders.

"That's a perfectly normal question to ask. It's not weird."

"You don't even know if she grew up around here, Cait."

Caitlin glanced at her phone. It had been silent all day. "That's kind of my point. I know she played basketball and must have been good because she got a scholarship, so if she's from around here, you'd probably remember her."

"Do you have any idea how many girls I played against throughout high school? Oh, that's right. Of course you don't. You wouldn't know what to do with a basketball if Mallory smacked you in the face with it."

Caitlin debated smacking Lina in the face with her weight but decided that wasn't a very good idea. Lina had driven them there, after all, and Caitlin couldn't drive her damn stick shift Wrangler. Alas, Lina had a point: Caitlin was not known for her involvement with athletics. She'd spent her high school years in band and orchestra, supporting athletic activities from the sidelines with the pep band, but never participating in them. She still marveled at the fact that she and Lina, coming from such different worlds, had crossed paths during their sophomore year and managed to maintain and grow their friendship even though they'd had so little in common back then.

Pausing her workout to watch Lina execute perfect upright rows, Caitlin felt a surge of pride for her best friend. Lina hadn't had it easy growing up and she had a fractured relationship with her family now, but she was one of the best people Caitlin knew. Being out in high school when they were teenagers wasn't cool. It wasn't dangerous, exactly, but it was a quieter and more secretive venture than it was now. *Except for kids at Vanderbilt*, Caitlin mused. Lina had faced the adversity of coming out at sixteen with her head held high, and when her mother threatened to disown her, she took it in stride and moved in with her aunt. It was around that time that Lina and Caitlin's friendship took off; Caitlin hadn't yet realized her sexual preference, but she knew she admired Lina. They were both thankful that their closeness was more sisterly than anything else; it made their friendship a hell of a lot easier, not having old sex baggage clinging to them.

"Stop staring at your phone," Lina grunted.

Caught. Again. Caitlin sat back down on the weight bench and pushed her phone toward the end of it. "She hasn't said a word," she said, dragging the toe of her sneaker on the ground. "It's driving me crazy."

"Do we have to go over this again? She said she's seeing someone."

"Okay, fine, but since when does that mean she can't respond to my text asking how her night went?"

Lina gave Caitlin a pointed look. "Perhaps because her night hasn't ended yet?"

"Oh for fuck's sake, Lina. Come on." Caitlin's stomach clenched uncomfortably. That wasn't something she'd considered, nor was it something she wanted to consider.

"You need to face the facts, Cait. She was honest with you."

Caitlin laid back on the bench, dangling her feet off the end. "She likes me."

"That's only part of it. Don't be an ass. You'll only hurt yourself if you don't face the truth of that conversation."

"Okay, but Lina. Seriously. She almost kissed me. We were *this close*," Caitlin held up her finger and thumb just barely apart for emphasis, "and then I licked my lips like a total idiot and she ran away."

"I highly doubt she ran away because you licked your lips. She ran away because, as she flat-out told you, she's seeing someone. That means she can't kiss you."

"I think it's also obvious that she wants to kiss me."

Lina shoved Caitlin's legs, forcing her to sit up so Lina could drop down next to her. Lina pushed her sweaty golden-brown hair off her face before grabbing Caitlin's shoulders and turning her so they were looking at each other.

"Dude, you literally put your sweaty hands on my skin."

"Get over it. Listen to me." Lina shook Caitlin's shoulders once, hard. "Mallory was honest with you. That tells you she's a good person. Yes, she said she likes you, but she also admitted she doesn't really know you, and we all know that once she does know you, she'll run away for real."

Lina deftly blocked Caitlin's attempt at punching her side. She clapped Caitlin's shoulder once more. "Bottom line is, Cait, she's involved with someone else. That's not a path you want to go down, and I know you know that."

As usual, Lina had a point. A valid one at that. Caitlin, as a practice and a credo, did not mess with people who were already involved with someone else. She didn't want the bad karma that came along with that. And yet...

"I hear you. And I agree with you. But there's something there, Lina. I can feel it. And I think she does, too." Caitlin's eyes snapped over to her phone even though she knew it didn't have anything to show her.

"I'm going to drop one of those twenties on your phone." Lina reached over for a weight and Caitlin slapped her arm. She then swung her right leg over the bench so she was face-to-face with Caitlin. "I don't want to see you get hurt. You get that, right?"

"Of course. But I don't think–"

"No. Listen. Maybe there is something between you two. Honestly, it sounds like there is and I haven't even seen you interact with her. But Caitlin, you've gotta sit back and let Mallory go through whatever she's doing with the person she's seeing. The more you interfere with that, the less likely it is that you and Mallory will have a chance with each other. At least, a chance that's pure and not weighed down with someone's regret."

Caitlin saw the burst of sadness that crept over Lina's features. "We're not talking about me anymore, are we?"

Lina shifted and stood, abruptly ending the conversation as Caitlin had known she would. But Caitlin was really, really tired of Lina walking away when the conversation got difficult.

"Lina, stop. Level with me. I'm your best friend and I have no idea what's going on with you."

"We are not talking about this here," Lina said through clenched teeth, her eyes scanning the room repeatedly. There were a couple guys over in a corner adjacent to them but otherwise the gym was empty. It was, however, filled with someone's terrible 1980s heavy metal playlist, so there was no chance the Army guys across the gym could hear them.

Regardless, Caitlin knew Lina's boundaries. "Fine. But we are going to talk about this."

She received another grunt in response and then Lina was off to some machine that looked vaguely like a torture device for thighs.

Twenty minutes later, Caitlin was dripping with sweat and beyond ready to leave that torturous place. It was past one and she was starving. In fact, she was going to command Lina to stop somewhere and buy her lunch on their way home.

As Caitlin packed her towel into her duffel bag, she couldn't resist tapping on her phone's screen to see if Mallory had texted. She hadn't. A piece of Caitlin deflated, and she took a deep breath to combat the sadness blossoming inside her.

"Ready?" Lina appeared next to Caitlin and yanked on her messy, sweaty ponytail. "Gross."

"You're not much prettier right now, Sarge."

"Sweat equity," Lina said, flexing her arm.

"Great. And when exactly will my arms look like that?" Caitlin flexed, poking her sad little muscle. "This looks somewhat bigger than it did this morning."

She braced herself for Lina's inevitable crack, but nothing came. Lina's eyes were locked on the couple that had just entered the gym.

Candice Barrows and her husband, Steve, were standing just inside the door. The group of guys had noticed them and were already calling over for Steve to join them. Caitlin couldn't take her eyes off Steve; he was insanely hot, even to a lesbian. He pulled off macho without being gross. It was strangely intoxicating.

Meanwhile, Lina couldn't take her eyes off Candice, who in return was doing everything she could not to look at Lina.

"Is there a back entrance?" Caitlin whispered, careful not to move her lips too much, lest Candice was an expert at lip reading from twenty feet away.

"No." Lina's voice was gruff and edged with the tone that came wherever Candice was seen or mentioned.

"Well, buddy, 'the best way out is always through.'" Caitlin tugged at Lina's arm. "Let's get this over with."

The two women walked toward the exit, toward Candice Barrows, who was wearing skin-tight cropped black leggings, black Nikes, and a Dri-FIT race shirt. Her body was phenomenal; not as cut as Lina's, but strong and sexy and damn good for being fifty. Candice's chin length blond hair was pulled into a small ponytail that stuck out through the back of her baseball hat.

"Hey! Hi…" Oh shit. What the hell was she supposed to call a retired Army official? Caitlin blanked and looked to Lina for help.

"Candice," Barrows said with a tight smile for Caitlin. "Hi, Caitlin."

"Ma'am," Lina said. She was still rocking that Candice-only tone that Caitlin hated. It was so…cold. Impersonal. And obviously trying to hide a whole lot of hurt.

"Sergeant. Nice to see you."

"Likewise."

Caitlin ping-ponged between the two of them. Talk about an uncomfortable interaction. Candice's eyes didn't stay on Lina for more than a second; she peered behind them, keeping her gaze steady on her husband.

"Wow, Lina, we need to get going. We have that–"

"Birthday party for your parents' dog," Candice said drily. "Have fun."

She stalked past them and Caitlin dragged Lina out of the gym. They made it into the Wrangler without further incident. Caitlin let Lina sit with her angry silence for a few minutes, then gently suggested she turn on the Jeep so they could leave the scene of the crime.

"Now I know why you actually come here," Caitlin said lightly.

"Drop it, Caitlin."

"Actually, Lina, I'm tired of you telling me to drop it. Clearly there's something still going on between you two and I'm tired of you keeping me in the dark."

Lina's grip on the steering wheel tightened and her knuckles turned white. "There's nothing going on between me and Candice."

"I don't believe you. You still love her."

"So what?"

"So, I don't–"

"It's too much for me to get into," Lina interrupted. "Okay? Can you please accept that?"

Caitlin watched her friend carefully. "Are you still seeing her?"

"I said no." Lina glanced at Caitlin, fear present in her eyes. "Please, Caitlin. I can't do this right now."

They drove in silence, Lina focused on the road while Caitlin focused on the passing landscape. She resisted the urge to look at her stupid phone, knowing the silence extended beyond the Wrangler and all the way to Mallory, wherever she was, with whatever she was doing other than not replying to Caitlin's text. Or whomever she was doing. Caitlin ditched that unpleasant but realistic thought as fast as she could. Her stomach growled but she decided to hold off until she got home. She could tell by Lina's silence that she wanted to be alone.

As Lina pulled down their street, their homes in sight, she glanced over at Caitlin.

"Did you quote Frost back there? I thought you hated him."

Caitlin groaned. Fucking Valerie and her little Frost lesson. "Let's pretend that never happened, okay?"

# CHAPTER FIFTEEN

Leaves crunched under Caitlin's feet as she jogged through the silent, softly lit streets of her development. While she normally preferred a change of scenery when running, she was grateful this very early morning for the clearly marked four-mile trail that circled and dipped between packs of condos. It was barely six a.m. and she was closing in on a slow but much-needed three miles. She was shocked that other people were also out walking and running at this hideous time of day. Caitlin was only here because she'd woken up at three a.m. and been unable to go back to sleep.

After checking her pace on her watch, Caitlin tried concentrating on her breathing in an effort to push away the winding thoughts in her head. It was no use; she was stuck on the unanswered thread of Mallory's disappearance last weekend that had carried over into an obvious distance during the work week. Sure, Caitlin saw her at work, and they were teaching together every other day, but that was it. Mallory had never responded to Caitlin's innocuous text, and they had been nothing but professionally cordial with each other. Even their shared prep period had been a place of avoidance for Mallory, who claimed to have meetings and "other things" she needed to tend to. She'd made a point to make an off-handed comment to Caitlin that "the unit is fully planned and we have only one more week teaching it, anyway." Caitlin felt that sting but had retreated into her classroom instead of pushing the issue.

Also weighing on Caitlin was a disturbing dream she'd had about Becca. This wasn't unusual; Caitlin's subconscious loved to drag up all sorts of unresolved dirt when she was sleeping. She didn't consider her relationship with Becca to be unresolved, though. It was the connection between Becca and Mallory that had her rolling in her thoughts.

Having reached her front door, Caitlin sat down on her front steps to catch her breath and cool down before getting in the shower. She rested her elbows on her knees and stared into the dimly lit streets. *Becca and Mallory. Mallory and Becca.* It didn't make sense—or Caitlin didn't *want* it to make sense. She knew that she didn't know Mallory that well (yet), but she did consider herself a bit of an expert on Becca. Their personalities meshing in a romantic relationship? Caitlin couldn't fathom it. Over the course of their marriage, Caitlin had learned that Becca preferred a more subservient partner, someone who went along with whatever Becca wanted. Caitlin had filled that spot in the early stages of their relationship but had grown out of it over the span of their years together. Nothing that she knew about Mallory indicated that she would be a subservient partner. Nothing that she knew about Mallory indicated that she would even get along with someone like Becca. And yet, it seemed that Caitlin was wrong about something.

Then again, as Lina had said to Caitlin several times (and made her repeat back to her in the way that only Lina could do), Caitlin didn't know for certain that Mallory was seeing Becca. Seeing them out in public together twice could mean myriad things.

Caitlin exhaled loudly and gazed up at the sky. She wanted things to go back to friendly-normal with Mallory. That couldn't be too much to ask, even if Mallory was dating Becca. Just two friends. Two lesbian friends. Two lesbian friends who liked each other and nearly kissed a week ago. Not a problem at all.

\* \* \*

The air in Caitlin's classroom was tense. Even the kids seemed out of sorts—while some were working effectively, the majority seemed distracted and antsy. Even Hailey, Caitlin's pride and joy, was spending more time off-task than she was engaging with her group. No matter how many times she was redirected, Hailey's focus wandered and the whispering started up again.

Caitlin hunched over her laptop at the front of the room as she entered homework grades. She snuck furtive glances over at Mallory, who was sitting with a particularly uninterested group of students. She'd been there for over fifteen minutes, and from what Caitlin could tell from her vantage point, no progress of any sort was being made. She thought about interfering but didn't want to make it awkward for Mallory. For all Caitlin knew, it was something deeply historical that they were trying to work out.

"Ms. Gregory? Can you come help us find something?"

Caitlin practically leapt toward the group of quiet girls asking for her help. She'd just found the letter from Abigail Adams that they were searching for when a shrill alarm sounded in the classroom, startling everyone.

Kids jumped from their seats and grabbed their phones before heading to the classroom door. They were happy to leave everything else behind to burn in the potential fire, even though it was likely only a drill. Caitlin tugged on her jacket as she followed the pack of students out the door and down the hallway toward the nearest exit. She peered over and around the students' heads, searching for Mallory.

Out in the fresh air, Caitlin was thrilled to find their large group of students standing together in the designated area for Caitlin's classroom. Managing students during an outdoor emergency drill was a nightmare for teachers, but Vanderbilt somehow made it easy for everyone to follow directions. Caitlin did a quick head count when she reached the group, noting that Mallory was standing nearest to the curb with her arms crossed.

"Gotta love these surprises," Caitlin said breezily as she walked up next to Mallory. "I'm surprised admin didn't send an email to warn us."

"They need to do a true drill every so often." Mallory's tone was clipped and she continued to stare across the street.

Caitlin bit her lip anxiously. "Hey," she started quietly, doing her best to avoid attracting student attention. "Is everything cool?"

The cold stare that Mallory aimed at Caitlin nearly leveled her to the ground. "Why do you ask?"

Gone were the pleasant, stirring friendly emotions tinged with attraction. The chill that spiked Mallory's words froze Caitlin's skin.

While she weighed her response, again unsure of whether she could play this off with a joke or go for sincerity, whistles blew near the building and kids started slowly filing back into the school. Caitlin was surprised to notice that Mallory hung back with her at the curb while their students dispersed.

"This isn't the time for us to talk," Mallory said.

"So something is going on."

"I'm not having this conversation right now." With that, Mallory stalked away, leaving Caitlin to follow her.

Back in the classroom, Caitlin kept her jacket on, needing a buffer to ward off the extra chill emanating from her coteacher. Mallory went right back to working with that same group. Caitlin checked in with the Abigail Adams group, making sure they had the information they needed, before wandering over to Hailey's group. It was the best group to go to since Hailey and her friends were as far across the room from Mallory as possible.

"He may have been a womanizer, but he made a lot of contributions to society," Hailey said as she flipped through websites.

"Nothing wrong with loving the ladies."

Hailey shot a withering glare at Devon. "Ew, Devon."

"What? He wasn't married, right?"

"Ben Franklin did have a wild social life before and after he was married," Caitlin mentioned as she squatted down next to their desks. "There was a pattern of illegitimate children in his family."

"His wife stayed with him after he cheated on her?" Ashley, a girl Caitlin didn't know very well, asked this with an appropriate amount of disgust in her voice.

"Not only did she stay with him, but she also raised the son he had with another woman."

Groans and gasps rose from the group. Nothing like a little Revolutionary Era gossip to get the kids interested.

Caitlin continued working with Hailey's group as they sorted through Franklin's political connections. They began listing the historical documents he'd signed, trying to sort through how involved he was.

"So Franklin wrote the Constitution?" Devon asked. He looked utterly confused.

"No, he didn't write it. But he was a part of its creation," Caitlin explained. "Many other–"

"No he wasn't." The group stilled. Caitlin felt her heartbeat nervously kick up a few notches.

She slowly stood, her aching knees crying for mercy, and turned to face Mallory, who had silently crept up behind her. "Sure he was. Many of the Founding Fathers, including Franklin, were at the Constitutional Convention and helped to create the document."

"Just because he was present doesn't mean that he had input," Mallory said coldly. "James Madison is credited with writing the Bill of Rights as well as framing the Constitution. It's a bit irresponsible to give Ben Franklin credit for the Constitution when there's no historical proof of what he contributed."

*Don't push her. Let her be the expert.* Caitlin knew this wouldn't end well if she tried to reframe the matter at hand. She was shocked and embarrassed that Mallory was correcting her—and it wasn't even a valid correction—in front of students, but this was not the time to address it.

"You're right." Caitlin turned back to the group. Their faces were comically shocked, and Caitlin would have laughed had she not felt like vomiting or screaming. "Just make a note that Franklin signed the Constitution. You don't have to go any deeper than that."

Without another glance at Mallory, Caitlin slipped away to her desk. She took a long drink of water from her Nalgene and checked the clock. Twenty minutes. Okay. That was doable.

She just had to find every way possible to stay the hell away from Mallory in those twenty minutes, quite the feat in a classroom this size.

# CHAPTER SIXTEEN

As she walked across the parking lot toward her car, Caitlin mentally congratulated herself for having gotten in her run early that morning. Now she was free and clear on a Friday afternoon and could grab a much-needed drink with Valerie and Drew before heading home to replay that awful exchange from class.

Caitlin paused a couple feet away from her car. She'd been so caught up in daydreams of vodka tonics that she hadn't noticed Mallory walking several paces ahead of her. The embarrassed anger rose up once more and Caitlin picked up her pace.

"Hey," she called. Mallory continued walking. "HEY!"

As though it was the most painful move in the world, like her body would actually crumble to pieces if she completed the revolution, Mallory slowly turned in Caitlin's direction. She kept her eyes focused somewhere near Caitlin's feet and didn't say a word.

"Remember how you said I gave you the gift of bluntness? Any chance you could do the same for me right now and explain what's going on?"

Caitlin waited, watching Mallory as she closed her eyes and blew a small breath out from her lips. She hitched her bag further up her shoulder and pulled it across her chest as a barrier to further separate them.

After several strained moments, Mallory spoke. "I don't think this," she gestured to the space between them, "is a good idea."

"You're going to need to be more specific, Mallory. In case you've forgotten, there's a couple layers to *this*."

Mallory took a deep breath and looked over Caitlin's shoulder. "Not really. I told you I'm seeing someone. I'm sorry if you somehow misinterpreted that, but that was my way of saying that you and I will be friends, and that's it."

"If this is how you treat your *friends*, it's no wonder no one stuck around after high school." Caitlin shut her eyes. "Okay, that came out a little–"

"Harsh? You think?"

Caitlin swallowed what felt like four glasses worth of shards. Mallory wasn't wrong, per se. But that moment in a different parking lot last week had spoken louder than Mallory's actual words and Caitlin couldn't let it go.

"I understand that you're involved with someone. I don't know how serious your relationship is and I don't want to interfere with that, but you're giving me some mixed signals, Walker."

"I don't mean to. That's not…I don't do that. Look, Caitlin." She pulled her bag even tighter across her chest and continued to avoid eye contact. "We can be friends. But that's where the line ends."

"But Mallory, you said you're attracted to me. I thought…I don't know, it really seems like there's more to this than just friendship." Caitlin bit her lip against the surge of regret that flooded after her words. It was true but she should have kept that in her head or vented it to someone else.

"Whining, Caitlin, is not a good look on you."

The line, familiar as it was, stabbed Caitlin directly in the gut. Mallory hadn't used any of Caitlin's teasing qualities to deliver that dagger. She was stone cold, rigid, and sealed up vacuum tight.

"Right," Caitlin said quietly, already backing away even though her car was behind Mallory. "Message received, loud and clear." She spun around and halted, realizing she had to turn back around and walk past Mallory in order to execute this escape. Wonderful.

Mallory remained stock still as Caitlin stalked past her, careful not to come more than two feet into her space. At the safety of her car, Caitlin rummaged in her bag for her keys, cursing herself for not having already had them in her hand. So much for a quick escape.

"You weren't wrong about Ben Franklin."

Keys found, her harried exit just moments away, Caitlin couldn't help but to respond to that abrupt statement. "I know. What I *don't* know is why you felt the need to correct me in front of forty of our students."

Mallory had turned around and was finally looking directly at Caitlin. She'd lost some of the rigidity, but all of her features remained closed up tight. "They didn't all hear it, Caitlin."

"That really doesn't matter. You could have waited until after class and addressed it with me privately. Instead, you nitpicked me directly in front of a group of students, and if you think they won't tell everyone else in that class, never mind the rest of the junior class, you are dead wrong." Caitlin stood her ground, the suppressed anger rising and holding her in place.

"I know. And I'm sorry. I could have handled that better."

"If better means not saying a fucking thing while we're in a room full of kids, then yes. You could have."

Mallory bristled. "That mouth is going to get you into trouble. I'm surprised it hasn't already, after what I heard."

Caitlin yanked open her back door and threw her bag in, then stomped over to Mallory, stopping less than a foot in front of her. "Excuse me?"

"As you said, the kids talk." Mallory shrugged and smirked at Caitlin. *Smirked.* It didn't do much to mar her otherwise gorgeous features, but Caitlin didn't care about how pretty

Mallory was at that moment. This passive aggressive behavior reminded her far too much of a certain woman she'd once been married to.

"I don't have the energy for this kind of bullshit. Either say what you want to say or don't bring it up."

Mallory rolled her shoulders, giving the completely false impression that she was loosening up. Her eyes remained locked on Caitlin's. "Brice told me all about your choice words in class a couple weeks ago."

Caitlin cringed; while she obviously knew what had happened and what she had said, she didn't trust a damn thing that came out of Brice's mouth.

"I thought you were better than that, Caitlin," Mallory went on. "But to say 'fuck' in front of a room full of students?" She shook her head, disdain rolling from her in waves. "I'd expect that from a first-year teacher, maybe. Not from someone who claims to have experience teaching."

Oh, okay. This was how Mallory wanted to destroy any and all attraction Caitlin had for her? With nasty subtext and outright criticism of her teaching? Great, brilliant. Perfect.

"I don't know what Brice told you, but it sounds like it wasn't factual," she said, trying to maintain control. She didn't know why she felt the need to defend herself other than to try to get the truth out there. "It's not like I told them to fuck off."

The laugh that came from Mallory sounded like something straight out of a cartoon villain's mouth. "You wouldn't be standing in this parking lot if you'd said that. It's bad enough that you used the word at all."

"It was in context. I was redirecting them." Caitlin felt flustered, her defense slipping away. "No, not redirecting. I was addressing the fact that they were cursing and it was inappropriate."

"I thought you were better than that." As cold as her words were, the sentiment still hit in a strangely warm way, almost like a bad backhanded compliment.

"Mallory, it's not like I said something they never hear. They'd just used the word themselves!"

"You're expected to be a role model."

"Last time I checked, even role models have flaws."

Mallory scoffed. "Not in a classroom."

Caitlin steadied herself. "What's the real issue here? You're throwing all these random things at me right now, and I don't–"

"This, Caitlin. *This* is the issue."

Finally at an impasse, Caitlin and Mallory stood inches apart. Not a single piece of Mallory looked like she had just one week ago, in a moment Caitlin could have sworn was going to end in a heated kiss that they both wanted.

"You know what?" Caitlin took a deep breath, feeling herself bouncing between screaming and going silent. She backed away toward her car, needing the distance. "Just forget it, Mallory. All of it. Just *fucking* forget it."

She slammed her car door and jammed her keys in the ignition. Fuck all of it, including Mallory Walker.

The boisterous happy hour environment of Ollie's was precisely what Caitlin needed after that parking lot throwdown. When she arrived, Valerie and Drew were sitting with some people Caitlin didn't know but they graciously splintered off and grabbed a table just for the three of them. Valerie took one look at the expression on Caitlin's face and told Drew to grab two vodka tonics from the bar.

"I still don't understand why you won't drink a double," he said to Caitlin as he set down her two single vodka tonics. "It's the same thing."

"No it's not," Valerie and Caitlin said in chorus. Drew raised his hands in submission.

Valerie waited until Caitlin had taken a few big sips of her first drink before asking "Do you want to talk about the reasons behind that look on your face?"

"Absolutely not." Caitlin chewed on the straw. "Not one bit. Please fill my ears with mindless school gossip."

Because they were good friends *and* keepers of the best Vanderbilt secrets, Valerie and Drew obliged. Caitlin tuned in and out, her attention diverting when Drew began a lengthy explanation of why the math and history departments were innately corrupt. She wondered if Mallory's name would come up and wasn't sure if she wanted to hear Valerie slam her some more, or if that would make her sad.

Caitlin knew Mallory had ice in her veins. Nothing about her suggested that she was warm and open and willing to put her heart on the line. But the way Mallory had turned on her that afternoon was not sitting well with Caitlin. There was an edge to her that was new and painful—an edge that didn't seem rational. There had to be something else going on there.

As though she'd felt the brain waves of Caitlin's thoughts from however many miles away, Mallory chose that moment to send Caitlin a text. Seeing her name flash on her phone didn't bring Caitlin any sense of joy. She debated ignoring it, leaving it for when she got home, but curiosity got the best of her.

Before she could open the text, Valerie grabbed Caitlin's phone and held it as far away as her arm would stretch. "Nope."

"Valerie, give me my phone."

"Nope. That look on your face is making me very angry and if Walker has anything to do with it, I'm going to be livid."

"Aren't very angry and livid basically the same words?" Drew asked thoughtfully, tapping his finger to his stubbled chin.

"Ooh, look at Mr. Math Man flexing his lexicon." Valerie brought Caitlin's phone a bit closer and peered at the screen. "Okay, I'm gonna need your passcode real quick."

"Not happening." Caitlin scooted off her chair and grabbed for her phone. A small but enthusiastic struggle ensued, squeaks coming from Valerie and plenty of cursing coming from Caitlin. In the end Caitlin emerged victorious, holding her phone like a swaddled baby.

While Valerie busied herself with fixing her unruly hair and complaining about Caitlin's weird superhuman wrist strength, Caitlin opened Mallory's text. Its contents weren't surprising but reading the words somehow made her feel even worse.

There was no need to respond. That wasn't Caitlin's MO, but after that parking lot encounter, she wasn't feeling the need to placate Mallory or be her usual chipper, joking self. She wasn't the type to send a snarky response (though it was tempting) but she hoped her silence would say more than enough.

Valerie tapped a frighteningly long manicured nail on the side of Caitlin's second drink. "Do I need to release the hounds?"

"That won't be necessary." Caitlin did her best to fix her face with a normal-looking smile. "We've reached the point in our unit where we don't need to be teaching together all the time. She was just clarifying that."

Well, Mallory's actual words were: *It's best if we stay in our own classrooms, with our own classes, from this point forward.*

Kind of lacking in the kindness department but probably not the coldest way she could have said it. Regardless, Caitlin felt the sting. She tried to soothe the burn with her vodka tonic, but more than anything she wanted to be at home, under a blanket, with her phone in another room.

Feeling the threat of tears pushed Caitlin into escape mode. She pushed the remainder of her drink toward Valerie, dropped some money on the table, and got up.

"No! You're not leaving!" Valerie grabbed Caitlin's arm. "I knew she upset you. Tell me everything."

"It's fine," Caitlin said, wiggling her arm free from Valerie's grasp. "I need to get home."

Valerie eyed her suspiciously but dropped it. "Text me when you're home safe. And don't give that bitch a second thought tonight."

While Caitlin would love to eject Mallory from her brain, she knew all too well that the damn woman would be flooding her thoughts all evening.

# CHAPTER SEVENTEEN

By the time Monday morning rolled around, the hurt from Mallory's words had dissipated but Caitlin hadn't fully gotten over Friday's events. She'd spent some time over the weekend doing some casual cyber-stalking, trying to find any clue that would explain the sudden and dramatic shift in Mallory's behavior toward Caitlin. It was no use—just as she was in person, Mallory's online presence was locked up tight. The one piece that did please Caitlin was figuring out that Becca and Mallory were not friends on any social networking platforms. Other than that, she came into Monday just as confused as she'd been on Friday.

Adding to her subpar mood was the fact that Mallory had gone as far as to close her classroom door, which she resolutely never did. At six fifty, Caitlin stood in the hallway between their rooms, gawking at the shut door. The metaphor was not lost on her, but it was yet another stab in her side.

And it wasn't as though Caitlin had been entertaining fantasies of walking down the aisle toward Mallory's smiling face. Sure, she thought she was hot and she liked her quirky, challenging personality. Yes, she daydreamed about Mallory's lips capturing hers in heated kisses. Mm-hmm, yeah, she took those daydreams further. But the bigger hurt that dominated Caitlin's heart was that Mallory had lost respect for her as a teacher and didn't even want to be her friend.

"Her loss," she muttered as she scrawled the day's agenda on the whiteboard. The notion of the spoken balm didn't quite reach Caitlin's aching heart.

By the time Caitlin's second block class began filtering into the room, she'd heard the rumor that Mallory was absent. That was surprising since Mallory seemed like the kind of teacher who would miss school only if she was actually dying.

Ashley, one of Hailey's friends and group members, tapped Caitlin on the shoulder. "When is Ms. Walker's class coming over?"

Caitlin gritted her teeth. So nice of Mallory to be out on the day they needed to transition their students back to working in their own classes. "We're not going to combine today, Ashley. You should be at a point where you can get some work done without your entire group being here."

"Oh." The young woman looked around the room nervously. "But my entire group is in the other class and I really need them for the part I'm working on."

Both Caitlin and Ashley turned to the door as a very tall, bearded man entered and called out a greeting. They glanced at each other, equally confused, as he approached Caitlin.

"You're Ms. Gregory, I presume?"

"Yes. That's me. What can I help you with?"

Ashley squealed and darted away from Caitlin. She peered around the strange bearded man and noticed a stream of students—her students—filtering into the room from the hallway.

"The sub plans said the classes combine?"

Caitlin resisted the urge to laugh or scream—she wasn't sure which would come out if she dared open her mouth. Instead, she nodded to the substitute teacher and watched as her students located their group members and picked up where they'd left off on Friday.

"Well, looks like you've got this under control! I'll be in the other room if you need me." The bearded interloper left as quickly as he'd arrived, leaving Caitlin alone with two classes' worth of students. Now she had to split her attention among forty-plus kids. Her brain charged ahead, knocking all Mallory-related distractions aside. She couldn't have been happier.

\* \* \*

The week passed quickly, if strangely. Mallory was absent again on Tuesday and when she returned on Wednesday, she avoided Caitlin as much as possible. From the glimpses Caitlin got in passing, she noted that Mallory *looked* fine. Her color was good; she didn't appear to have lost a ton of weight from a volatile stomach bug; she hadn't gotten a new unfortunate haircut... Nope. In a brief hallway update about the last two days of the kids working in Caitlin's room, she noticed that Mallory didn't even sound stuffy or raspy.

It was all well and good, Caitlin figured, since tomorrow was Friday and that was the day of the group presentations. While Mallory kept her word and her kids in her classroom on Wednesday and Thursday, she'd have no choice but to reunite with Caitlin for the final day of the unit.

And then, they could put this shit show to rest and pretend they'd never thought it was a good idea to work together.

The thing was, it wasn't a shit show. As Caitlin explained to Marcy and Valerie after school on Thursday, the unit had gone exceedingly well. Better than she or Mallory had expected, truly.

"I'm impressed, Caitlin," Marcy said as she sat down heavily in a chair. She looked tired; Caitlin didn't know the details, but there was quite a bit of English department drama going on about inconsistent grading practices. "You two did a knockout job from the looks of it."

She and Caitlin looked around the room at the various projects lining the walls. Valerie was moving between them, getting a closer look.

"Thanks! Overall I'm pleased with how it went."

"Marce, just say what we're both thinking," Valerie said as she joined them and perched on the desk next to Marcy. "We can't believe you managed to work with Walker for this entire unit without either quitting because of her arrogance or at least telling her off for being such an uptight bitch."

As Marcy gasped and reprimanded Valerie, Caitlin felt a flush rise up her neck. On one hand, she was happy that word hadn't gotten out this last week about them not working so closely together. Then again, a very small part of her wanted to acknowledge that she would love to say some choice words to Mallory's face—words that would undoubtedly delight Valerie.

"Believe it. We did it." Short and sweet would have to do the trick.

Valerie opened her mouth, likely to spew some more vitriol, but Marcy cut her off. "The real reason I'm here is to check on you. You were upset when we spoke earlier."

Earlier that day, Brice had struck again. Caitlin had had a feeling she wouldn't escape the rest of the year without another encounter with him, but this one had caught her off-guard. Her third block class had been unusually talkative—likely because they were mostly finished with their projects and slipped off-task—and Caitlin had been making the rounds, checking in to see who needed what before Friday. When she was with Hailey's group, minus Ashley who was with Mallory and likely complaining about it, Caitlin noticed that Brice's group was getting louder by the second. She tried to tune them out and focus on Devon's question about Ben Franklin and his creative stint as Silence Dogood, but Brice's voice carried.

Admittedly, Caitlin didn't hear the full sentence. All she caught was "stupid dyke teachers" and the hum of silence that followed. She was relieved she wouldn't have to say 'fuck' in front of her class again but felt nauseous once she realized she might have to address the fact that she was, in fact, a dyke (though not a stupid one) and Brice needed to open his goddamn mind and accept—okay, no. She'd stop much earlier than that.

Before she had a chance to hop on her soapbox and begin her LGBTQ+ rights speech, Hailey spoke up.

"Shut up, Brice. Seriously."

Not one to be admonished by a female, especially one who was his age, Brice retorted immediately, his voice flashing with anger. "Of course you'd defend the dyke."

Caitlin tasted that morning's oatmeal at the back of her throat. Maybe if she projectile vomited, the conversation would end and everyone would forget about it. The stench of vomit would clear a room faster than Caitlin admitting she was gay even in this closeted school.

"You know what they say, Brice. People who have major problems with others being gay are usually gay themselves and too afraid to face it."

For the second time that year, and hopefully the last, Caitlin's class gasped and laughed at the expense of Brice Bradford. Caitlin wished she'd stopped this dead when she'd heard Brice's initial comment.

"Enough," Caitlin said firmly, glad her voice was still intact and not shaking like her hands. "That is enough."

She'd practically raced to Marcy's office after class ended, near tears and certain this would be the axe that murdered her stint at Vanderbilt. Marcy had been compassionate and reassuring; she'd suggested Caitlin schedule a meeting with Brice, his parents, and his guidance counselor as soon as possible in order to squash this issue. Caitlin had numbly followed the instructions, then spent the rest of her prep period sitting at her desk, staring out the window.

"I'm better now, thanks." Caitlin ran her hands through her dark hair, pushing it behind her ears. "And Valerie knows, so you don't have to be vague about it."

"I am literally going to punt that kid through the goal post," Valerie said through gritted teeth.

"Marcy, has anyone ever brought up starting a GSA here? I think that could help alleviate some of the, um, gay problems."

Valerie snickered. Marcy looked thoughtful. "No, I don't recall ever hearing about that. It's certainly something I can bring up at my next meeting with the principals."

"Just so you know, I'm not going to lie to my students. I'm only here for another seven months anyway, so if anyone has a problem with me being out, then…well, so be it."

"No! Don't talk about the impermanence of your time with us!" Valerie thrust her hand against her forehead. "I simply can't handle it." Her eyes widened and she turned to Marcy. "I know! Let's ditch Nicole and keep Caitlin!"

Marcy laughed and patted Valerie's knee. "I know that would make you very happy."

Staying at Vanderbilt wasn't something Caitlin had allowed herself to consider. Not yet, anyway. She knew there was a slim possibility that Nicole wouldn't come back from maternity leave, but even beyond that, acquiring this spot as a full-time position was out of Caitlin's control.

"Speaking of lesbians," Valerie started.

"Nicole's not a lesbian," Marcy said, confusion crinkling her eyebrows.

Valerie pointed at Caitlin. "No, this one's a lesbian."

"Well I know that, she just said she is!"

Caitlin and Valerie exchanged an amused look. "I saw your girl Walker out this weekend." Valerie whistled, low and slow. "She was with some hot little number."

There went that clenching in Caitlin's stomach again. "Good for her," she said lightly, turning to organize an already organized pile of vocabulary quizzes on the desk.

"They were having a very passionate encounter." Valerie's voice was far-away, as though she was reflecting so hard she'd transported herself back to the moment. "Not the sexy kind, though. Man, I have never seen two women argue like that. It seemed like her sexy friend was a little drunk, maybe, but Walker looked like she was ready to explode from pent-up anger."

*Interesting*, Caitlin thought. It seemed Mallory had already moved on from Becca to some "hot little number," sidestepping Caitlin on the way. Maybe that whole I-like-you-I'm-attracted-to-you thing had been in her head.

"I've gotta give you credit, Caitlin. Walker's a walking time bomb. I have no idea how you put up with her for almost an entire month."

"She's a great teacher," Caitlin said, her voice strong. "I have a lot of respect for her."

"Yeah but even the kids can't stand her!"

Marcy put a calming hand on Valerie's knee.

"That's not true. I've seen her interact with kids and they might be a little intimidated by her at times, but they respect her. And I can name several kids who clearly like her very much."

Valerie looked at Marcy, her barometer, and Marcy shook her head in response. "Okay. I'll drop it. But I swear to God, Caitlin, if she was mean to you last week, I'll–"

"She wasn't. We had a miscommunication and worked it out." It was one hell of a miscommunication, but Valerie and Marcy didn't need to know that. "We worked well together, and while I'll be glad to have my classes back to normal, I'm going to miss working so closely with Mallory. I learned a lot from her."

Caitlin's sincerity seemed to stun both Valerie and Marcy into silence. That or they were genuinely shocked that perhaps Mallory wasn't as bad as they thought she was.

Several minutes later, Caitlin had the room to herself once more. She double checked the set-up of the room, ensuring it was ready to go for tomorrow's presentations, then packed up her bag.

She couldn't help but notice that Mallory's classroom door was open. She pushed aside her desire to poke her head in and focused instead on locking her door. Just as Caitlin turned to walk down the hall, she heard Mallory call her name.

She was standing in the doorway of her classroom, a blank look on her face. She motioned Caitlin to come closer.

"I heard what you said."

*Fucking fantastic.* "Okay…" Caitlin trailed off.

"I wanted to thank you for defending me."

Caitlin snapped her head up to look at Mallory. "What are you talking about?"

She motioned toward Caitlin's classroom. "I was coming back from the office and heard Valerie. She's pretty loud, you know. I know she hates me, so I wasn't surprised to hear her questioning your ability to work with me."

Caitlin waited, not wanting to say too much. She had no idea how much Mallory had overheard.

Mallory cleared her throat. Her eyes were now more blue than black, Caitlin noticed. They held a look of embarrassed sincerity, a new emotion to add to Mallory's ever-evolving file.

"You didn't have to defend me, especially after our conversation last week. But you did."

"My feelings for you haven't changed, Mallory." Caitlin cringed and quickly put both hands up in front of her chest. "I didn't mean it that way. I respect you as a teacher and we did work well together, so I told the truth."

A beat of silence worked its way between them. Caitlin chewed the inside of her cheek, forcing herself to stay quiet.

"We did," Mallory agreed. "I'm happy we decided to do this unit together. And I'm looking forward to the presentations tomorrow."

"Me too, on both accounts."

"Great." Mallory hesitated. She flinch-smiled. Oh, wow. Caitlin hadn't realized how much she'd missed those flinch-smiles. "I'll see you tomorrow."

Caitlin smiled and nodded. When she was no more than five steps away, Mallory called her name once more. Caitlin turned and waited.

"For what it's worth, I'm really sorry about our miscommunication last week." Aha, so she'd heard more than Caitlin thought. Mallory's expression was still serious and— whoa—warm. Heated, almost. "Really sorry," she repeated, remorse evident in her tone.

"I am too," Caitlin said, then turned and left before she said something she'd regret in the morning.

# CHAPTER EIGHTEEN

Little changed over the next two weeks, much to Caitlin's disappointment. She and Mallory concluded their unit and received accolades from a couple administrators who stopped by to check out the kids' presentations. Mallory handled everything stoically, not breaking her controlled facade even when the administrator in charge of curriculum and instruction outright gushed about how much she loved what the two teachers had created together.

Now that they didn't have a unit to plan or fine tune, Caitlin and Mallory reverted back to casual greetings in the hallway between classes. It weighed on Caitlin, like losing an opportunity for something amazing but not even knowing if the opportunity had ever really existed. She didn't like having loose ends; in truth, the divorce from Becca should have happened earlier but Caitlin kept thinking things would change. She'd needed the entire disaster of their relationship neatly tied up before she was able to walk away.

Another disaster Caitlin was ready to walk away from was Brice Bradford. The thought and reality of facing another seven months with him brought her zero joy. It was Brice's bullshit, however, that got Caitlin a singular moment of heightened emotion with Mallory earlier in the week.

The meeting with Brice and his parents had gone better than expected. Caitlin was shocked when she discovered that his parents didn't appear to be raging homophobes who spread their antiquated views to their son. Quite the opposite—Brice's mother apologized profusely for her son's behavior in class, going as far as to note that her own brother was gay, and Brice was well aware of that. While Brice's father didn't say much, he did state that he was deeply disappointed in Brice. The student being debated stayed surprisingly quiet, speaking only to apologize to Caitlin.

Despite the meeting going well, Caitlin was still shaken up when she made her way back to her classroom afterward. She closed the door behind her, wanting privacy for her thoughts, and turned on a playlist stocked with songs that lifted her mood.

Not fifteen minutes after she returned, her door opened without a cursory knock. She whipped her head around to find Mallory stomping toward her. She looked like she was on a mission.

"You should have told me it was Brice."

Caitlin's head swam, trying to catch up. "How did you–"

"Why didn't you tell me?"

"Because it wasn't your battle to fight, Mallory," Caitlin said, recalling their conversation from a month ago. She also remembered the fire in Mallory's eyes, how quickly she'd jumped to protect Caitlin.

"I won't fight your fights." Her voice was firm but warm. "I wouldn't do that to you, Caitlin." She released her breath in a whoosh. "Brice told me what happened but conveniently neglected to identify his role in it. But I really wish you had told me it was him."

"What difference would that have made?"

Mallory shifted her gaze to the window. "I know his family. It's a long story, but I could have run interference."

"You just said you won't fight my fights."

"And I meant that." Mallory fidgeted with her lanyard as she brought her eyes back to Caitlin. "I *mean* that. I could have helped. That's all. I could have been there for you and made this easier for you to deal with."

Caitlin still wasn't sure how running interference with her student's family wasn't fighting her fight for her, but she was willing to let it go. After all, she'd been craving a human encounter with Mallory, and if Brice was the catalyst for it, so be it.

"I appreciate that. Really. But I didn't want anyone else involved in this. I had to deal with it on my own."

Mallory nodded, holding Caitlin's gaze. "I respect that. Just…just know that you don't have to deal with stuff like that on your own. If you don't want to, I mean."

Caitlin's brain continued to swim, doing its best to match this Mallory with the Mallory of several weeks ago. How could one person flip back and forth so dramatically, and about incredibly similar topics?

"You're listening to Taylor Swift," Mallory said softly.

Sure enough, Caitlin's playlist was in the Taylor zone. "I do like some of her songs," she admitted. "Maybe not quite to the extent that you do, but…"

Mallory smiled, a genuine one that filled her face with warmth. "It's kind of hard to out-fan me when it comes to Taylor. I'd let you win, though." Her expression switched off as fast as it had flipped on and she began edging toward the door. "Okay. I just wanted to tell you that. Right, so…see you tomorrow."

\* \* \*

"And you let her leave like that?"

Caitlin shot Lina a look that she hoped conveyed her utter annoyance. "Yes." In retelling the story of that interaction, Caitlin had to admit—to herself—that she wished she'd stopped Mallory from making her quick escape.

Lina tapped her fingers against her chin, a thoughtful look on her face. "That seems out of character for you, Cait."

A loud sigh escaped Caitlin's lips as she glared at Lina. She stretched her legs out down the sofa and gently poked her bare toes into Pepper's floof, satisfied when her sweet cat began purring immediately. "You may recall you're the one who told me to let it go. Let *her* go."

From her position on Caitlin's living room floor, fully stretched out with her arms cradling her neck, Lina emitted a noise that sounded like "ehhh."

"Lina Ragelis, I swear to God. You did!"

"I know. But I meant in the moment—you were obsessing over whether or not she was going to text you. And the whole part about her being involved with someone else, yeah. You need to back away from that. But! There's no reason why you can't be friends with her."

"In what world has being friends with someone you're interested in ever worked out?"

Lina laughed a little. "Fair point. I still think it's weird that you didn't pull a Caitlin on her."

"I'm sorry, what? Pull a Caitlin?"

Sitting up, Lina grinned at her. "Yeah. That's what I call it when you get all straight-forward and blunt with people. It's one of your best qualities, but it's also a little scary." She leaned forward and pulled open a drawer in the end table. "Do you have any floss?"

"First of all, I don't like that you have this term created. Secondly, why would I have floss in my living room? Normal people keep things like that in their bathrooms."

Caitlin tugged her hair out of a messy bun and ran her fingers through it, working out some knots. She readied herself for whatever verbal barb Lina was certain to lob back at her, but Lina had gone silent. Caitlin peered over Lina's shoulder and gasped, then scrambled to grab the picture frame from her hands.

"Give it to me now," she said through gritted teeth. The fight was no use, of course, as Caitlin's upper body strength wasn't even a contender for Lina's. Lina pulled the frame from Caitlin's wimpy grasp and scooted across the floor for a closer look.

After a moment of inspecting the picture, Lina looked sternly at Caitlin. "Why, and I cannot emphasize this enough, *the fuck* do you still have this picture?"

There were several lies Caitlin could whip out and try to convince Lina of, but it would be useless. "I, uh, think it's a good picture of me."

"Jesus Christ," Lina muttered before bursting into laughter. "How about you give it to me?"

"Oh no. I need a closer look at this."

The picture in question was burned into Caitlin's mind. It was from a couple years ago, before her marriage had totally gone to shit. Caitlin and Becca were arm in arm and Lina was standing next to them, trying to look cool next to Candice Barrows. It was the only time the four of them had done anything social together, and it had taken a lot of teeth-pulling on both sides to make it happen.

Caitlin watched Lina's features soften as she focused on herself and Barrows. If her math was correct, the picture had been taken during a much simpler time for them.

What Caitlin would never admit to Lina was that she'd kept this picture purposely because she thought she *and* Becca looked great in it. Individually and together. They were both tan, healthy-looking, and wore real smiles. Caitlin obviously found Becca attractive, but this picture made her remember that sometimes Becca looked downright hot. Her short strawberry blond hair was tousled and looked like she'd spent the day on the beach. Her green-blue eyes were aglow and nothing hateful lurked in her expression. This picture was better than any of their engagement or wedding photos combined.

"I think it's time to dispose of this," Lina said abruptly, jumping to her feet with the picture in hand. She strode to the kitchen and tossed it into the trash.

Caitlin, fumbling for her phone which had just vibrated, didn't put up a fight. She wasn't an idiot. She had a digital copy of the picture saved.

From the kitchen, Lina started blabbering on about something Army related, complaining about drill weekend or something like that. Caitlin couldn't hear her over the rush of thoughts in her head. She stared at the text in utter confusion with a side of unhealthy excitement.

*Hey. Are you busy?*

Four words had never brought Caitlin so much curiosity and excited wonder. She made no hesitation in responding with *Nope. What's up?*

She was sure Lina was still talking in the kitchen, but all Caitlin was listening for was the buzz of Mallory's response. When it came, she gawked at her phone. If she'd been confused before, that was nothing compared to what she felt now.

Lina flopped onto the sofa next to Caitlin and grabbed her phone from her hand. "What's this?"

"Great question. It appears to be an address."

"This is Mallory?"

Caitlin nodded, watching the three dots bubbling at the bottom of the screen.

*Meet me there at 3.*

Lina turned to Caitlin, her light brown eyes wide. "What kind of serial killer move is this?"

"She's not a serial killer." Caitlin took her phone back and responded that she'd see Mallory then and there. "It's probably something school-related."

"You want back up?"

"That's not necessary." Caitlin checked the time. "Also, go home. I have to get in the shower if I'm going to get there on time."

Lina stayed on the sofa as Caitlin headed for the stairs. "I don't like this, Cait. She's been blowing you off and sending mixed signals. Now she's telling you to jump–"

"And I'm asking how high." Caitlin paused on the landing and weighed Lina's statements. "I hear you. I do. Can you please trust me on this one?"

"You're not going to give me a choice, are you?"

Caitlin bounded upstairs, hoping that would suffice as her response.

# CHAPTER NINETEEN

"No reason to be nervous, kiddo," Caitlin said as she gave herself another once over in the mirror. Why Mallory had sent her to a Starbucks in Bordentown she had no idea, but she was early and thankful for the ability to steal a few moments with a mirror. The change in seasons had made itself known and Caitlin had happily hopped into her fall wardrobe. For this surprise and mysterious excursion, she'd decided on dark skinny jeans that had a couple rips in them, worn-in brown boots, and an oversized forest green sweater. The temperature was in the low 50s but there was a chilly breeze, so she'd thrown on a light but warm quilted vest.

Satisfied that her hair was perfect in that curated messy bun way, Caitlin left the bathroom and sat down at a table in front of a bank of windows. She checked her watch. Okay. Mallory should be here any moment. No problem at all.

The uncertainty of *which* Mallory would show up gnawed at Caitlin. Her gut instincts were pretty decent and she'd had a positive feeling about Mallory from the start, but she couldn't disregard some of their interactions. More accurately, it was the confusion from the interactions that left Caitlin most unsettled. Everyone was entitled to a couple bad days and poor social interactions, after all.

Mallory's entrance into the coffee shop coupled with Caitlin realizing she hadn't eaten since eight a.m. when her stomach rumbled uncomfortably. As she looked up at Mallory, she wasn't sure which feeling was dominating her belly: hunger or...well, *hunger*.

The dark blue jeans Mallory wore accentuated every curve of her long, toned legs. A peek of a red and grey flannel shirt hung below a form-fitting black jacket. But it wasn't the outfit, or even the body beneath it, that got Caitlin's emotions stirring.

The look on Mallory's face as she gazed down at Caitlin was one she had never seen before and truly never expected to see. Warmth radiated off Mallory, her cheeks rosy and a tentative smile on her face. Those inky, deep eyes were practically twinkling.

Caitlin took her time standing up, trying to get her bearings before turning face-to-face with this confounding and intoxicating woman.

"Thanks for meeting me here," Mallory said. "Would you like a warm drink? We're going to be outside for a while."

"Aha, so this random Starbucks isn't the final destination?"

Mallory laughed. It was a rare and gorgeous sound that Caitlin wanted to hear every day. "I do like my privacy, but if all I wanted was to buy you coffee, we could have done that a lot closer to home. Come on. Let's grab drinks."

Several minutes later, warm drinks in hand, Caitlin followed Mallory out into the cool fall air. Mallory had already asked her twice if she would be warm enough, pointing out that the little looping holes in Caitlin's sweater might let too much air in.

"If you get too cold, tell me. We can switch outerwear."

Caitlin bit her lip against her growing smile. This Mallory was freaking adorable. "I think I'll be okay but you'll be the first to know if I get a chill."

Satisfied, Mallory nodded and led the way down the street. They were in that golden fall period between Halloween and Thanksgiving and the quaint town had shown up with a harvest flair. Store fronts were decorated with garlands of leaves and cheeky pumpkins. A florist shop had a beautiful array of fall flowers practically hiding its entrance, creating a trellis archway that lured customers in. Caitlin remained clueless about where they were going but at least the scenery was pretty.

"I grew up around here," Mallory said, almost as an afterthought. "I've always had a thing for small towns."

"I was wondering if you were Jersey born and raised."

"Can't you tell by my obnoxious accent?"

Caitlin elbowed Mallory gently. "Takes one to know one. But for what it's worth, I don't think either one of us has a Jersey accent."

"That's because we sound normal to each other. Once we cross the border, we sound like the mafia."

"You say that with such conviction."

Mallory shrugged, a smile tugging at the corners of her mouth. "I went to college in Delaware. I wasn't there a full week before people started knocking on my dorm door, asking to hear my Jersey Shore accent."

"That fucking show," Caitlin mumbled. "Oh. Sorry about the cursing."

Mallory stopped in the middle of the sidewalk and turned to Caitlin. "Don't apologize. I like your filthy mouth—just not at school."

A blush lit like fire across Caitlin's cheeks as they resumed their stroll. She fought against the urge to catch Mallory's swinging hand in hers and squeeze it, then reminded herself to yell at Lina later. There was no way she could pull off casual friends with Mallory, not with an attraction this strong.

Caitlin cleared her throat. "So you grew up in a small town and it seems like you liked it. Tell me about your family."

Instantly, Mallory's posture stiffened. Her eyes trained forward as she responded. "Also small."

Detonate the bomb or sidestep it? They'd driven separately, so if this went poorly, Caitlin didn't have to suffer through an awkward drive home. She decided to cautiously detonate.

"How small? Small is such a connotative word."

The tension slipped from Mallory's frame. Caitlin practically felt her loosen up.

"Very small. It was just me and my dad. My mom died when I was about two years old, so I don't have many real memories of her. Only things my dad and grandparents have told me."

"Oh, Mallory. I had no idea. I'm so sorry."

"It's okay. It's just weird, you know? Losing someone so important at an age where you can't even understand what happened. I wish I could remember more of her but then I'd miss her more and hurt more and…maybe it's best that I was so young."

Caitlin took a small risk and moved closer. Their shoulders brushed together as they walked, and Caitlin pressed gently into Mallory. It was the lamest attempt at a hug she'd ever made, but until Mallory gave her a clear signal, it would have to do.

"I don't think it's easy to lose a parent at any age, regardless of memories."

"Yeah. That makes sense. My dad and I have a great relationship, though, so I've never felt alone."

Caitlin pictured the male version of Mallory and smiled to herself. She was willing to bet Mallory's dad was a total stud.

"Okay. We're here."

Mallory's slightly nervous voice kicked Caitlin out of her Mr. Walker imaginings. She looked up and squinted. They'd moved out of the downtown area and had ended up in a suburban part of town via a park they'd cut through to arrive at their destination. Caitlin had missed the plaque containing its name. Otherwise surrounded by houses, they were standing behind a statue, but nothing was clicking in Caitlin's head.

"I wanted to bring you here earlier, before we did the unit or even during it, but that didn't exactly work out."

Mallory looked expectantly at Caitlin who was doing her best to figure out what she was looking at. From this angle, it was a nicely sculpted butt. While Caitlin appreciated fine works of butt art, she knew there was more to this venture than a good metal ass. She stepped around to the front of the statute, took a harder look, and gasped delightedly.

"Are you serious? I had no idea this existed!"

Standing before Caitlin in all his metallic, sculpted glory was Thomas Paine. One foot was propped up on what appeared to be a pile of papers and he was leaning forward, gesturing as though he was always ready to disseminate a political message.

"I love it," Caitlin exclaimed. Then she paused, the self-doubt kicking in. Should she have known this statue existed within driving distance of both home and school?

"I almost told you about it when we were working on the unit, but I thought you'd prefer to see it in person," Mallory said, her voice warm and soft.

"I bet you bring your kids here every year," Caitlin said quickly, worried Mallory thought she was an idiot who had no idea how rich New Jersey was with historical content and statues.

Mallory's already rosy cheeks flushed even more. "No, actually. I've never been here before. I, uh, know how much you like Thomas Paine so I thought it would be cool if I brought you here. So we could both see it. Together."

Maybe this was her opening? Caitlin studied Mallory, who was avoiding eye contact, wondering if she could finally kiss her. But no—she wasn't doing a damn thing until Mallory stated she was single and wanted Caitlin to kiss her.

"I love that. Thank you."

"Really? This isn't too nerdy?"

Caitlin squeezed Mallory's arm. "It is so nerdy and that's what makes it so perfect."

Pure elation spread over Mallory's pretty face as she met Caitlin's eyes. "Thank you for trusting me with a random address in a text. Especially when we haven't been talking as much lately."

Caitlin sidestepped that little bomb as she took a couple pictures of the statue, including one of Mallory posing next to it. Mallory then insisted Caitlin do the same. On a whim, Caitlin suggested they use the self-timer to take a couple shots together with Thomas Paine. She was surprised and overly happy when Mallory enthusiastically agreed. It was a good excuse to put their arms around each other, too. Caitlin couldn't help but to notice how good it felt to be that close.

Satisfied with their pictures, they stood in front of the statue, each wondering what happened next. Caitlin was nearing starvation and was about to ask Mallory to join her for an early dinner when Mallory spoke up.

"I've missed talking with you."

"That is a very mutual feeling, Walker."

Mallory scuffed the toe of her shoe against the sidewalk. "I don't want you to take this the wrong way, but you are the only person in that school that I feel like I connect with."

"How would I take that the wrong way? That's a nice thing to say."

"I don't want it to make you think that's the only reason I like you."

*Oh, okay. Back to the I Like You stuff.* Caitlin channeled as much patience and boldness as she could. "Are we going down the mixed signals path again?"

"We are not." Mallory shook her head for emphasis. "I would like to go down a very different path with you."

Caitlin felt her move before she saw it out of the corner of her eye. Mallory reached over and grabbed both of Caitlin's hands with a gentleness that made her stomach whirl. Face-to-face, they looked at each other openly and curiously.

"I've also missed having made up reasons to look into your beautiful multicolored eyes," Mallory said.

"Did you know Alexander the Great is rumored to have had heterochromia, too?" Caitlin blurted out.

If Mallory was shocked or put off by her ridiculous nervous outburst, Caitlin would never know. She watched as a slow grin moved across Mallory's face then disappeared into a look burning with intensity.

Caitlin would replay the moment over and over again, and she would never know for certain who leaned in first. She liked to think they moved in synchrony; however it happened, their lips pressed together with the coupled feeling of deep arousal and the sensation of coming home.

Moments into the absolute best kiss of her life, Caitlin's brain lit up and she pulled away.

"Wait. Wait." Caitlin pushed Mallory away with the utmost tenderness. "You're seeing someone. I won't be this person."

Mallory shook her head and pushed an escaped strand of Caitlin's hair behind her ear. "And I told you I don't do mixed signals. I'm not seeing her anymore. It's done."

Could it be that simple? Caitlin searched Mallory's eyes for more information but came up empty. That kiss, quick as it was, felt far too good to abandon. She'd have to trust Mallory.

"Promise?"

"I promise, Caitlin." Mallory took a deep breath. "I cannot and will not push away my feelings for you any longer."

"So you really like me, huh?"

Mallory grinned. "You could say that." She leaned in and kissed Caitlin, her tongue swiping at Caitlin's bottom lip. Passion inflamed their already heated kiss and there before the Thomas Paine statute, Mallory and Caitlin made out like they'd been deprived of kissing since 1776.

As the kiss slowed, Caitlin started to giggle. She took a small step back and gestured toward their voyeur. "But Mallory. What would Thomas Paine think?"

Mallory leaned in and brushed her lips against Caitlin's, a teasing promise of more to come. "I think he'd be into this."

# CHAPTER TWENTY

Kissing was good. Kissing was *amazing*. Somehow, in the time since the beginning of her marriage's deterioration and the final nail slamming into its coffin, Caitlin had forgotten how unbelievable it was to kiss someone she was madly attracted to—both physically and intellectually. Emotionally, too, but Caitlin wasn't quite ready to go there.

With Mallory Walker's lips meeting hers on a regular but not-quite-enough schedule, Caitlin vowed never to forget how wonderful kissing was.

It turned out that Mallory was a busy person. Caitlin already knew how devoted she was to her teaching duties, which expanded beyond the classroom after three p.m., but she was learning how devoted she also was to her father. They had dinner together at least three times a week, and since Mallory kept herself on a strict sleeping regimen, that didn't leave much time for her to hang out with Caitlin outside of school.

Add to that the fact that winter sports season had arrived. As the assistant girls' basketball coach, Mallory's responsibilities didn't seem to be that much less than the head coach's. At the approach of Thanksgiving break, Mallory was the one running most practices. Caitlin admired her dedication to the team but also wondered if Mallory wasn't getting the short end of the stick. The head coach didn't seem all too interested and often deferred to Mallory. Because Mallory seemed fine with this, only sharing information and not complaining about it, Caitlin decided to keep her opinions to herself.

Weekends weren't much better. Vanderbilt apparently had a very good girls' basketball team and weekend morning practices were common. It was turning out to be the worst possible time to strike up a romance with a basketball coach, Caitlin realized. She wasn't going to let that stop her, and neither was Mallory, who did her best to cut out little blocks of time for them to be together. Unfortunately, most of that time was spent grading, talking about school, or talking about basketball (which, for the secret record, Caitlin was getting crash courses on from Lina). When those topics were exhausted, they spent their time learning about each other.

On the positive side, when all that working and talking was complete, the kissing entered the room and stayed until they had to part ways. And Caitlin really, truly loved the kissing.

* * *

As Thanksgiving break arrived, Caitlin was more than ready for a much-needed six-day vacation from school. Her grading was caught up and she was in the middle of a unit, so she had zero school work to do. She was hopeful that she'd get some quality Mallory time but also realistic: there were two basketball tournaments on her coaching agenda, with a possible third if a transportation issue got resolved.

Lina, best friend that she was, had already offered to go to one of the tournaments with Caitlin, but Caitlin was hesitant to accept the offer. Lina's presence wasn't the issue—it was Caitlin not knowing if she and Mallory were officially together, and regardless if they were, would Mallory even want her there?

"You're being stupid," Lina said through a mouthful of pizza. "Why don't you ask her if she'd like you to be there?"

"Ehh." Caitlin stared down the pizza box, daring it to suggest she stop at two pieces. "She didn't say anything about today's tournament, so I'm thinking she won't mention tomorrow's either."

"My point exactly. You need to bring it up."

Caitlin kicked her feet against the stool in Lina's kitchen. They were carbing up for Caitlin's big 5k tomorrow. Well, Caitlin was doing it for the 5k; Lina claimed to be doing it for moral support but really she just loved pizza.

"How was Thanksgiving?"

"Smooth subject change," Lina grumbled. "You know how it was. Same old shit. Everyone played nice but no one could wait for me to leave."

"You should have come to my parents' house like I *and* my mother suggested."

"And you know that would have been even worse for me." Lina was right. Her family would have given her hell for not coming to their hosted event even if they acted like they didn't want her there. "You ready for tomorrow?"

"I think so. I mean, I better be."

"You'll be great. Do me a favor and kick your loser brother's ass."

"You can literally kick his ass if you'd like. He and Jenna are picking me up so we can ride together."

Lina gaped at Caitlin. Half-chewed pizza sat between her teeth. Caitlin reached over and pushed Lina's jaw shut.

"And we wonder why you're single."

Chewing and swallowing complete, Lina retorted. "I'm not technically single and furthermore, who is this woman who has stayed with your brother for more than a week?"

"Excuse me? Not technically single?"

Lina pointed to the clock. "Jesus Christ, would you look at the time! You need to get your rest! Big day tomorrow!"

She grabbed Caitlin up from her stool and pushed her toward the door.

"I'll bill you for the pizza. Good night! Sleep tight!"

Caitlin tried to fight off Lina and yelled at her the whole way to the door, but it was no use. She found herself standing on Lina's front porch listening to Lina lock the door as she yelled out another "Good night and good luck!"

Why she chose to be best friends with such a bizarre, secretive human being, Caitlin would never know.

Saturday morning dawned bright and chilly. It was great running weather in the sense that it wasn't windy and it definitely wasn't hot, but Caitlin wouldn't have minded if the temperature rose a few notches. She bounced on the balls of her feet, trying to keep her blood moving. Jenna and Miles were beside her, engaged in an elaborate stretching routine. Caitlin had nearly gagged when she'd gotten into the car earlier and found that Miles had color-coordinated with Jenna. Their matching lime green long-sleeved Under Armour Coldgear shirts were blinding. It was cute but super gross, and Caitlin couldn't wait to mock her brother when Jenna wasn't around.

"Might wanna stretch those hamstrings, big sis," Miles said from his bent over position. "We wouldn't want you to cramp up mid-race and have to quit."

"I'm not a quitter, *little bro*, and you know it." Caitlin casually moved her right foot over her left foot and gave her brother the satisfaction of stretching—but just a little bit.

"Caitlin, Miles told me this is your first race. Are you excited?"

Caitlin shrugged, fiddling with the sleeves of her shirt. "I guess so. It's something I set out to do when I started running. I'm not fast, so I'm not angling for a big win. I just want to do it."

Jenna started to say something else, but Miles cut her off like the proper asshole he was. "Now that you've lost like a hundred pounds, this should be no sweat."

A swift punch to the ribs caught her brother off-guard and he swore. Jenna stifled a giggle then tried to look compassionate for Miles's sake.

"What I was *going* to say, Caitlin, is I think it's awesome that you got into running. The satisfaction of completing any race feels amazing and I'm excited you're going to experience that today!"

Jenna may have continued, but her words disappeared into the melee surrounding them as Caitlin was officially distracted by a familiar, sexy, athletic body moving in her direction. She shook her head, feeling both excited and confused.

"What are you doing here?" They spoke in sync, matching happily perplexed looks on their faces.

"I thought you had a tournament," Caitlin added.

"That's tomorrow." Mallory cocked her head. "I thought you were doing that shopping thing with your mom."

"That was yesterday."

They grinned at each other, amazed at how wrong they'd both been. Nerves started shooting through Caitlin's body as reality set in. She was *not* ready for Mallory to witness her lack of athletic ability, even though she considered herself a decent runner. *Please don't suggest we run together*, Caitlin thought anxiously.

"My girls are here," Mallory said, gesturing behind her. "We always do this race between tournament days to keep them moving."

Great! Not just Mallory, but also a handful of Vanderbilt students! They were all here to witness Caitlin's racing debut. This day could not get any better. SO GREAT.

"Oh, wow, that's a good idea." Caitlin stumbled over her words, nerves getting the best of her. "I bet you're the pace keeper for them."

"No, Hailey's taking the lead today. They're way up with the seven-minute pacing group. This may shock you, but I'm not the fastest runner." Mallory peered behind Caitlin, where Miles and Jenna were not hiding their eavesdropping. "Hi," she said with a wave. "I'm Mallory."

"Oh fuck," Caitlin said under her breath. She liked Mallory too much for her to be exposed to Miles at this point. But here they were.

"That's my brother Miles and his girlfriend Jenna. Guys, this is Mallory. We…we work together."

If Mallory was fazed by that awkward introduction, she didn't show it. "It's nice to meet you both. Mind if I steal Caitlin away for a minute?"

"Feel free to keep her forever," Miles called after them as they walked a few feet away. Caitlin flipped him off.

"He seems lovely," Mallory remarked.

"A true gentleman. I'm shocked to see you."

"A good shock, I hope?"

Mostly, yes. But beneath that, Caitlin was muddling through her nervousness. She did not feel sexy while running, nor was she sexy after completing a run. She wanted Mallory to appreciate what sexiness she did have, and was worried that would be stomped on if they ran anywhere near each other during this race.

"Absolutely," Caitlin said. "But, um, you *are* going to run with the team, right?"

Confusion wrinkled Mallory's features. "I usually do, but I told them I'm not running seven-minute miles so…did you want to run together?"

"Not really!" Caitlin blurted. "I'm what you'd call a lone wolf when it comes to running. You should definitely run with the girls or, you know, with whatever pacing group you prefer."

"I can't interest you in a little friendly competition?" Caitlin watched Mallory's eyes light up with her suggestion, an alluring smirk spreading across her lips.

Around them, people began streaming toward the start line and falling into place at their pacing marks. Caitlin eyed the group standing at the 10:30 pacer sign and flicked her eyes back to Mallory. She was not a quitter, nor could she turn down a competition.

"Fine. Let's do this."

Mallory extended her arm. "Lead the way."

Begrudgingly, but not wanting to put herself in a pacing situation she couldn't handle, Caitlin walked over to the 10:30 group. This was a comfortable pace for her, and though Lina had warned her that she'd probably run faster than normal, something about the energy of running with a lot of people, Caitlin wasn't here to impress Mallory by strolling to the 9:00 group or even the 10:00 group.

Suddenly worried she was going to make an ass out of herself, Caitlin clammed up as she listened to Mallory chatter about yesterday's basketball tournament. In the middle of a description of a spectacular three-pointer made by a freshman on the varsity team, Caitlin interrupted.

"Is this, like, foreplay for you?"

Mallory's mouth froze in a gape. "Wha-what? Talking about basketball?"

"No," Caitlin gestured around them. "This. Racing. A friendly competition."

Her features softened and she moved closer to Caitlin, their faces inches apart. Caitlin felt the buzzing energy between them and put her hand over her mouth to stop herself from kissing Mallory.

"Maybe. I guess you'll find out." Mallory winked at her and moved so that they were standing next to each other with their shoulders pressed firmly together. As Caitlin tried to bat down the increasing sexual buzzing, she felt a soft brush of fingers against her butt.

She gawked at Mallory, lips still secured behind her hand. "Did you just touch my butt? Here? In front of all of these people?"

"What? Oh, you had some dust on your pants," she said, her voice low and her lips dangerously close to Caitlin's. "Are your shoes tied tight? You might want to bend over and check them."

Caitlin turned slightly and pressed her hand against Mallory's stomach. "If you're trying to distract me, it's not going to work."

Mallory laughed and touched Caitlin's hand. "I want you to be safe. That's all."

"Likely story."

Before Mallory could respond, the national anthem began playing. Caitlin resumed her bouncing, readying her body for the task awaiting it.

Moments later, the shot went off and the crowd slowly surged ahead. Caitlin was expecting a mad dash to begin. Instead, being in one of the later pacing groups, they walked as a clump until they hit the start line and then finally began running.

Not twenty steps in, Mallory started talking about the weather.

"Nope." Caitlin thrust a hand in Mallory's direction. "I don't talk and run. You're on your own for conversation, Walker."

"As you wish. See you at the finish line, hot stuff."

With that, Mallory picked up her stride and waved to Caitlin as she propelled past her. Caitlin shook her head and pressed on. She enjoyed her quiet solitude as her feet pounded the streets, checking her watch every so often to track her pace. Lina was right—she was running faster than she normally did, but she felt good and went with it.

Around mile two, Caitlin found Mallory in the pack. She was a bit winded but looked to be putting up a good fight.

"Pushed a little too hard there, huh?"

Mallory huffed. "Thought you didn't talk and run."

"I don't. See you at the finish line, sexy."

She had no desire to show off, so Caitlin didn't zoom past Mallory. She kept her pace and focused on the ground beneath her. It wasn't until she hit mile three that she realized Mallory was nowhere around her.

Crossing the finish line was a moment of pure satisfaction for Caitlin. Not only had she run her first 5k, but she'd also come in a solid two minutes faster than she'd expected. She grabbed a bottle of water from a volunteer and scanned the crowd for her brother and Mallory. Miles and Jenna should be easy to spot in that horrific, matching lime green set, but Caitlin couldn't see them. She was certain they'd finished well before her. Not seeing Mallory either, Caitlin sent Miles a quick text.

"You're probably wishing we'd made a bet." Mallory appeared suddenly, flushed and sweaty but smiling.

"I am, and I'm also wishing my brother wasn't such an idiot." Caitlin stabbed at her phone as she replied to Miles's text.

"What's wrong?"

"He left. He drove me here, and he left."

Mallory shook out her hair before retying her ponytail. "Why would he do that?"

Caitlin scoffed and pushed her phone back into the pocket of her running tights. "He claims he heard you say you'd take me home." Realizing how presumptuous that may sound, Caitlin quickly backtracked. "But it's fine. I can have my mom come get me." She winced. Yes, because she was fifteen years old.

"I'll take you home. It's no problem."

"But I'm so…" Caitlin waved her hands down the length of her body.

"Beautiful? Yes you are, even when you're soaked in sweat." Mallory bit her lower lip. "Let's get out of here."

# CHAPTER TWENTY-ONE

For two people who loved talking and verbally poking at each other, one more stoically than the other, the car ride home from the race was oddly quiet. When they'd gotten into Mallory's sensibly gay Subaru Outback, Caitlin had burst out laughing as Taylor Swift predictably blasted from the speakers as soon as Mallory turned the key. She'd earned a withering glare for her laughter, and Mallory had swiftly changed the music to a playlist of jam bands. That surprised Caitlin into silence, and after entering her address into the navigation system, she tried to get comfortable and not drip her sweat all over Mallory's pristine car.

When the navigation informed them that their destination was ahead on the left, Caitlin watched as Mallory's body language shifted. She started toying with her ponytail, then tapped her fingers on the steering wheel before absently scratching at the same spot on her chin for ten full seconds. Not once did she look over at her passenger, but instead kept her eyes trained on the road before her. She cleared her throat a few times, increasingly so as the calculated distance ticked downward and Caitlin's house neared, but no words came.

When Mallory pulled into the driveway, Caitlin felt a rush of excited uncertainty. She half expected Mallory to have a reason to leave immediately, but was hoping she could convince her to come inside for at least a little kissing before she had to leave, probably to see her dad.

"Would you like to come in for a glass of water?"

Mallory looked pointedly at the half-full bottle of water in the console between them. *Of course. Smooth, Caitlin. Real smooth.*

"How about coffee? Tea? Or a replenishing sports drink to refill your electrolytes?"

That won her a smile. "Actually, I…"

"Right, of course. I'm sure you have to go." Caitlin yanked on the door handle.

"Stop," Mallory said quietly. Caitlin stilled.

"I have a change of clothes. How about we shower and go get brunch?"

Thoughts of being naked and wet in the shower with Mallory sent Caitlin's racing heart into overdrive. Yes, she liked this plan.

After they walked inside, Caitlin talked herself out of propositioning shower sex—surely that wasn't what Mallory had meant by "how about we shower"—and led Mallory upstairs to the guest room, which had direct access to the hallway bathroom. With a parting smile, Mallory disappeared into the bathroom and closed the door behind her. Caitlin stood for a moment, weighing the option of barging into the bathroom and slipping into the shower with her.

"Be cool," she whispered and headed to her own bedroom and bathroom. Their attraction was palpable, and Caitlin had reached a point of believing that it was mutual, but she wasn't yet convinced that Mallory wasn't going to run again. If that meant she had to wait for sex, then so be it. She could wait. Patience was her favorite waiting game.

Once she was in the shower, lathering up her own curvy body with her own dumb hands, standing alone under the hot spray and imagining Mallory's soft and sturdy hands sliding down her sides and pulling her in before pushing her up against the tiled wall—only then did Caitlin realize that patience was stupid and waiting was even stupider.

She grumbled as she searched her closet for her favorite pair of jeans. She swore they were right there at the top of the pile… until she remembered that they were in fact freshly washed and folded on top of the dryer. Which was down the hall. Next to the guest bedroom.

Pulling her towel tighter around her damp body, Caitlin slowly opened her bedroom door. She stuck her head into the hallway and, confident that the coast was clear, tiptoed down to the closet that held her washer and dryer. She eased open the perennially squeaky door and grabbed her jeans. She whipped around as she closed the door and felt a fresh burst of cool air hit her skin. *All* of her skin. She spun back to the closet doors. There hung her towel, clasped between the squeaky door and the door that had been stuck since she bought the place.

"Fuck!" Much louder than she'd intended, the word burst from Caitlin's mouth as she scrambled to retrieve her towel.

"You and that dirty mouth." Mallory's voice, thick with a new emotion, came from the doorway next to the offending laundry closet. Caitlin froze, forgetting her towel. She felt Mallory's stare land on her, felt it travel and linger. Caitlin expected to feel exposed, maybe even uncomfortable, but she felt like a fucking goddess under that gaze. She half-heartedly held her jeans up in front of her but it was too late. Mallory had seen it all.

"This is an unfair advantage," Caitlin managed.

"It is. We should level the playing field." Mallory leaned in the doorway, fully dressed with a smug look on her face.

Caitlin arranged the jeans against her naked body, doing her best to cover up the good parts. She ended up with a leg of her pants tucked between her thighs.

"Don't do that."

She looked down. "Do what?"

"Don't cover yourself up."

"Fine." Caitlin dropped the jeans and put her hands on her hips. "Then level the playing field, Walker."

The corner of Mallory's mouth rose into a half-smile. "Come here," she said. "I want you to do it for me."

Caitlin leaned forward, grabbed Mallory's hand, and pulled her back down the hallway into her bedroom. She pressed Mallory against the shut door and kissed her hard. Mallory's hands wasted no time in drifting to Caitlin's naked body, stroking her skin gently before pressing her fingertips into her hips. She tugged Caitlin's hips and a breath escaped from Caitlin's mouth as their hips pressed together, a pulsing vibration throbbing between them.

"The clothes," Caitlin whispered between kisses. Mallory relaxed enough for Caitlin to quickly strip her. Skin to skin, they stood before each other with nothing left to hide.

Mallory walked Caitlin backward to the bed. She gently eased her down before lying next to her, a guiding hand on Caitlin's hip turning her to face Mallory as they lay side by side. Mallory's lips captured Caitlin's in a searing kiss, her teeth nipping Caitlin's upper lip before her tongue danced against her lower lip. With a soft moan, Caitlin opened her mouth so their kiss could deepen.

The gentleness of Mallory's touch was surprising. She slid her hand from Caitlin's clavicle to her breast, slowly circling her nipple before gently rolling it between her thumb and finger. Caitlin arched into Mallory, sliding her leg between Mallory's thighs. Her shower fantasy had done half the work, and now she was combustible from Mallory's actual touches.

In a swift motion, Mallory pushed Caitlin onto her back and hovered above her. "You're not in charge right now," she said with that lustful smile. Her mouth dropped to Caitlin's breast, taking her nipple captive.

Caitlin gasped, relishing the sucking and biting. She reached up and cupped Mallory's small, firm breasts in her hands and stroked her thumbs over both nipples. Mallory increased her biting, drawing a guttural groan from Caitlin. The sensation shot an electric current from Caitlin's nipple directly to her clit, which was nearly throbbing with arousal.

"Please fuck me," Caitlin whispered. She couldn't stand how wet she was, and the fact that after all this kissing and touching, Mallory's hands had yet to venture down her body.

Mallory drew her head up slightly to look evenly at Caitlin. "I like it when you beg."

She dropped her mouth back to Caitlin's breasts, lavishing them with attention. Her hand began a tantalizingly slow descent to Caitlin's vagina. Fingers swirled against her inner thighs, dipping just enough into the folds of Caitlin's arousal to drag her wetness back over her quivering thighs. When Mallory's finger slid the tiniest bit inside of Caitlin, her body jumped and Caitlin nearly grabbed Mallory's hand and pushed more fingers inside. She was dying for this woman's touch, dying for the release that would come from it—dying for Mallory to give her that release.

After a long, passionate kiss, Mallory slid down the length of Caitlin's body, kissing, licking, and nipping along the way. "Your body is amazing," she said reverently, her hands following the path of her lips. "Absolutely gorgeous."

Caitlin watched Mallory's descent under hooded eyes. She'd been so overcome by her own arousal that she hadn't been able to fully admire Mallory's body yet.

Thoughts of that sexy body were eclipsed as Mallory's tongue began a torturously slow stroke against Caitlin's clit. Sparks exploded behind Caitlin's closed eyes. Every lick and stroke sent her body into another quiver. Mallory's mouth felt amazing, and Caitlin wanted nothing more than to keep it there for hours, but it had been so long and it felt so damn good. She knew she wasn't going to hold out for very long.

As her tongue stroked from side to side over Caitlin's hard clit, Mallory slid a single finger into Caitlin, who gasped as her muscles contracted and her body began to shake.

"Fuck! Oh fuck, Mallory." Caitlin felt her muscles tense further, then stilled, and she exploded into orgasm, clutching the sheets in her fists as Mallory's tongue pressed against her clit. "Holy shit," she breathed, riding out every last bit of her incredible release.

"You're sexy when you come," Mallory said, not moving from her position between Caitlin's thighs.

"Oh, now you like my dirty mouth." Caitlin took a deep breath, trying to ground herself.

"I've always liked your dirty mouth, but never as much as I do right now."

Aroused energy flooded through Caitlin as she sat up and grabbed for Mallory. Moments into another fiery kiss, Mallory pulled away.

"I thought you wanted me to fuck you," she said, a devious glimmer in her eyes.

"You had your chance, Walker. This is my time now."

To Caitlin's surprise, Mallory acquiesced and allowed her to nudge her back onto the bed without a challenge. When Caitlin's hand dropped below Mallory's taut stomach, she realized why there'd been no fight.

"Holy shit, you're soaking wet," Caitlin breathed in wonder. Her fingers were instantly covered with Mallory's slick arousal. It was the sexiest thing she'd ever experienced.

"It's what you do to me," Mallory said softly.

Still, Caitlin took her time. She lavished Mallory's breasts with kisses and sucking bites. She trailed her tongue over Mallory's stomach, taking a moment to gaze back up at Mallory as she lay on the bed. Her eyes were following Caitlin's every movement, their dark blue hue shining powerfully. Her mouth was slightly open, and her cheeks were flushed the sweetest shade of pink.

Caitlin swallowed hard as some choice words sprung up from deep inside of her.

She focused then on her tongue and lips as they moved across the innermost part of Mallory's tight thighs. With each trail of her mouth, she eased closer to Mallory's vagina, the scent of her arousal luring Caitlin even closer. Finally she allowed her tongue to slide across the outermost edge of Mallory's wetness, drawing a sharp gasp from her.

Caitlin pulled back and knelt before this beautiful woman, tucked neatly between her legs. She shifted so she was straddling a thigh before easing two fingers into Mallory. The gasp was louder this time, and Mallory's back arched immediately. Caitlin found a rhythm that Mallory's body rapidly responded to, flicking her fingers up just enough to hit Mallory's core. Her groans came faster and louder, she somehow became even more wet, and Caitlin slid a third finger in as Mallory opened up to her.

"Oh God, Caitlin, please."

Caitlin increased both the pressure and speed of her fingers, pushing Mallory closer and closer to orgasm. Her ecstatic cries arrived with the tensing of her body, the orgasm taking her hard and fast. Caitlin rode the wave with her fingers still inside, the little pulses slowing as Mallory's body relaxed, before she moved back up the bed.

"You're fucking incredible," Mallory said, her mouth buried in Caitlin's damp hair.

"I can't believe you just said fuck."

"I'm not a prude, Caitlin."

"I think that's fairly obvious." Caitlin smiled and kissed Mallory, pushing all of her stored-up emotions into that kiss, hoping Mallory would feel them too.

A bit later, aglow from all the kissing and sex, Caitlin propped herself up on one elbow and looked down at Mallory. She'd never seen her look so peaceful. That post-orgasm glow really enhanced her already beautiful features.

"I have a question."

"Lay it on me."

"Why the hell do you have a random change of clothes in your car?"

Mallory laughed and ran a finger down the side of Caitlin's face. "It's my go-bag."

"Explain."

"I always have it: a change of clothes, toiletries, bottle of water, granola bar. It's like an emergency bag."

"For all your random hook-up sleepovers?"

"You know that's not who I am, Caitlin."

Mallory pulled Caitlin down and kissed her, soft and slow.

Caitlin pulled away, needing to be sure. "So I'm not random? Or a once and done?"

Those bottomless eyes turned darker and more serious. "Never think that. You are so much more than that to me."

Questions and words died out on Caitlin's lips at the sound of a disgruntled thump against her bedroom door.

Mallory startled, sitting up and grabbing the sheets against her naked body. "What the hell was that?"

Caitlin was already at the door. "Just my cat." She opened the door, and Pepper bounded in, meowing loudly and fairly pissed off at having been excluded from this love-fest.

The gasp that flew from Mallory's mouth was Oscar-worthy. She followed it up by clamping her hand over her mouth, trying to keep the laughter inside.

"I'm sorry, is something funny?" Caitlin stood with her hands on her hips, trying to pull off anger in her state of sex-glow nakedness.

"Your cat," Mallory mumbled, her hand still over her mouth. "It's quite…large."

"First of all, my cat is a *she*, and her name is Pepper." Caitlin tapped her foot as Pepper wound through her legs, still mewing pathetically. "And secondly, she is perfectly sized, thank you very much."

As if to prove her owner's point, Pepper shimmy-shook her rear until the jumping power centered in her back haunches. She then jumped with all her might onto the bed, landing directly next to Mallory.

"Caitlin, the bed is tipping."

"Oh my God! She can hear you!"

Pepper sniffed Mallory, her dainty paws carefully prodding the sheets that Mallory still had pulled up tight.

"You don't have to be afraid of her, Mallory. She's a sweet girl." Caitlin sat down on the edge of the bed, giving Pepper reassuring pets.

"She's just so…"

"Careful." Caitlin glared at Mallory. "I am the only person who is allowed to comment on her voluptuous nature."

"Pretty," Mallory finished, giving Caitlin a winning smile. "Such a pretty girl, that Pepper."

Caitlin rewarded Mallory with a kiss. "That's better."

Mallory grabbed Caitlin's forearms, letting the sheets slip back down, not letting the kiss end. "Does Pepper have a hobby she can entertain herself with? In another room, perhaps? I'm not done with you."

"Many hobbies, yes." Caitlin ushered Pepper out of the room, cooing loving words as she shut the door behind her rotund, protesting, furry body. Cat removed, she made her way back to the bed, trying her damndest not to sprint back into Mallory's arms.

# CHAPTER TWENTY-TWO

A soft, persistent ache in Caitlin's thighs woke her the next morning. As she eased into a waking state, she realized her left arm was tingling and nearly dead asleep. A moment of panic rose inside of her—did Pepper sneak in again and sleep on her arm?—until she felt a brush of hair near her wrist and the warm breath of a human, not a cat, blowing gently across her forearm.

Mallory was sprawled out, taking up most of the queen-sized bed, with the majority of her upper body weight thrown over Caitlin's arm. She also had a tight hold on Caitlin's left hand, grasping it between both of her own. Her butt was smushed up against Caitlin's stomach, and she was fast asleep.

Caitlin took advantage of the opportunity and let her gaze travel the length of Mallory's body. It was just as perfect as she'd imagined it would be. Mallory's muscles were nicely toned without being bulky, especially her thighs and calves. Those incredible legs were topped with an even more amazing tight ass. Her skin was satin-soft and pale, almost giving the impression that it rarely saw the sun, unlike Caitlin's skin, which had permanent tan lines. Mallory was by no means curvy, but her hips carried the subtlest pop of femininity.

Unsatisfied with simply looking, Caitlin let her fingers glide down Mallory's side, slipping into the tiny dip between her waist and hips. Mallory didn't stir, so Caitlin resumed her travels, shifting slightly so she could spread her fingers over Mallory's ass, cupping the side of it with a bit more force than she'd intended. She'd never considered herself an ass-person before, but Mallory's butt was impossible not to touch.

A barely audible moan escaped from Mallory's mouth. She remained still as Caitlin continued exploring her naked body, moving her fingers down those sculpted thighs. After smoothing over Mallory's taut hamstrings, Caitlin stroked the delicate skin behind her knees, then eased her hand between slightly parted thighs. Stroking upward with the slowest movements she could muster, Caitlin moved closer to the spot she was dying to touch again—because several times the previous day and night somehow hadn't been enough.

Mallory let loose a louder moan as Caitlin's fingers found her wetness. She was beginning to think Mallory was always ready to go, and it was the hottest thing Caitlin had ever experienced in bed. Unable to resist this beautiful body and the amazing human it belonged to any longer, Caitlin moved down the bed and gently pressed Mallory's legs apart before settling between her damp thighs.

"Is this how you say good morning?" Her voice was sleepy and sweet but layered with desire.

"Mm-hmm" was all Caitlin was willing to say, as her tongue was already circling Mallory's hardening clit. She wasted no time, knowing Mallory was going to soon realize what time it was and bolt from the bed. Her tongue moved quickly, forcefully; her fingers dug into Mallory's outer thighs, holding her open. Mallory writhed, bucking against Caitlin's mouth. She gasped as her orgasm started, elbows digging into the tangled sheets. Caitlin held on as Mallory's body shook and trembled.

"My God," Mallory mumbled, reaching for Caitlin as she scooted back to the top of the bed and wrapped her arms around

Mallory's still-quivering body. "I didn't think I had anything left after yesterday, but that was intense."

"I may have done things a little differently than I did last night because I know you're in a time crunch."

"A time crunch? Did I promise you breakfast in the haze of incredible sex?"

Caitlin leaned over and angled the clock so it faced them. "Not exactly…more like you have a tournament to get to?"

Instantly Mallory tensed and shot up, knocking Caitlin to the side. She apologized profusely but Caitlin waved her off.

"Go get in the shower. I'll make you a quick breakfast to go–"

"Caitlin, I can't. I don't have any of my coaching gear with me." Mallory jumped out of bed and frantically pulled on her clothes. "Oh my God, I am *never* this irresponsible."

A pit of worry began expanding in Caitlin's gut. It must have shown on her face because Mallory rushed back to the bed and kissed her hard.

"I am so happy your idiot brother stranded you at the race. The last twenty hours have been amazing, and believe me, I do not want to leave this room right now." Mallory cupped Caitlin's face. "I hate to leave like this, sweetheart. But I really do have to go."

"It's okay." Caitlin flushed at the unexpected term of endearment as she yanked on sweatpants and a T-shirt so she could walk Mallory to the front door without scaring her neighbors with her nudity. "I understand and I'm not upset. A little disappointed that you have to leave, but I get it. I promise."

Mallory smiled warmly and took Caitlin's hand in hers. She led the way downstairs, giving Caitlin a nice view on the way, and wrapped her into a big hug at the front door.

"I don't want to leave," she said, her voice muffled against Caitlin's hair.

"I don't want you to go, but…Get out of here before you're late. We both know you won't handle that well."

With a knowing grin, Mallory kissed Caitlin fully, taking a moment to run her fingers through Caitlin's messy, morning-after hair. She placed a tender kiss on Caitlin's forehead before slipping through the front door.

Caitlin leaned on her door frame, watching Mallory hop into her car and waste no time in backing out of the driveway. She knew not to take it personally; over the past couple weeks she had discovered Mallory ran a tight schedule. Caitlin had managed to disrupt it for nearly an entire day. The change in schedule was over for the time being, and it was game-on now, quite literally with the girls' basketball tournament starting in three hours.

As Caitlin began to close the front door, a flash of movement in Lina's driveway caught her eye. Curious, she leaned her head out and narrowed her eyes. *No way. She wouldn't dare.*

A slow inhale and even slower exhale held Caitlin in place until the car pulled away from the curb and drove off. Once it was out of sight, Caitlin jumped onto her front porch. She was ready to bang on the front door and verbally accost Lina, but decidedly not ready for Lina jumping toward her at the same time from her own front porch.

They pointed at each other, accusatory looks on their faces.

"Are you fucking kidding me?" Caitlin yelled.

"Who the fuck was that?" Lina exclaimed.

A barking dog across the street startled them as they came to the slow realization that they were both standing outside, neither properly dressed for such a spectacle. Caitlin held her glare, hoping it was threatening enough to get Lina to confess to her crimes.

Lina sighed in defeat. "Okay. Fine. Come in."

Caitlin gracelessly hopped the railing separating their porches and followed Lina inside. Her condo was the mirror opposite of Caitlin's, but whereas Caitlin's home spilled over with her quirky personality, Lina's was more modern and frankly a bit stark. She had the least comfortable sofa known to womankind, but the two captain chairs in the living room made up for it, and that's where they found themselves after Lina fixed herself a mug of coffee, and one of blackberry vanilla tea for Caitlin.

"You first," Lina said, her tone stern.

"That was Mallory."

Lina's eyebrows shot up. "No fucking way."

"Yep. We ran into each other at the race, and when Miles the Mega-Asshole left without me afterward, Mallory brought me home…and stayed till this morning." Caitlin didn't bother hiding her triumphant smile.

"I should have known that was her. She had big lesbian energy."

"I'm sorry, what? No. That's not a thing. Don't make that a thing."

Lina laughed. "But seriously, I didn't know you two had gotten so close."

"It's been slow going because of her schedule, but believe me, I think that slowness is now a thing of the past."

"Aha, so you're in love."

Caitlin sputtered, nearly choking on her tea. "No. I didn't say that. That's not what I meant, Lina."

"I can see it all over your face." Lina leaned forward and peered at Caitlin. "Oh, never mind, that's–"

"Okay! Now that I've spilled it, it's your turn!" Even though she was pretty sure Lina was messing with her, Caitlin rubbed her mouth with her sleeve.

"I'd love to hear more about Mallory, actually. This is so exciting! She's very pretty, by the way. Will she be back later? I'd love to meet her."

Caitlin allowed Lina to carry on for a while, wondering how many more inane things she could rattle off in an attempt to avoid her own disclosure. Once she hit the topic of marriage, Caitlin cut her off.

"Enough. It's time for you to tell me why Candice Barrows just left your house at eight a.m. on a Sunday morning."

Lina sighed heavily, avoiding eye contact. She bowed her head and placed her coffee mug on the end table.

"Please don't judge me," she said quietly.

"Lina Ragelis, when have I *ever* judged you? By the way, I'm still pissed your parents never gave you a middle name."

Lina laughed bitterly. "Don't think they ever will, especially with their disgraced lesbian daughter continuing a potentially career-ruining affair with a married woman who outranks her."

Caitlin whistled. "We're really going for the drama here, huh?"

"What about this situation isn't dramatic?"

"I'll give you that. Let's focus on the part where you're still sleeping with this woman after you swore to me, a *year ago*, that you were done."

Lina slumped lower in her chair. "I was done. For a while. But then she came back and said she was leaving Steve. I didn't believe her because she'd said it before and we both know how many times she's lied to me. I shut her out as best as I could but, you know, work interfered. So when news came down of her retiring–"

"Wait, are you saying she didn't tell you she was retiring?"

"Correct. I heard it from someone else and didn't believe that either, but then it happened. It was so fast. She won't tell me the whole story, but I think something else was going on that made it all happen so quickly."

Caitlin nodded, putting the pieces together. "And if she retired, the ranking thing wouldn't be an issue anymore."

"Also correct. The marriage thing, though: still an issue." Lina paused, raking her fingers through her short hair. "Until she texted me and asked me to help her move."

The day at the gym popped into Caitlin's mind. "Hang on. Did she move out, or move somewhere else with Steve?"

"She moved into that new complex outside of West Grove. Steve stayed in the house. That day I helped her move, she told me that she had officially separated from Steve and was planning on moving forward with the divorce."

"Seems like Steve didn't get the memo," Caitlin muttered, flashing back to seeing the couple together at the gym.

"Steve refuses to get the memo. He's not making it easy on her, and honestly, Caitlin, I don't know if she's strong enough to go through with the divorce." Anguish crept over Lina's features, darkening her eyes. "I have tried to stay away from this woman. You know I have. But she has this insane ability to keep pulling me back in."

"The sex must be off the chain," Caitlin remarked, thinking about her own recent encounter.

Lina snorted as she took their empty mugs to the kitchen. "I'm not responding to that. But I will say that I love her."

"Holy what the shit fuck." Caitlin fumbled for an appropriate response. Lina didn't fall in love. She didn't *do* love. And such a bold, stark, unprompted statement? What was going on?

"Yeah. I said it. Now forget it."

Caitlin stared at her best friend as she moved through the lower level of her home, staying as far away from Caitlin as she could manage.

"I'll try to forget it, but Lina…what are you going to do?"

Lina paused between the kitchen and the dining room, dragging her hand over the half-wall. "Figure it out. Like I always do. Now, tell me more about Mallory. I'm so stoked for you, Cait." Lina sent a grin across the room, Candice momentarily forgotten—or more like promptly avoided as Lina loved to do. "Was the sex amazing? All that built up tension and wondering?"

Caitlin allowed a rather smug look to cover her face. "Yeah. You could definitely say it was amazing."

# CHAPTER TWENTY-THREE

Feather-light flakes of snow spun down from the thick gray sky. Caitlin tried with all her might not to give the flurries her attention, hoping against all rational hope that her students wouldn't notice the sudden sky avalanche, but it was futile. Moments after the first handful of flakes descended, the sixteen- and seventeen-year-olds in Caitlin's classroom were practically jumping out of their seats with joy and rumors of an early release.

"I hate to be the spoilsport here, but you do remember you already have a half day today, right?" Caitlin gestured toward the whiteboard and its display of the modified class times.

A groan from her first block students sounded loudly, quickly replaced by chattering hopes for an outright blizzard that would cancel school the following day. Caitlin shook her head as she listened and moved around the classroom. She'd forgotten how excitable kids got as soon as they remembered the mighty role winter weather played in their school attendance. Since Briarwood had a residential population, snow days hadn't been a factor in working there. If the weather was truly treacherous, a third of the school wouldn't be there, but the other two-thirds was plenty demanding of attention, even with a blizzard raging outside.

Caitlin could admit that it was nice being back in the public school excitement of snow days and late starts, even early dismissals. If this storm turned into something and they did have off the following day, this would be the final day she saw her students before Christmas break began.

Thoughts of a long break prickled Caitlin's skin with excitement. Sure there would be basketball practice and another tournament to contend with, but other than that, Mallory had promised they'd spend as much time together as possible. The past three weeks had been hit or miss with Mallory's schedule, though Caitlin recognized an increased effort to make time together. They'd spent all of the previous weekend at Mallory's house, exploring and learning each other with copious sides of incredible orgasms. Caitlin discovered Mallory's obsession with board games—she had a specific interest in Parcheesi—and her undying love for a good drama-soaked reality TV show. Though Caitlin never watched reality TV, much preferring true crime and other crime-filled dramas, she supported Mallory's love for it by sitting through four episodes of *Love is Blind* and even, to her chagrin, becoming invested in one of the budding romances.

Having two weeks off for Christmas break—a lovely gift from Christmas and New Year's falling on Wednesdays—sounded like the perfect time for Caitlin and Mallory to continue their growing…relationship? Romance? Sexy flirtationship? Friends with benefits-ship? Caitlin pressed her lips together. Okay, maybe this holiday break was the perfect time to define what they were doing with each other.

The soothing class-ending chimes sounded, jolting Caitlin out of her thoughts. Her students scattered from the room before she could properly wrap things up. Another thing she'd forgotten: students mentally checking out before holiday breaks even began.

Second and third blocks passed quickly; having her classes for shy of an hour instead of the usual ninety minutes was a major adjustment, especially when it came to material to cover. Caitlin managed to get everything done that she'd planned, but by the time her prep period rolled around, she was worried she'd missed something vital in every class.

She was staring at her lesson plans when Mallory poked her head in the door. Just seeing her sent fireworks shooting through Caitlin's veins. They'd agreed to keep it as low-key as possible at work, which had translated into barely talking to each other. Although Caitlin was decidedly *not* a fan of that, she respected Mallory's wishes. After the Brice debacle, Caitlin wasn't too keen on giving her less-accepting students any additional ammunition anyway.

"Hey you," Mallory said quietly as she crossed the room. She'd double checked that Caitlin was alone before entering, something Caitlin wasn't sure she'd be as careful to do if the roles were reversed.

"Hi yourself." Caitlin pointed to the windows. "I haven't looked. Tell me. How bad is it?"

"Barely a coating and it's stopping. I don't think the kids are going to get their wish for an extra day tagged on to break."

"So sad for them. I almost wish it had gotten bad; can't say I'm looking forward to trying to teach tomorrow."

"You could do what everyone else does and just show movies."

Caitlin narrowed her eyes. "Yeah right. I'd never hear the end of that from you."

"That's possible," Mallory said lightly. "But it's also your choice. It's your classroom."

"You know technically it's not."

Mallory abruptly stopped fidgeting with a pen she'd picked up from the desk. "You're not really going to make a decision on showing a movie based on my potential reaction, are you?"

The short-term nature of Caitlin's employment at Vanderbilt was something Mallory continued to avoid. In truth, there wasn't much to discuss: Caitlin would either be there next year or she wouldn't. And if she wasn't, it was her responsibility to find another job. It was a strange place to teeter, though. Caitlin liked having the professional connection to Mallory but continually wondered what their relationship would be like if they didn't work in the same school.

Caitlin rolled Mallory's comment back through her head. No, she wasn't going to make a decision based on Mallory's potential reaction, but hell if the potential fallout from showing a movie wasn't poking her in the brain.

"I'll do whatever feels right tomorrow. I have a couple ideas." Caitlin shuffled some papers, trying to make herself look prepared for all potential classroom moods and vibes. "What's on your professional development agenda today?"

Mallory groaned. The pen landed with a tiny thud on the desk. "The online trauma training everyone's doing and then the awful task of aligning our sequence of studies."

"That doesn't sound much better than the scope and sequence I have to work on."

"Hmm." The deliberate pause seemed uncomfortable. "So you'll be with Valerie all afternoon?"

Caitlin bit her lip against the sigh that threatened to emerge. While she desperately wanted Valerie and Mallory to get along as well as their rhyming names did, she hadn't pushed the issue with either one because they were both stubborn assholes when it came to their vendetta against each other. Other than Valerie's laissez faire approach to teaching and Mallory's outward arrogance, Caitlin hadn't come any closer to figuring out the root of their issue. She had high hopes of getting them together socially, with other people-buffers present of course, to try to ease the tension, but just the thought of that event gave *her* anxiety so she hadn't planned it yet.

"I sure will!" Caitlin said jubilantly.

Mallory took the cue and dropped the subject. "About tomorrow…"

This time Caitlin did sigh. She knew what was coming. She also knew her official invitation had been a shot in the dark. In the distance, the chimes jingled, signaling the end of the students' half day. A different bell rang in Caitlin's head.

"Coach McKinney is holding practice after school. I really thought she wasn't going to," Mallory rushed, "but she already told the girls."

Tomorrow was Caitlin's first foray into a Vanderbilt social hour. It was the holiday extravaganza, an event much hyped up by Valerie, Drew, and Marcy, which included an open bar for the first two hours. That was a rather dangerous gift for teachers, who had a rightful reputation of enjoying many drinks to celebrate school events such as the beginnings of breaks. Valerie's exact words were "total shit show" when describing the late hours of these events. Caitlin was curious and excited and had asked Mallory to go, knowing that she normally avoided such events. She'd originally given a non-response, but here was her official no.

"It's fine. I understand."

Before Mallory could beg forgiveness (likely story), Valerie whooshed into the room, her wild hair and oversized bag trailing after her.

"Let's get this shit done so I can go get laid!" she exclaimed, tossing her bag onto a desk. "Oh. Walker. So nice to see you."

Caitlin admired the quick shift in Valerie's tone before she remembered she should be annoyed by it.

"West. Wish I could say the same." Mallory nodded at Caitlin before stalking out of the room. The door shut behind her with a bit more force than was warranted.

Valerie eyed Caitlin as she twisted her hair into a bun. "I don't know how you–"

"Don't." Caitlin picked up her laptop and moved next to Valerie. "Let's get traumatized before you start picking apart my relationship." Caitlin's cheeks colored, and she hoped Valerie would let that one go.

Surprisingly, she did. Long enough to get through the trauma training and twenty minutes of scoping and sequencing eleventh grade skills, anyway.

Caitlin was silently assessing the best time to teach semicolons and colons when Valerie's held-back words burst forth.

"So. You used the r-word."

"I really think it would be better if we taught commas before this auxiliary punctuation." Caitlin tapped furiously at her keyboard. "Who came up with this ridiculous timeline? It's back-assward."

Valerie reached over and shut Caitlin's laptop, briefly trapping Caitlin's hands. "Stop. Nothing ever changes with that bullshit. Don't waste your time on that; gossip with me instead, please."

With a sigh, Caitlin turned slightly in her chair so she was facing Valerie. Might as well get this firing round over with so Valerie could go get laid and Caitlin could...well, not get laid, since of course there was a basketball game that night.

"We haven't had the talk," she said, her shoulders lifting into a small shrug. "So I don't have much to say."

"Fine, but you literally just called it your relationship." Valerie poked Caitlin's arm. "I can't believe this is a thing with you two. You're so different."

"Maybe that's what makes it work."

"I mean, what do you even get someone like her for Christmas? An igloo to store all her icy feelings?"

Caitlin glared at Valerie. "She's not as bad as you want her to be. I've already told you this. She's...different with me."

"Okay, I accept your claim she's different with you, but she still doesn't want to say that you're together, right? I don't like that, Caitlin. Not one bit."

The theme of this conversation felt familiar to a recent chat Lina had dragged Caitlin into. Everyone around her wanted Mallory to permanently label their...situation...and okay, maybe Caitlin wanted the security that came with the r-word, but even she knew calling something a relationship didn't give it much more power than simply letting things exist as they were. It was just a label.

Then again, she could admit to herself that she wanted Mallory to introduce her as her girlfriend.

"We're getting there, okay? We've only been seeing each other for a month."

"Yeah, but you lesbians have the whole U-Haul thing, so don't try to tell me you don't want this to speed up."

"First of all, rude stereotype even if it tends to be true." Caitlin paused, thinking about something Mallory had said over the weekend. It had come seemingly out of nowhere when Mallory said she'd like to keep things casual and see where they went. She reinforced how much she liked Caitlin and loved spending time with her but then threw in a line about being "gun-shy" about relationships. Caitlin knew Mallory had been burned, and she didn't fault her for being cautious or nervous. She hoped she was different from Mallory's past, but truthfully neither of them could know that yet.

"Mallory and I are taking things as they come. And that's that." Valerie didn't need to know the specifics of that brief chat, especially since Caitlin was still processing what it meant, hence the need for a more official talk.

"But she's hiding it," Valerie observed.

"At work? Yes. And I'm totally fine with that. No one here, kids certainly included, needs to know about either of our private lives, especially when they're intertwined."

"Well that I can understand. I wouldn't want the kids to know about my sex life either."

"Would ya look at that?" Caitlin pressed her chin into her hands and gave Valerie a wide smile. "We finally agree on something about Mallory."

"Tell no one."

"And poke a hole in your everlasting feud? I wouldn't dare."

Caitlin looked pointedly at the papers strewn in front of them. With a dramatic huff, Valerie started talking about punctuation, and they managed to get some work done in the final half hour of the day.

As they packed up their things, Valerie gave Caitlin a nervous look. It was so utterly out of character for her that Caitlin startled.

"What? What is it?"

"I don't want to say this."

"So your face indicates."

Valerie hiked her shoulders up high before releasing them. "What if you remind her of Amy and that's why she's holding back and avoiding labels, and if that's the case then I'm worried for you because that situation was so bad and I know she told you about it but really Caitlin, it was so so so bad, and I feel like maybe she didn't specify how bad it was." The words flooded out in a mad rush, Valerie's cheeks pinking with the release.

Caitlin slid her laptop into her bag. She let the words cascade over her, unsure of how to respond. It was a thought that had already crossed her mind, but Valerie didn't need to know that. Caitlin understood that Valerie was trying to protect her. It was sweet. But it wasn't her place to do so.

"Say something," Valerie pleaded.

"I hear you," Caitlin replied, her tone simple and light. That familiar stone of worry was growing in her gut again, and she wanted nothing more than to go home and process her feelings and concerns privately. "Thank you for sharing your concerns."

"Oh fuck, don't be mad–"

Drew burst into the room, his tell-tale gossip smile shining on his face. "You are *not* going to believe what I just heard in my department meeting."

Valerie shifted her gaze from Caitlin to Drew. Gossip was the preferred discussion at the moment, especially since it dissolved the awkwardness that had bloomed between them.

"We're dying to hear it, Gossip Man," Caitlin said as the three teachers left the classroom.

# CHAPTER TWENTY-FOUR

The intensity of the decorations surprised Caitlin, but as she slowly spun around the private room of the restaurant hosting the Holiday Shit Show Extravaganza, she found that they were getting her in a playful Christmas mood. The Vanderbilt social club, composed of several divorced middle-aged teachers and counselors who were rumored to occasionally sleep with each other, had done a knock-out job of glamming up the place with red and green streamers and some random pictures of holiday scenes that captured a number of religious beliefs. The pictures were clearly printed at school, but the effort was nice. A giant blow-up Santa was creeping in the corner, and a reindeer had already been trotted across the room by numerous teachers. An inflated snowman by the bar was looking a little deflated already, but someone was pumping more air into him.

"Hi! Here's your welcome shot!" Caitlin jumped slightly when one of the science teachers—Bethany, if her memory was correct—pushed a tray in front of her. Sure enough, the heavy silver platter was covered with green and red Jell-O shots.

"Wow, thank you so much." She picked a red shot off the platter and went to work on it, not so delicately circling the tip of her tongue between the Jell-O and the plastic cup.

"You're Caitlin, right?" At her nod, Bethany went on. "The kids just love you. I hope you're able to stay at Vanderbilt next year!"

Having dislodged the shot and swallowed it whole, Caitlin opened her mouth to say thank you, but found that Bethany had already flounced off to another group of incoming partiers. After stopping at the bar to take advantage of the free drinks, Caitlin scanned the crowd. She finally spotted Valerie and Drew holding court in the corner near Santa. Valerie looked up and waved her over.

The gossip-fest was in full swing, and Caitlin was amazed at how quickly these people, her colleagues, were throwing back drinks. She tried not to gawk when Mike Wilcox sat down with two full glasses of beer and began sipping from each of them, one after the other. He caught Caitlin's eye and grinned.

"Two hours of free drinks goes faster than you think." He nodded at her gin and tonic. "Might want to grab yourself another one now."

Caitlin worried that if she did she'd start cracking wildly inappropriate jokes about his unfortunate name.

"Hello my darling," Valerie said, giving Caitlin a loud smacking kiss on the cheek. "What took you so long?"

"This started at three thirty. It's three forty-two."

"Uh, yeah, but most of us were here by ten after three."

"Funny, I didn't get that memo."

Valerie bumped her shoulder against Caitlin's. "Are you still salty about yesterday?"

Honestly? Maybe a little. But Valerie was being a concerned friend, and though Caitlin believed she was acting in her best interest, she wasn't thrilled that she'd spent last night obsessing over Mallory and Amy's relationship, wondering how similar it was to what she and Mallory had. It didn't help that Mallory hadn't even called last night; instead, she'd sent a simple "Missing you. Goodnight sweetheart" text that felt warm and lonely all at once.

"It's all good," Caitlin said, bumping back into Valerie. "But it would be even better if you would scamper your sexy self over to the bar and get us both more drinks."

In Valerie's absence, Caitlin pulled out her phone to double-check Mallory hadn't changed her mind and decided to come after all. Wishful thinking, she knew. Mallory hadn't texted, but Lina had. Caitlin looked around. It was difficult to know if all the people here were Vanderbilt people or if some partners/spouses had shown up as well. Valerie had mentioned that some usually trickled in, often not till the end of the night when their significant others needed to be dragged home.

She sent a short text to Lina, telling her where she was and suggesting she stop by later if she wanted. Caitlin knew things with Candice were tense because of the holidays, and she didn't like the idea of Lina sitting at home sulking.

It only took two and a half strong gin and tonics for Caitlin to loosen up to the point where she was ready to make her Vanderbilt karaoke debut. The small machine was tucked away in a part of the spacious room where Caitlin reasoned maybe not everyone would hear her. Plus, it was Mike Wilcox's fault. When he came back with his third and fourth beers, he struck up a conversation with Caitlin about the best duets, and after a heated argument, he announced that Caitlin had to join him for a duet in order to redeem her love for Elton John and Kiki Dee's "Don't Go Breaking My Heart."

And so it was that Caitlin found herself crammed into a small space with a man she barely knew but felt a delightful buzzed kinship with, crooning "Summer Nights" from *Grease* which, for the record, hadn't even made Caitlin's list of acceptable duets. She was impressed with Mike's ability to land that final weird high note, igniting rousing cheers from their audience. With the fire of success burning steady beneath her, Caitlin flipped through the book and picked a song that made her feel a confusing number of emotions.

After Bethany and one of the guidance counselors ripped through Meatloaf's "Anything for Love," Caitlin found herself alone at the karaoke mic. She threw back the rest of her drink and shot a meaningful look at Valerie, who scampered off for a refill. That two-hour window was closing in just as fast as Mike Wilcox had warned it would.

The opening notes of "Blank Space" popped out of the speakers and a couple of rowdy teachers cheered. Caitlin ignored them and closed her eyes, waiting for her big entrance into the song. She didn't need the scrolling lyrics; this one had been cemented in her memory for years.

Her four minutes of glory ended with a rush of applause and whooping cheers. Valerie and Drew screamed for emphasis, something like "that's our girl!" It wasn't until Caitlin hopped off the miniature makeshift stage and accepted her fresh drink from Valerie that she got the distinct feeling she was being watched.

Figuring it was Lina, Caitlin looked around for the familiar flop of golden brown hair. Not seeing her, Caitlin shrugged and turned to watch the next bold performer.

And there she was. Not Lina, but Mallory, leaning comfortably against the wall. She was standing in shadows by herself, a bottle of beer hanging from the tips of her fingers. Caitlin's heart tripped over itself as she scanned the emotions fluttering across Mallory's face. They eyed each other from ten feet apart, each waiting for the other to make a clear move. Caitlin stood stock still, knowing this was Mallory's move, but worried that if she didn't do something, Mallory would stay in the shadows all night.

Caitlin took a tentative step toward Mallory who immediately put up her hand as if to say "stop." She then jerked her thumb to the side. Caitlin craned her neck and saw a small sofa sitting outside the larger groups of socializing teachers. She moved toward it and sat down.

Mallory eased herself down a moment later, keeping a safe distance between them. "I knew you were a closet Taylor fan," she said, her voice low and unapologetically sexy.

"Oh God. You saw that?"

"It was amazing. *You* were amazing." She smiled warmly at Caitlin. "I had no idea you could sing like that."

"Okay, it wasn't *that* great. I think you're biased."

"I may be. I may very well be."

Caitlin fought the urge to kiss Mallory, and judging by the way Mallory was gripping her half-empty bottle with both hands while her eyes locked on Caitlin's, there was a mutual fighting of urges happening.

And then it dawned on Caitlin; she'd later blame the gin and tonics for her delay. "Wait. What are you even doing here?"

"I convinced McKinney to cancel practice. We'll see the girls plenty over break; after last night's game, they needed a rest." She offered a small but genuine smile. "And I wanted to come here. To see you. To be with you."

"Well I'll be damned, Mallory Walker," Caitlin drawled. "This is very interesting, indeed."

"The fact that I want to be here with you?"

"Uh, yeah. Hello. That's major."

Mallory shrugged. "It's not if we don't make it major. We can be cool."

The gin and tonics in Caitlin's stomach did a nasty little jig. "Sure, sure. Cool," she retorted.

If Mallory noticed the bite in Caitlin's tone, she didn't let on. Instead, she gently elbowed Caitlin and stood up.

"Let's go socialize."

Caitlin stared at Mallory in confusion and wonder. Yet another piece of the Magical Mallory Puzzle.

Mallory's definition of socializing meant standing around and talking with people from her department and a few math guys who seemed to only converse with the history teachers. Caitlin felt a little out of place at first, but Joe Donnelly, Drew's department chair, drew Caitlin into a conversation about Chaucer that threw her off until she gained her footing.

During the consumption of her second beer, Mallory moved closer to Caitlin, allowing their bodies to touch here and there. Their circle had widened a bit; even Valerie and Drew were at the fringes, though they didn't dare get too close to Mallory. Valerie gave Caitlin a questioning look and she shrugged in response, still unclear about what was happening here.

Caitlin had just returned with glasses of water for both herself and Mallory when Mallory put her arm around Caitlin's waist and squeezed gently. Caitlin nearly dropped her glass.

"Is this okay?" Mallory whispered, her lips brushing Caitlin's hair.

"It's okay with me if it's okay with you," she said cautiously.

"I think it is," Mallory said, her hand tightening on Caitlin's hip.

No one blinked an eye at the change in their posture. Caitlin decided not to point that out; she was well-versed in the rumor mill of public schools, and in a school as small as Vanderbilt, she had a solid hunch that their romance was already old news.

As seven p.m. approached, Caitlin was stifling a yawn as she chatted with Mallory and three other teachers whom she didn't know very well. They were women that Mallory often spoke about and seemed to trust. Mallory's hand was resting on Caitlin's thigh; it wasn't a scandalous touch, but it was far more than friendly. Caitlin felt the heat of arousal coupled with the warmth of Mallory being open about their connection. She'd worried this day would never come. She absently ran her fingers over Mallory's hand, enjoying their open closeness.

"Damn. I missed the free drinks, didn't I?"

Caitlin twisted in her chair and grinned at Lina. "If you'd shown up when I texted you, you wouldn't have."

"Yeah well, work intervened. Point me to the bar?"

Caitlin felt the abrupt departure of Mallory's touch. She glanced over and found her focused intently on Lina. Caitlin could practically see the wheels spinning.

"Hey, Lina? This is Mallory." Caitlin turned to Mallory and touched her shoulder. "Mallory, this is my best friend Lina."

"It's great to meet you," Lina said with a grin, extending her hand. Mallory looked at it for a split second, seeming to think it was an explosive, before tentatively giving it a firm shake.

"It's nice to meet you." Caitlin flinched, hearing the sheet of ice suffocating any warmth in Mallory's voice.

"I'll walk you to the bar," she said, standing up and collecting their empty glasses. "I'm ready for my last drink. Mallory? Can I get you a beer?"

"I'm good," came the response, still laden with a distinct chill.

At the bar, Caitlin shifted from foot to foot as Lina talked about her day at work. She wracked her brain, trying to find a cause for Mallory's obvious change in behavior. It was possible they had become so caught up in each other that Caitlin hadn't said much about Lina other than that she was her best friend, but that didn't explain the cold reaction to meeting her. No, Caitlin *knew* she'd mentioned Lina, multiple times in fact. This didn't make any sense.

"Is she normally so…" Lina's voice trailed off, the right word escaping her.

"Only when she meets new people?" Caitlin's voice upticked out of nervousness.

Lina peered at Caitlin as she sipped her beer. "You good?"

Caitlin took a deep breath, moving so that she and Lina were next to the bar instead of in front of it. "Yeah. I'm good. I didn't expect her to be here, and I'm so happy she is. I really don't know why she was weird about meeting you, though."

"Must be my shocking good looks." Lina winked.

"Unfortunately that may be the case," Caitlin muttered. She supposed Mallory could be jealous. Lina was very attractive, after all. But their friendship was just that: friendship.

"Oh my God!" A vibrant squeal came from behind them. "Is this the Lina I've heard so much about? In the actual flesh?"

Now *that's* the kind of reaction Mallory should have had, Caitlin thought, then smiled. She'd never, and Caitlin knew it.

"Lina, meet Valerie West, my favorite English teacher other than myself. Valerie, yes. This is finally Lina."

Valerie threw herself into Lina's arms and greeted her with an overly zealous hug. "This is the best day of my life. We have *so* much to discuss."

As Valerie dragged Lina away, Lina waved to Caitlin, not a fleck of fear in her eyes, though it was anyone's guess as to what Valerie intended to do with her. Caitlin looked over to the spot where she'd been sitting when Lina arrived and found only two of the women remained.

Neither one was Mallory.

Caitlin slowly wound her way around the space, making small talk here and there as she looked for Mallory. Circuit complete, the little pit of worry that had shown up in her gut yesterday started growing. She positioned herself next to the reindeer, patting him gently on his soft plastic head.

She wouldn't have left like that, Caitlin reasoned. Without even saying goodbye? Sure, Mallory could get frosty, but she had warmed to Caitlin so much over the past month that a silent departure now seemed completely out of character.

"You lookin' for Walker?"

Caitlin nodded sullenly.

Drew gave her a compassionate look. "She left a couple minutes ago. Maybe you could catch her in the parking lot?"

Caitlin steadied herself against the reindeer, not her best idea since he wasn't exactly a sturdy decoration. "Nah, I think she had a basketball thing she had to get to." The lie was weak, and Drew likely saw straight through it, but Caitlin couldn't bear looking like a complete loser.

And on the flip side, she reminded herself with a shaky breath, Mallory wasn't even supposed to be there in the first place. This was Caitlin's time to have fun, with or without Mallory Walker. She slapped a smile on her face, took a long sip of her drink, and made her way back to the karaoke stage to find and sing the absolute antithesis to Taylor Swift.

# CHAPTER TWENTY-FIVE

"There's no moping allowed on Christmas." Caitlin's dad came up behind her and handed her a mug of rich, homemade hot chocolate. "What do I have to do to get you to turn that frown upside down, kiddo?"

Caitlin groaned. "You can start with avoiding cheesy lines like that."

Paul Gregory took an offended step backward, placing his hand over his heart. "When did I become cheesy?"

"Somewhere around fifty if I recall correctly."

He scoffed and moved toward his favorite chair in the corner of the living room. Caitlin watched as he eased himself down and propped his legs on the leather ottoman. The fire sparked and flamed next to his chair, sending warmth and the unmistakable scent of smoldering wood into the air. Caitlin's mom had outdone herself, as usual, with the Christmas tree. It was sparkling with white and gold lights, trimmed with matching ornaments. Prior to Miles and Caitlin reverting back to their innate childhood natures and making a mess of unwrapping their gifts, the presents had been piled thoughtfully under the tree, wrapped in matching white and gold paper. No holiday in the Gregory household was complete without a picture-perfect scene to capture memories.

Now, presents unwrapped and tucked away in their cars, the room was glowing with post-present success. Not a scrap of paper or ribbon was anywhere to be seen; Paul had gleefully used his new vacuum cleaner to rid all evidence of the great present explosion. Rigby was snoring under the tree, one of his new toys clutched in his paws.

Caitlin settled into the corner of the leather sofa and tucked her feet under her. She took a tentative sip of the steamy hot chocolate, a childhood favorite, and savored the bold flavors.

"Do you want to talk about what's bothering you?" her dad asked as he turned down the New Age Christmas music trickling from the speakers.

Bright and early that morning, before Caitlin had even forced herself out of bed, Mallory had texted. Caitlin had stared at her phone for several moments, unsure of whether or not she wanted to open the message. Their communication following Mallory's ghosting at the happy hour had been sparse. Over four days, Caitlin had texted seven times. She'd never begged Mallory to talk to her. She hadn't poured out concern or drama. She'd simply asked what happened on Friday. She'd suggested they get together and talk. She'd offered to come to Mallory's house; she'd stated that she really wanted to talk face-to-face. She'd said she missed her. Mallory's responses had been short and noncommittal to the point that Caitlin had decided, late Christmas Eve night, to give one solid push and see what happened.

So at ten thirty the night before, she'd called. To her surprise, Mallory had answered.

"What's up?"

Caitlin's veins flooded with icy shards. Having moved so far past their initial conversations, "what's up" now felt like such an un-Mallory thing to say, so "just friends" that it hurt.

She cleared her throat. "I'd like you to tell me why you left the party in such a rush. And why you didn't bother to tell me you were leaving. Or contact me afterward, for that matter."

Silence wafted through the phone. It went on for long enough that Caitlin double checked her phone to make sure the call hadn't dropped.

"Mallory? Just tell me what happened." Caitlin waited another couple of seconds, and nothing but Mallory's soft breathing came from the other end of the line. "Were you uncomfortable with people seeing us together? I thought you were okay with the physical contact at the party." Caitlin paused, rethinking the evening. "Uh, you must have been okay with it because you made the contact happen. Anyway. Did someone say something to you? I'm really at a loss here, Mallory, and any insight–"

"No one said anything."

"She speaks," Caitlin said lightly, forcing a smile even though Mallory couldn't see her.

"Caitlin, this isn't a good time. I'm sorry."

That time the weighted silence on the other end of the phone was due to a dropped, or hung up, connection. Confused and angry, Caitlin had shoved her phone under the empty pillow next to hers and curled up to fall into a dreamless sleep.

When her phone buzzed with Mallory's text before seven a.m., she'd contemplated searching the internet for a way to delete a text without seeing the teaser that popped up in the messaging app. She almost got out of bed and banged on Lina's front door to make her screen the text, but had eventually decided she was a grown ass woman and could handle whatever that damn text said.

*Merry Christmas, Caitlin. I hope you have a wonderful day with your family.*

Caitlin had stared at the words, willing them to jumble into something more meaningful. But there it was, in blue and white. Simple. Kind, but simple. Kind and simple, but lacking absolutely all of the passion and intensity that Caitlin had felt growing like a wildfire between them.

She hadn't responded, and that weighed on her now as she sipped from her mug of hot chocolate. Caitlin wasn't rude or spiteful, but she was feeling hurt and, admittedly, a little embarrassed for reading the situation so wrong.

"Kiddo?" her dad prodded.

"Nope, I'm good. I just remembered a text I need to send."

She slipped from the cozy room and picked up her phone from the kitchen island. Mallor-Elsa could shoot ice at her all she wanted, but Caitlin wasn't about to let that stop her from showing Mallory how much she meant to her.

After some deleting and careful editing, Caitlin pressed send on her final product: *Merry Christmas to you, Mallory. I hope your day is filled with warmth and happiness, and I hope you enjoy the time with your dad. I'm thinking of you and wishing you were here with me.*

She took a staggered breath after the text went through, hoping that wasn't too much. "Fuck it," she mumbled, putting her phone back in the kitchen, where she would take pains to avoid it. She was tired of holding back for Mallory's sake.

Despite her best attempts to ignore her phone, Caitlin peeked before she and her family sat down to Christmas dinner. No response. She shook it off, reminding herself that she'd done what she could, and sat down to stuff her face with her mother's incredible cooking.

"More stuffing please," she said, grabbing for the bowl even though it was out of reach.

"Mom, is it too late to send her to etiquette school? It's like eating dinner with a caveman."

Caitlin glared at her brother. "Really, Mr. I Can't Chew With My Mouth Closed to Save My Life?"

Jenna stifled a giggle. She was seated next to Miles, rounding out the table for six. Oh, right, the table for *five*, since the seat next to Caitlin was obviously empty. The last person to have sat in that seat was Becca, and the thought of her ghostly image with its elbows on the table made Caitlin shudder.

"My table manners are fine," he retorted, spooning himself more cranberry sauce.

"Your sister does have a point," Jenna said thoughtfully. "Sometimes you chew so loudly that I can't hear myself think."

Caitlin pointed her knife toward Jenna. "See? She tells it like it is, Miles. We like her. You should keep her."

Had Caitlin not been looking at Jenna in that moment, she would have missed the quick glance shared between her brother and his girlfriend. But she caught it, and she knew immediately what was coming next.

"No way," she said quietly, mostly to herself, but Jenna heard her and gave her a big smile.

"We have news," Miles said. Caitlin was impressed to hear his voice shake nervously. Maybe Mr. Confidence had a soft streak in him after all.

"Oh dear," Leslie said, pressing her hand to her chest. "You're not…"

"We're not quite ready for grandkids, son, but we'll do our best to support you." Paul let out a deep sigh.

Caitlin bit her lip, trying to hold back laughter. She liked Jenna very much, but watching her squirm through her parents' poor acting was highly entertaining.

"No! God! We're engaged, not pregnant!" Miles blurted.

A chorus of surprised gasps, two-thirds of which were exaggerated and fake, sounded from around the table. Caitlin's real gasp stuck in her throat, and she reached for her glass of water.

Miles narrowed his eyes at his mother, then his father. "Why are you being weird?"

"We may be of retirement age, but we're not blind, Miles." Paul gestured toward Jenna's hand, resting delicately on the table. Caitlin followed his gesture and finally noticed the sparkling halo diamond ring sitting on Jenna's finger.

Leslie leaned forward and patted Jenna's arm. "Are you sure you're not pregnant, honey?"

"Mom, what the hell! Stop! No one is pregnant." Miles was bright red, but Jenna was laughing.

"I'm definitely not pregnant, Mrs. Gregory. We know it's a little fast, but when you know, you know, right?" She looked lovingly at Miles.

Somewhere inside the swirling shock Caitlin was feeling was genuine happiness for her brother. He was a shithead, for sure, but she liked Jenna, and Caitlin had a good feeling that if

Miles had proposed, it meant he'd finally found someone who could put up with his shit.

"It's kind of funny," Miles began with a sly smirk that showed his frustration had worn off, "typically it's Caitlin's people who get engaged so quickly. And yet here she is, alone."

Caitlin balled her fists against her thighs. Christmas dinner was a terrible time to deliver the decades-planned total beatdown to her little brother. After dinner would be fine; get the dishes done first. She could wait.

"Miles," their father warned.

"But Caitlin could have someone here!" Jenna said, her voice filled with delight. Perhaps Caitlin didn't like her as much as she'd thought she did three minutes ago.

"Oh yeah!" Miles exclaimed, tapping his fork on the table. "How's it going with that hot basketball coach from the 5k? Why isn't she here? You scare her off already?"

"Who are they talking about, honey?" Leslie asked.

"No one," she said quickly, shooting her brother a threatening glare. "Just my friend, Mallory." She stumbled over her own words, wishing they were something else.

"Friend? Looked like more than that."

"Miles, if you could please shut up, I'll consider that next year's Christmas gift in advance."

Jenna looked worriedly at Caitlin. "I'm sorry. We just assumed…"

"It's okay." Caitlin exhaled loudly. "I was hoping things would turn out differently with her, but I'm pretty sure we're not on the same page, and there's currently no indication that we will be."

The dining room lapsed into silence, the only noise coming from Rigby's paws tip-tapping across the hardwood floor. The silence was worse than her family pestering her.

"It's not a big deal," she continued. "Carry on."

"Caitlin, I'm sorry. I thought–"

"Well, we hate her," Leslie announced, standing up to begin clearing the table.

"Mom! No. Don't be ridiculous."

"So we…shouldn't hate her?" Paul asked, his features lined with confusion. Caitlin couldn't tell if this was more bad acting from her parents, but she was pretty sure it was.

"No. No hating. She's a great woman. I think…" Saying it out loud would make it more real, Caitlin realized. "I think we want different things. And that's why she's not here." Well, that and the fact that Caitlin hadn't invited her because Mallory had made it clear she would be spending the day with her father. Maybe she could have come here for at least an hour? Caitlin shook the thought from her head. She knew how much Mallory valued her relationship with her dad.

Leslie leaned down to kiss the top of her daughter's head. "Give it some time, honey. Maybe the holidays are rough for her."

Caitlin leaned back in her chair, stunned by her mother's words. It hadn't occurred to her, but her mother may be on to something.

Later that night, home safe and mostly unharmed from another Gregory family holiday, Caitlin curled around Pepper and wondered what Mallory was doing. A response to her text had never arrived, and though it hurt like hell to admit it, Caitlin recognized the truth in what she'd said over dinner. Being in two different places, wanting two different things, was no way to forge a relationship of any kind. She wanted more than casual. It wasn't what she'd thought she wanted, but now that she'd gotten to know Mallory, now that she'd felt that intense spark between them, Caitlin knew casual would never work for her.

Falling in love was the only next step she could take with Mallory, and there was no point in being alone in that feeling. Maybe she should have let this go before it even started; who was she to think she could scale Mallory's frozen tower of self-protection? She nudged her phone further away and laid her head down, letting Pepper's soft purring snores lure her to sleep.

# CHAPTER TWENTY-SIX

"I'm going to have to ask you to turn off this music."

Caitlin looked up from her position on the floor. Lina was over, helping Caitlin assemble the TV stand her parents had gotten her for Christmas. It was the first step toward redecorating her living room, a process Caitlin had anticipated would wait till the summer, but now that she had Mallory-free time on her hands over Christmas break…well, no time like the present. Lina had chided her for not painting before assembling furniture, but Caitlin was impatient and hated the sight of the hulking box sitting in the corner of her living room.

"What's wrong with my music? I thought you liked these artists."

"I do, but not when I'm forced to listen to a collection of their greatest sad song hits. Caitlin, seriously. This is painful."

Everything But the Girl's "Before Today" was streaming through the speakers. So it wasn't the happiest song. Big deal. Caitlin ignored Lina's complaints and waited for the next song to come through. Surely it would be better.

"Absolutely not!" Lina yelled.

Caitlin couldn't blame her. "You Had Time" by Ani DiFranco wasn't exactly an uplifting jam to build furniture to.

Lina grabbed Caitlin's phone and fast forwarded. The next six songs were nixed, "Party of One" by Brandi Carlile earning an exaggerated groan, and finally Lina threw the phone at Caitlin.

"Fix this or I'm leaving."

Caitlin thumbed through her other playlists. Choosing the one titled "She Never Loved You" had been a poor choice for today, even if it was true. She settled for a playlist full of 80s classic rock, knowing Lina would be satisfied enough to pick up the screwdriver she'd thrown to the floor during her tantrum.

"Did you stay up all night making that emo playlist?"

"No," Caitlin huffed, reaching around Lina for a shelf that was ready to slide into place. "That's a divorce playlist."

"Wooowww." Lina drew out the word and followed it with a low whistle. "You're taking this pretty hard, huh? And here I thought you said you didn't love her."

"Lina! I don't." Caitlin banged the shelf into place with more force than necessary. "It's not about that. It's about me and my shitty choices in women."

"Don't do that."

"It's obvious that's the problem." Caitlin read from the mental list she'd composed when she couldn't sleep the night before. "Mallory is a cold person. She's burned from her relationship with a teacher years ago. She doesn't even want a relationship; she wants a casual fling because she's too fucking scared to let that self-serving wall of ice down. And here I am, thinking I can melt her. Or whatever." She cringed at her pathetic use of imagery.

Outburst complete, at least for the moment, Caitlin rocked back on her heels until she was in a seated position.

"No, Caitlin. I mean it. Don't do that. This isn't your fault."

"Uh, yeah, I know. That's what I just said."

Lina dropped down next to Caitlin and gently took the hammer from her hands. "Give me this before you do some real damage. Now listen to me." She grabbed Caitlin's chin and forced her to make eye contact. "You like her. And she likes you."

Caitlin waited for Lina's sage words of wisdom to continue, but that seemed to be the end.

"Now hand me that long piece to your left. I think that's the next step," Lina continued.

"Not until you finish your little speech, Sergeant."

Lina leaned over Caitlin and picked up the piece she'd requested. "I did. You like each other. You've been dating, or whatever you want to call it, for a month. A *month*, Caitlin. Let it figure itself out."

Dumbfounded, Caitlin stared at her best friend. It couldn't be that simple.

A couple hours later, after they'd managed to finish building the TV stand without injuring each other or the furniture, Caitlin was snuggled under another Christmas present from her parents: a fleece-lined blanket that promised to keep her toes warm even on the most blustery of New Jersey winter nights. While it was only forty degrees outside and nowhere near blustery, the blanket was doing an excellent job of soothing Caitlin with its coziness.

She'd just gotten settled and pressed play on a new true crime series when there was a knock at her door. Grumbling, she got up. Lina had left a couple of her tools behind and the woman hated to be without her prized possessions.

Tools in hand, Caitlin pulled open her front door. "You really couldn't wait?"

Mallory stood before her, snow stuck in her dark hair. She was bundled up in a thick coat and her face was pale in the cloudy darkness.

"No. I couldn't," she said, her voice soft and tinged with emotion.

Caitlin stared at her, blinking rapidly to be sure she wasn't hallucinating. The cold winter air swirled around them, flurries glinting like silver stars as they danced from the overcast sky.

"Can I come in?" Mallory asked.

"You can't just—what are you doing here?" Caitlin stuttered.

"I wanted to see you. And I want to talk to you, face-to-face, like you asked. You were right. We need to do that."

Caitlin continued staring, conflicting emotions tussling inside of her. She was happy, excited even, to see Mallory, but a part of her was pissed that Mallory had the audacity to show up unannounced. It was presumptuous. It was arrogant. And it was exactly who the woman was.

"Come in," Caitlin finally said, allowing Mallory to walk past her into the house.

After Mallory shrugged out of her jacket, she and Caitlin sat down on the sofa. Each took an end, leaving ample space between them, which Pepper immediately took advantage of.

"How was your Christmas?"

Caitlin shook her head. "No. We're not doing small talk. Let's do the hard talking first and see where that leads us."

A flinch-smile skittered across Mallory's face. "You stopped reaching out," she said simply, as though that was the answer to all of Caitlin's unasked questions.

"I...me? You're putting this on me?"

"No, I'm not. But that's why I'm here. Because you stopped reaching out." Mallory twisted her hands together. "I guess you've figured out that I'm not great with asking for things that I need."

"You could say that."

"Okay. I deserve that." She shook her hands out, nervous energy emanating from her. "Caitlin, I needed space. And I didn't tell you that, which was incredibly stupid of me. I let the dead air speak for itself and didn't consider how that might hurt you." Mallory took a breath as she collected her thoughts. "I was wrong when I told you that I want something casual. I don't. I don't think I can even *do* casual with you. But I wasn't wrong about being scared, and the reason I left the holiday party so abruptly is because I was confronted with one of my biggest fears."

Caitlin scrolled through the events preceding Mallory's departure. Nothing stuck out, other than her slaying a song by Mallory's favorite musical artist.

"It was my rendition of 'Blank Space,' wasn't it?"

"No, that was actually quite good." Discomfort splashed across Mallory's features as she said, "It was Lina."

A weight dropped onto Caitlin's shoulders. Of course. It was always Lina; Becca had had an issue with her, too. The fact that lesbians couldn't handle their girlfriends having platonic relationships with other lesbians drove Caitlin mad.

But this wasn't Becca, Caitlin reminded herself. Instead of jumping in with a defense, she waited to hear Mallory's concerns.

Mallory went on even though she looked like it physically pained her to do so. "I don't understand why you invited her there. It was a work function. The only non-Vanderbilt people there were spouses. Correct me if I'm wrong, but Lina is not... your spouse."

"No. She's my best friend. That's all she's ever been, and all she ever will be. As for why I invited her, that's a matter between me and Lina, and frankly, it's none of your business."

Mallory leaned forward and rested her elbows on her knees. "Will you please just tell me why you invited her?"

Anger began slowly pricking at Caitlin's skin. She forced herself to stay calm as she crafted a response that left out personal details. "Lina needed a night out and Valerie suggested I invite her. She wanted to meet Lina. I wanted Lina to get out and have fun. That's all there is to it."

When Mallory didn't respond, Caitlin looked at her more closely. Her eyes were trained on the floor and her fists were clenched. They may have only had a month of intimately learning each other, but she knew Mallory well enough to see that there was something she was holding back.

"Whatever it is, Mallory, say it. Things between us won't go anywhere unless–"

"Have you ever slept with her?"

The anger flared up so fast that Caitlin couldn't tamp it down. "Why is that even a fucking question? I just told you she's my best friend and that's it. Period. End of story. Don't make this into something it isn't, Mallory. I don't do jealousy in relationships or whatever this is between us."

Mallory looked at Caitlin, the pleading coolness of her eyes shifting Caitlin's anger. "Hear me out, okay? I know you probably don't want to hear this, but I am so tired of holding it in."

Caitlin pulled back further into her corner of the sofa and held a pillow firmly in front of her. "I'm listening."

"I dated your ex-wife." She paused, seeming to expect some kind of outburst or reaction from Caitlin, but none came. "You…that doesn't bother you?"

"I had a feeling. I saw you out with her once or twice." While it wasn't news to Caitlin, it still felt gross having Mallory say it out loud.

"We thought you might have known." The use of "we" hit Caitlin harder than Mallory's previous admission. She'd hoped it wasn't that serious between them, but that little pronoun indicated she was wrong. She resisted the urge to flee by focusing on hearing Mallory out.

"Becca…You know what, this isn't important." Mallory stood up. Pepper mewed in protest. "You told me you haven't slept with Lina, and I'll take your word for it."

"Sit down and finish," Caitlin said firmly. "I can already tell I don't want to hear this, but I think you owe me this gift of bluntness."

"You just…" She stuffed her hands in her pockets, discomfort radiating off her. "You want me to tell it to you straight?"

"Get it out, Mallory, so we can move on."

She nodded and sat back down, this time facing Caitlin. "From the moment I met Becca, she had nothing nice to say about her ex-wife. In hindsight, that should have been the first red flag. But she never used your name until she figured out that we both teach at Vanderbilt, which is completely my fault." A look of embarrassment passed over Mallory's features. "That night we were all at Ollie's, I mentioned my coworkers were there. I didn't know until later that night you were the ex-wife she so freely talked about."

Knowing that Becca was running her mouth about Caitlin didn't feel awesome, but it didn't surprise her either. Knowing that Becca talked shit on her to Mallory, however, made Caitlin want to punch a wall.

"I told her we were working on a unit together and she didn't like that. She was kind of insane about it even though at that point, I barely knew you. I just wanted to work with you. But she wouldn't let it go. The things she said…" Mallory shook her head. "That's the first time I cut off my relationship with her. We weren't that serious, and I couldn't handle her jealousy and nastiness."

Caitlin smiled wanly. "You don't have to explain that part to me. I'm well versed in that area."

"I thought you might be. But there's more." She looked for a sign to continue and Caitlin nodded. "You got under my skin. It's like she had a sixth sense, Caitlin; I think she knew it before I did. I started liking you, and she would not leave me alone. I may be kind of cold–"

"Oh, so you know you're an icy woman?"

"I prefer guarded, but I'll let you have that." She risked a small smile in Caitlin's direction. "Anyway. I couldn't block her number and be done. That's not who I am. I tried to be nice, but it kept backfiring. That day we went to Beanie's after school, she texted me and said she needed me. I should have ignored her. I wish I had," she said, regret in her tone, "because that's when everything fell apart."

Caitlin's stomach twisted. This was more to take in than she'd expected, and her emotions were warring internally. She fought the urge to tell Mallory to stop, that she'd heard enough and they could move on.

Mallory absently picked at her short nails. "She must have known I was getting closer to you, because that's when she let out her full assault." She cleared her throat. "Becca told me that you and Lina carried on an affair over the last year of your marriage and that was the reason for the divorce. She had so many stories, so much 'evidence,' as she called it. I didn't want to believe her, but she was persistent and unbelievably convincing."

The twisting knot in Caitlin's stomach had gone hard and cold. "She's lying," she said, her own voice chilly around the edges. "Not a word of what she told you about me is true, especially anything suggesting more than friendship between me and Lina." Even as she said it, Caitlin realized Mallory must have believed much of what Becca claimed to be true. Her actions and behaviors had shifted so dramatically after that post-tea almost-kiss, and Caitlin had spent all that time thinking she was the problem.

Of course Becca was the problem. She always was. But to pull a move like this? That was low, even for her. Caitlin's blood began to boil and her mind raced with ways to confront Becca.

"I believe you," Mallory continued. "But can you understand why seeing Lina that night made me–"

"Freak out? Run away? Bail without explaining or asking? Act like a child? Shut me out for absolutely no good reason? Sure. I can see why."

She hung her head. "Also deserved."

"Mallory, you're going to believe what you choose to believe. But I need you to remember that I have been nothing but honest with you from the get-go. Honest to a fault, even."

"I know. And that's why I'm here."

Their eyes met, and the familiar warmth between them tentatively rose once more. It wasn't insurmountable, this tear in their fabric, but it was one hell of a snag.

"You told me when we went to the Paine statue that you weren't seeing her anymore," Caitlin said. "Was that true?"

"Absolutely. After that horrible fight you and I had in the parking lot, I pulled back hard from Becca; it took a little while, but I finally got it through to her that I want nothing to do with her."

"And now?"

Mallory spread her hands out in front of her. "Zero contact. I blocked her." She grinned, clearly proud of herself.

"Do you believe me when I tell you that she told you a bunch of lies about me? Most importantly—do you believe me when I tell you that I have never done anything more than hug Lina?"

Mallory's nod was slow, but it came. "You think everything she said was a lie?"

Caitlin tugged her hair tie and shook her hair out over her shoulders. She had one hell of a headache building. "I'd put money on it."

Silence enveloped the two women as they sat facing each other, neither one risking moving closer. Pepper dozed, her furry ears twitching every so often, oblivious to the challenging conversation her human was moving through.

As Caitlin weighed her options for how to proceed, Mallory stood up.

"If it's okay with you, I think I should go now."

"The truth is I don't know what's okay with me right now," Caitlin admitted. "That was a lot to take in and while I'm happy we got it all out on the table, I'd be lying if I told you I'm not affected by it."

"I understand. I'm going to leave, but not because I want to. Because I need some time to work through that conversation, and I get the feeling you do too."

Caitlin stood and took Mallory's hand before walking her to the door. "Just because we're taking some time to process doesn't mean that I like you any less."

Mallory pressed her forehead against Caitlin's, her cool skin soothing Caitlin's growing headache. "I really like you, Caitlin. Please don't doubt that."

"Don't make me doubt it, Walker."

Mallory searched Caitlin's eyes for permission. Finding it, she kissed her forehead, her fingers lightly brushing Caitlin's hair behind her ear, with a gentleness that made Caitlin's legs feel like spaghetti.

"I'll talk to you soon."

The front door closed behind her, and Caitlin pressed her hand against the cool glass, wishing the night had gone differently but thankful for the truth finally coming out.

After Mallory's taillights disappeared down the street, Caitlin sat down at the bottom of her stairs, her head heavy in her hands. She heard the thud of Pepper jumping to the floor and soon her thick furry body slinked between Caitlin's legs.

"Come on, baby girl," Caitlin said, gently hoisting Pepper into her arms. "Come purr me to sleep."

# CHAPTER TWENTY-SEVEN

After two full days of silence between her and Mallory, Caitlin was getting antsy. She'd moved through her emotions with care, taking time to establish who she was most angry with (obviously Becca) and why she was a little mad at Mallory (too layered for her to understand, and not something she wanted to discuss with anyone else, so her decision was to simply forgive her for being an uncommunicative, cowardly ass). The Becca-anger was a tough one because there was no use in addressing it with Becca. As much as Caitlin yearned to scream all the injustices in Becca's face, she knew it would be a waste of her time and probably another blow to her self-esteem when Becca rebuked her or manipulated the situation to make herself look like the victim. Add to that the fact that she absolutely did not want Becca to know she still had the annoying ability to get under Caitlin's skin...

Yep. This was Caitlin's to work through alone.

Using a tactic Lina swore by, Caitlin alternated screaming into her pillow with punching her mattress in order to release her anger. It wasn't a perfect system, but after two days of vigilant bed-abuse, she did feel lighter.

It was proving interesting, this space thing. Caitlin's preferred method was to address things as they happened, which had *maybe* led to some discussions that didn't end well in previous relationships. Mallory was clearly a space-taker, and while Caitlin did not enjoy the silence, she did recognize the gradual shifts in her own emotions as the silent minutes ticked by.

When New Year's Eve dawned with a six forty a.m. text from Mallory, Caitlin surprised herself by waiting until eight to answer.

She was in the middle of making breakfast when her phone rang.

"I gather you're done with needing space?" she said coyly.

Mallory's chuckle was low and throaty. "I am. What about you?"

"I was done yesterday but figured I'd wait for you."

"That's sweet of you. You could have reached out, though."

Caitlin flipped her egg. "Nope. The space thing is yours to dictate. That's your coping mechanism, not mine."

"Okay, I can accept that. I know it's really last minute and probably makes me look like an idiot, but...do you have plans tonight?"

"I don't. New Year's Eve isn't a holiday I particularly enjoy, so it usually ends up being just another night for me."

"Good. I mean, well, yeah. Good. Can I see you?"

"Whew, I don't know. That might be rushing things, Walker. We just took all that space, and I–"

"Great, I'll be over around six."

Caitlin laughed, all the anxieties and residual anger lifting away. "Will you be staying the night?"

"Yes, if that's okay with you. Oh, and I'm bringing a new game my dad got me for Christmas." Excitement bubbled into Mallory's voice and Caitlin smiled, knowing it was likely more for the new game than the prospect of sex.

"I can't wait to see you."

"Good. Because I can't wait to see you, either."

* * *

"Want a beer?"

Mallory nodded, too absorbed in reading the directions for The Golden City, the game her dad had gotten for her. Caitlin was overwhelmed just looking at the board, but she was ready to give it a go, despite her concern that they'd be playing until the early morning hours.

When Mallory had arrived at five instead of six, claiming she couldn't wait any longer, she'd pulled Caitlin into a long, tight hug. They'd stayed like that for several minutes, both taking in and enjoying their closeness. When Mallory lifted Caitlin's chin and kissed her, any remaining worries fled the room and Caitlin leaned into that kiss with all her might. They'd snuggled together on the sofa, Pepper sprawled at their feet, talking here and there but mostly kissing and holding each other. The bliss was broken only when Mallory's stomach growled so loudly that even Pepper jumped. After a gourmet dinner of frozen pizza—the roads were icy, and the only good place nearby was takeout, not delivery—Mallory had whipped out her new game with a look of glee.

When Caitlin returned to the sofa, she tried to sit next to Mallory, but Pepper was commanding the space next to her with utmost authority. Caitlin sneered at the large feline princess as she handed Mallory her beer, then sat down on the floor across from Mallory, readying herself for the game.

Caitlin raised her bottle for a cheers, then waited for Mallory to tear her eyes from the directions before she said, "At the clink of these bottles, we are promising the following things. Ready?"

"Ready." The flinch-smile was gone, replaced by a dazzling real smile.

"We will not ignore each other. We will not believe what spurned exes say about us. We will talk instead of running away.

When we need something, we will ask for it instead of assuming the other person has read our mind."

"We will never mention Becca's name ever again," Mallory added.

Caitlin felt an unsettled pop of emotion. "Maybe one more clarification..." she trailed off.

"Whatever you want to know, just ask."

"It's not that I *want* to know, per se, but...umm..."

"The answer is no, sweetheart. That never happened." Mallory leaned over the coffee table, her lips inches from Caitlin's. "She was such a fucking nag about everything that I was afraid to sleep with her."

Caitlin shuddered. "Your foul mouth speaks volumes. I am now ready to never speak of her again. Anything else you want to add to the promises?"

Mallory tapped her finger against her lips, the very lips Caitlin was ready to start kissing again. "We promise to only kiss each other. And only sleep with each other."

In spite of her efforts to play it cool, Caitlin felt herself flush. Heat spread through her body, igniting little fires that had been cool and dormant for too many days.

"Mallory Walker, those sound like relationship promises."

"They are if you want them to be."

"I do," Caitlin said, then immediately groaned. "Fuck. I mean yes. I want them to be."

Mallory leaned further forward and pressed her lips lightly against Caitlin's. "Let's stick with a committed relationship for a while before we start exchanging vows, okay?"

"We promise not to speak of marriage," Caitlin added to the list.

"Cheers." Mallory smiled as their bottles clinked.

Caitlin took a satisfying sip of beer while looking at Mallory as she spoiled Pepper with chin rubs. "You two are friends now?"

"She's forgiven me for my inappropriate reaction when we first met."

"She's good like that."

"But Caitlin…exactly how much of your Christmas dinner did you feed to this cat?"

Caitlin gasped and clutched at her heart. "None! Now tell me how this game works before I claim to be too stupid to understand it and demand that you take me to bed instead."

With a flirty wink that promised non-board-game things to come, Mallory happily began rattling off directions, pointing out items on the board as she spoke. Suddenly she paused and gave a little laugh.

"We have a problem." She glanced at Pepper. "Exactly how smart is your cat?"

"You've met her. She prefers food over knowledge. What's the problem?"

"We, uh, need three people to play."

Mallory Walker, the rule-follower to end all rule-followers. Caitlin stifled a giggle at her utter distress. Then an idea formed.

"I do know someone who would probably come over and join us."

"Absolutely not." Mallory shook her head emphatically. "I can try to be nice to her, but I will not play board games with Valerie."

"Oh please. She's out with her latest boy toy; she wouldn't be caught dead at home tonight. I was referring to Lina," she said evenly.

A beat passed before Mallory relaxed and nodded. "Okay."

Caitlin lifted her phone cautiously. "You're sure? We could probably convince Pepper to play, but she's not exactly a worthy opponent."

"I think I'm surprised that Lina's available to come over," Mallory said, choosing her words carefully.

"You do know she's next door, right?" At Mallory's nod, Caitlin continued. "She doesn't do this holiday either. She has her own reasons." She bit the inside of her cheek, straddling that fine line between saying too much and not explaining enough. "Lina's in the Army. She's served a handful of tours overseas."

"Okay…" Mallory furrowed her brow.

"Come on, history teacher. Use that sexy Studier of Wars brain of yours and put two and two together." Caitlin tapped out a text as she waited for Mallory's synapses to fire. She wasn't sure Lina would be in the mood to come over, but it was worth a shot.

"And hurry up because she'll be over in less than ten minutes," Caitlin added after seeing Lina's reply.

"Is it a PTSD thing?"

"Ding, ding! I knew you had it in you—brains *and* beauty. Smoldering beauty, actually," Caitlin said, kneeling to kiss her girlfriend. Girlfriend. The word sounded funny in her head. Funny but incredibly right.

A knock sounded before the front door opened and Lina called out a hello.

"Don't mention the PTSD thing," Caitlin whispered as she scrambled to her feet. "She'd be upset if she knew we talked about it."

Mallory wouldn't notice, but Caitlin picked up on Lina's subdued mood right away. Her normally bold personality was hushed and mellow. Caitlin was glad the game required three people; it was obvious that sitting at home alone tonight wasn't good for Lina.

"This looks intense," Lina remarked as she sat down next to Pepper. She nodded over at Mallory. "Hey. It's good to see you."

"You too. Thanks for coming over. I tried to get Pepper to play, but," Mallory gestured toward the sleeping lump, "she wasn't interested."

"She prefers bird watching. She needs a lot of rest for that, as you may have gathered."

Caitlin watched from her spot on the floor as Lina and Mallory easily fell into a back and forth that she had hoped for but not predicted. Mallory's entire body lost its nervous tension as she animatedly explained the game to Lina, who was just as interested in it as Mallory was. Forty-five minutes into the game, which they were enjoying far more than Caitlin was, Lina excused herself to the bathroom. Caitlin and Mallory went to grab fresh drinks and some snacks from the kitchen.

Mallory pulled Caitlin into her arms. "You didn't tell her," she murmured, leaning her head against Caitlin's.

"There's no reason to, babe. The last thing I want is for you two to have Becca's bullshit interfering with your obvious ability to get along."

There was a twinkle in Mallory's eyes as she delivered a long, fiery kiss to Caitlin's waiting mouth. "Did you just call me 'babe'?" she whispered, her lips still brushing against Caitlin's.

Breathless from their kiss, Caitlin gently bit Mallory's lower lip. "Get used to it." Their kissing resumed, deepening, Mallory's tongue slipping past Caitlin's lips. Caitlin grabbed Mallory's arms and pulled her as close as she could, fitting their hips together as she slid a leg between Mallory's.

"Stop making out, you horny teenagers! We have a game to finish," Lina yelled from the sofa. "Disgusting," she muttered, loud enough for them to hear.

"We shouldn't keep her waiting." Caitlin tugged on the bottom of Mallory's sweatshirt.

"To be continued?" The dark passion in Mallory's eyes made Caitlin rethink her suggestion that they return to Lina and the game.

"I'll be waiting," she whispered, stealing one more kiss before pulling Mallory back to the living room.

# CHAPTER TWENTY-EIGHT

The front door had barely closed behind Lina before Mallory had Caitlin pinned against it, her lips and teeth alternating kisses and bites on the softest parts of Caitlin's neck. A pent-up moan escaped Caitlin's mouth as she dragged her fingers down Mallory's back.

"Upstairs. Now. You made me wait long enough."

"That's a feisty tone. You must really want me to take you to bed," Mallory whispered, her teeth raking across Caitlin's ear. "Or are you still mad about the music thing?"

Mad wasn't the word. Not even close. The moment Mallory was referring to was (so far, anyway) Caitlin's favorite moment of the night.

They were deep into The Golden City and everyone was getting along. Caitlin was monitoring the situation just in case, but after two hours of the three of them hanging out, everything seemed copacetic and she relaxed. As a small distraction from the tedium of the game, Caitlin had turned on music. Not ten minutes into her playlist, Mallory had looked up at Caitlin, her face crinkled in mild disgust.

"Caitlin? Can we maybe change the music? This is a little too sad."

A loud gasp burst from Lina as she threw up her hands in victory. Caitlin glared at both of them as she begrudgingly switched to a more upbeat playlist.

After that, she didn't care what music was playing. The fact that Lina and Mallory had bonded over Caitlin's predilection for slightly emo female singer-songwriters made her happier than any playlist she could have queued up.

Now, with Mallory's tongue moving at a torturously slow pace toward her collarbone, Caitlin moved Lina and the other memories of the evening out of mind. She wound her fingers through Mallory's and led her upstairs.

Once inside her bedroom, Caitlin shut the blinds, not wanting to give her neighbors a show. Before she could turn back toward the bed, Mallory moved behind her and wrapped her arms around her, pressing her palms flat on Caitlin's stomach. Her touch was firmer than usual, a pressing need emitting from her as her hands slid to Caitlin's hips.

The slow teasing of five minutes ago was gone, replaced with a series of sharp, deeply arousing bites to the back of Caitlin's neck. Each one grew in intensity and depth. When Mallory's teeth moved to the place where Caitlin's neck connected to her shoulder, the bite vibrated through her entire body and she fell back against Mallory. Strong hands caught her and smoothly spun her until the backs of her knees were against the edge of the bed.

A gentle but domineering nudge pushed Caitlin onto the bed, and Mallory wasted no time in stripping off Caitlin's jeans and hoodie. She hovered over Caitlin, taking time to admire the matching black lace underwear and bra, her fingertips grazing the fabric as her eyes drank in the sight before her.

"Did you wear this for me?" Mallory's voice was throaty, gruff with desire.

"I did. Do you like it?"

"You could say that."

Caitlin's heart rate sped up and she felt her breasts pushing against the fabric of her bra with each heated breath she took. Mallory took her time stroking and kissing Caitlin's breasts through the lace. Her nipples strained against the thin fabric as the tip of Mallory's tongue prodded them, teasing them, making them harder than they'd ever been before.

As Mallory's teeth captured her nipple and Caitlin cried out, Mallory glided her fingers down Caitlin's torso, drawing her pointer finger under the top of Caitlin's underwear. With great ease, as though she had all the time in the world, Mallory slid her finger out and then reached under Caitlin to squeeze her ass. Having moved to Caitlin's other nipple with her mouth, she moved her hand under Caitlin, fingers still cupping her ass while pressing her thumb against Caitlin's soaked underwear.

"Please touch me," Caitlin murmured. Her head was spinning with desire. She watched through hazy eyes as Mallory pulled back and stripped off her own sweatshirt and jeans, keeping her T-shirt and underwear on. Caitlin reached up to remove the rest of her clothing, but Mallory pressed her back against the bed.

"Not yet."

From her position above, Mallory let her eyes travel over the span of Caitlin's body, taking in its dips and hills, the tiny scars here and there, and the litany of birthmarks scattered across her thighs.

"I want you to know that it pains me to take off this stunning ensemble. But if I don't remove it right now, I'm afraid I'm going to rip it off."

Caitlin's breath hitched in her throat as Mallory made quick work of her lace intimates. Her mouth met Caitlin's in a passionate kiss. The energy between them was charged anew; Caitlin felt the desire radiating off of Mallory. Her hands moved from Caitlin's hair back to her breasts, rolling her nipples until Caitlin moaned. Before Caitlin had a chance to reach once more for Mallory's annoying T-shirt, Mallory shifted and delivered another searing kiss.

Caitlin squirmed beneath her mouth, digging her fingers into Mallory's back. Their mouths fit together so beautifully, the heat from the kiss adding to Caitlin's already impressive arousal. She sucked gently on Mallory's tongue as she felt Mallory's hand cup her wetness.

"Caitlin." Her voice was steady and strong, and it made Caitlin's body erupt in goosebumps.

"Mallory," she responded, slightly pushing herself against Mallory's hand.

"I want to fuck you. Can I fuck you?"

"Please."

Mallory's fingers pushed into Caitlin with careful force, as steady and strong as her voice. Caitlin grabbed at the sheets as Mallory's fingers filled her and moved into a heady rhythm. She arched her back and Mallory's strokes hit her most sensitive spot. Caitlin gasped and groaned all at once, her body rocking in sync with the thrusts that were bringing her so close to orgasm.

When Mallory added a third finger, Caitlin cried out. She felt the opening surges of her orgasm and seconds later, her body tensed before crashing into a shaking release. Mallory rode it out with her, her hand moving with each quake until Caitlin's body stilled.

Caitlin barely caught her breath before she felt Mallory's tongue gliding over her painfully hard clit. The sensation was intense and exhilarating; she wanted it to last for hours but knew she couldn't keep her orgasm at bay for very long. Mallory's tongue caressed Caitlin, her strokes as commanding as her fingers had been. Caitlin ground her hips down into the bed, feeling Mallory take her shift in stride, her tongue never losing contact.

A flight of stars burst behind Caitlin's eyelids and the hot rush of her second orgasm swept through her body, her thighs shaking with each of the aftershocks. She reached out for Mallory and pulled her down, holding her tight.

They lay in silence, legs sticking together with sweat and heat. Caitlin kept her arms locked around Mallory, loving the feeling of her weight holding her down.

"Happy New Year," Mallory said, loosening Caitlin's grip by lifting onto her elbows. She gazed down at Caitlin with a sweet smile.

Caitlin glanced at the clock. Sure enough, midnight had shown up a couple minutes ago and brought with it a whole new year. "Happy New Year to you. That was quite the celebration, by the way."

"What can I say? I wanted to give you fireworks at midnight."

Caitlin laughed and ran her fingers up Mallory's sides, pushing her shirt out of the way. "I had no idea you were such a dork."

"Don't tell anyone. You'll ruin my reputation." Mallory kissed the side of Caitlin's head. "Have I told you lately that I really, really like you?"

"Yeah," Caitlin smiled as she tugged Mallory down and rolled her over, moving to straddle her hips. She lifted the T-shirt, tugged it off, and threw it across the room. "I kinda gathered that."

* * *

Mallory rolled over and tugged Caitlin closer, smushing their naked bodies together. Caitlin threaded her fingers through Mallory's and brought their hands to her mouth, kissing Mallory's knuckles.

"Did I wake you?" came a sleepy murmur from behind.

"No, I can't sleep past seven. It's a curse of adulthood."

"I'm hungry," came the next murmur, this one a little whiny.

"Whining, babe–"

"I know, I know. It's not a good look on either of us." She yawned and burrowed her head into the nook of Caitlin's shoulder. "But you are going to feed me, correct?"

"Waffles and bacon sound good?"

"Oh my God. So good." She nibbled Caitlin's shoulder. "Did you want to invite Lina for breakfast?"

Caitlin stilled. She knew the two had reached common ground the previous evening, but this was unexpected.

"We can do that, if you're sure you're okay with it. Lina's a huge part of my life, but she's not a part of *everything* I do."

"I know. I just thought with her being in a rough place yesterday that you'd want to make sure she's okay today."

Caitlin flipped over and looked into Mallory's eyes. "Thank you."

Mallory wiped the sleep from her eyes. "For what?"

"For understanding. It means more to me than I can say."

Mallory wiggled her eyebrows, an adorable sight considering her messy bedhead and sleep-wrinkled face. "I can think of some ways for you to show me how much it means to you."

"Wow, we've really opened Pandora's box here, huh?" Caitlin ran her hands down Mallory's side, scratching gently along the way.

"I could make a really bad joke–"

Caitlin pressed her lips against Mallory's. "Yeah, yeah. I get it. Let's go have breakfast before the lesbians open any more boxes, okay?"

The sound of Mallory's laughter warmed Caitlin through and through; it was a sound she knew she would never tire of.

# CHAPTER TWENTY-NINE

The noise in the gym was deafening. The bleachers, packed with Vanderbilt fans on one side and Essex Junction High School supporters on the other, were filled to an alarming capacity. Valerie swore everything was regulation, but Caitlin was unnerved by the amount of people that had shown up for this playoff game.

They'd paused so Valerie could say hello to some teachers. Lina was next to Caitlin, trying not to fidget but doing a terrible job of it. Caitlin kept glancing around the gym, looking for both Mallory and an open space that would be comfortable for Lina.

Just as a feeling of dread was sinking in, Valerie grabbed Caitlin's arm and propelled their group to the far side of the gym. Halfway there, Caitlin noticed Mallory watching them. She was in coach mode, but when she made eye contact with Caitlin, a knowing smile warmed her otherwise stoic expression.

"Coach Walker," Valerie said by way of greeting.

"Valerie," Mallory said with a curt nod. "Hey, Lina. Thanks for coming."

Lina clapped Mallory on the back in a bro move that made Caitlin smile. She was thoroughly enjoying watching a friendship develop between her best friend and her girlfriend just as much as she was enjoying watching her own relationship evolve. January had been a whirlwind for Mallory and Caitlin as they found their footing in their new official relationship. Not much changed other than spending more time together, and even having some school night sleepovers. Mallory was still busy with basketball, which only got worse as they moved into February; Vanderbilt was doing exceedingly well, and in the middle of the month, they'd entered the playoff season.

Mallory had initially been surprised at Lina's dedication to coming to games, but once she realized it stemmed from Lina's genuine desire to be there, she loved it. When Caitlin had missed a game and Lina had shown up, Mallory hadn't even been upset about Caitlin not being there. A few times when Mallory was at Caitlin's, Lina had come over just to talk basketball with her. Caitlin had joked that Lina was her stand-in for girlfriend sports requirements, and with a shrug, Mallory had said, "I can deal with that."

It was sweet, the way Lina and Mallory got along. Caitlin couldn't have been happier, or more relieved, about it.

"Hey you," Mallory said now, her voice low but her smile warm. "I saved you seats behind us. I figured that way Lina could stand against the wall if she got uncomfortable," she added quietly.

Caitlin reminded herself of where they were so she didn't throw herself into Mallory's arms and smother her with gratitude kisses. She settled for saying, "You're the best. Thank you for doing that."

Mallory reached over and squeezed Caitlin's hand, taking her quite by surprise. "I'm really happy you're here. Both of you." She grimaced. "All of you," came through gritted teeth.

"Can't wait to let Valerie know that!" Caitlin nodded toward the open seats. "We're gonna go get settled. I'll be rooting for you. Kick some ass out there, Coach."

A quick nod let her know Mallory was slipping back into coach mode. Caitlin corralled her friends toward the bleachers.

The first half of the game went well enough. So Lina said, anyway. She pointed out specific plays and techniques, but neither Valerie nor Caitlin kept up their feigned interest in learning about the sport. Valerie spent most of the time on her phone or chatting with the group of male teachers nearby, while Caitlin locked her attention on Mallory.

She was extra hot while in coaching mode, Caitlin decided. Not only did she look unbearably sexy in navy khakis that showed off her muscular legs, but the white button-down shirt with its sleeves rolled carefully and neatly to her elbows fit her perfectly. The combined effect of the outfit was sexy authoritarian coach, and Caitlin was into it.

A whistle blew, followed by an eardrum-grating buzzer. Halftime had arrived while Caitlin was busy drooling over her girlfriend. She glanced at the score. Vanderbilt was in the lead, but only by six points. Essex Junction was proving to be a challenging foe.

Mallory looked back at Caitlin before jogging to the locker room. A knowing look passed between them, enough to warm Caitlin's insides and hopefully bolster Mallory with support.

"You lovebirds are so cute. It's actually kind of disgusting." Valerie stood and stretched, sticking her tongue out at Caitlin.

"I agree. Totally gross," Lina piped up. As Mallory had predicted, Lina had sat in the bleachers for a whole two minutes before moving to stand against the wall. She was close enough to call out all those explanations to Valerie and Caitlin, but with her back against a sturdy surface, there was no chance for someone to come to from behind and catch her by surprise.

Caitlin rolled her eyes, not giving either of her friends ammunition. Maybe it was gross. But she was happy, and she deserved it, dammit. Her phone vibrated.

*You look beautiful. I can't wait to fall asleep next to you tonight.*

A blush skittered across Caitlin's cheeks. She was still getting used to Mallory's romantic side—a side she hadn't expected to even be an option in her deck of personality cards. Caitlin had to admit that it was a pretty great side.

*And YOU look sexy as fuck. I'm in need of lots of kisses, FYI. Now go give a pep talk or whatever it is that coaches do.*

Valerie leaned over to spy, but Caitlin's cat-like reflexes—something she had not learned from Pepper—prevented Valerie from reading the gooey exchange.

Lina and Valerie soon went off to get drinks and Caitlin stayed put to save their spots. She scanned the gym floor, where handfuls of Vanderbilt students had gathered in clumps. She noticed Devon pacing behind the chairs where the team sat. His posture straightened and a dazzling grin appeared on his face as the girls' team jogged back onto the court, their resting period over. Caitlin watched Devon watch Hailey as she jumped in line to practice free throws. He cheered her on for every single move she made, and unfailingly, she gave him a little wave from her side each time she sunk a basket.

Their relationship, finally moving into the open despite Vanderbilt's terrible racial politics, was the cutest thing Caitlin had ever seen.

The second half began with a hard fight from Essex Junction. The difference in coaching between McKinney and Mallory was interesting to watch. McKinney was loud and pushy whereas Mallory was calmer, more focused and direct with her instructions. They balanced the team, and perhaps Caitlin was biased, but it was clear to her that Mallory was the superior coach.

Five minutes in and now down by fifteen, McKinney started to unravel. Caitlin watched as Mallory approached her and placed a firm hand on her shoulder. Words were exchanged, and McKinney visibly relaxed, but just a smidgeon. It was enough to get her to stop screaming at the girls, though.

"Ollie's after the game?" Valerie was tapping out another text.

"Nah. She's had a long night. We're just gonna go back to my place."

"Ugh. I should have known you'd be no fun when you're in loooooove." Valerie rolled her eyes then craned her neck to get Lina's attention. "Hey! Ragelis! You'll come out with me after the game, right?"

Lina waved Valerie off, her attention focused on the game.

"Was that a yes? It looked like a yes. Oh! Oh my God, that girl is here."

"What are you talking about?" Caitlin asked, her attention firmly focused on Carly sprinting down the court, ball bouncing just in front of her. How did she avoid tripping?

"Remember how I told you I saw Walker get into a big ol' fight with some hot girl? She's here. I wonder who she is."

Not one for subtlety, Valerie pointed to the gym floor where, sure enough, an attractive woman was lingering near the Vanderbilt bench.

And not just any attractive woman.

"This is not happening," Caitlin murmured, looking over to Lina, who was normally attune to everything going on around her but was currently focused so hard on the game that she didn't see Becca standing a mere five feet from Mallory. To her credit, Mallory was also focused on the game and didn't appear to have a clue about Becca's presence either.

"She's hot, right?" Valerie elbowed Caitlin.

"She's an asshole," Caitlin said curtly.

"Wait, you know her?"

The sound of Lina clearing her throat obnoxiously loud was a good enough indication that she'd noticed Becca. Caitlin risked a look over at her and nearly laughed at Lina's comical expression of panic.

Caitlin shrugged and shook her head simultaneously before responding to Valerie. "She's my ex-wife."

"Holy shit. I'll be right back; I need some popcorn for this drama festival."

Caitlin pressed her arm across Valerie, holding her to her seat. "I'm not going to say anything more about this, but I'm gonna need you to stay exactly where you are and not draw a single ounce of attention in this direction. Got it?"

"Yes, ma'am." Valerie giggled. "I like it when you're bossy."

For the rest of the half, Caitlin moved her glance between Becca, Lina, and Mallory. Any movement or realization of someone's presence could set off any number of bombs. There was a moment when Becca began turning around and Caitlin nearly jumped out of her skin. She had nowhere to hide. Fortunately, McKinney barked something at Mallory and that caught Becca's attention and kept it there.

When the buzzer rang, Caitlin sat, frozen. The correct course of action was unknown. She figured sitting still was better than making herself a moving target. Lina must have agreed; she slowly made her way from the wall to the spot next to Caitlin and sat stock still. Even Valerie was glued to the unfolding drama and was, for once, quiet.

Vanderbilt went through the high fives with Essex Junction's team before returning to their bench to celebrate their very tight victory; they'd pulled off a win by a mere two points. Caitlin got momentarily distracted when Devon picked up Hailey and spun her around before kissing her on the lips. While internally cheering for them, she flicked her eyes back to Mallory and willed her to look back.

And she did. Her gaze landed directly on Caitlin, but the flicker of confusion indicated she'd caught sight of Becca. Sure enough, after sending Caitlin a smile, she diverted her gaze and a wall of ice closed up her features.

"This could get ugly," Lina mumbled.

Becca wasn't dumb. She was observant and read people well. She noticed the varying emotions in Mallory, noticed where she had looked first, and took it upon herself to spin around and search the bleachers until her green-blue eyes settled on Caitlin and, naturally, Lina.

The look that crossed over Becca's face was annoyance coupled with fear. There was a touch of cockiness in her stance, as though seeing Lina sitting next to Caitlin proved all of her lies were true.

"What do we do?" Valerie said through closed lips.

"Nothing. We do nothing," Lina mumbled.

Caitlin decided against nothing, and since Becca's eyes were still locked on hers, she decided to give her a little wave. A heated anger flushed Becca's cheeks and she whirled around toward Mallory once more.

Mallory was waiting, arms crossed. Intimidation radiated off of her, but Becca wasn't deterred. They exchanged words, and when Becca leaned closer to Mallory, Mallory took a large step backward and recrossed her arms. The peanut gallery watched in awe as Mallory's lips moved faster, her posture never changing from its cold stance. When Becca spun around a second time, now pure irritation with a touch of embarrassment written all over her face, Lina and Valerie joined Caitlin in waving to her.

With a loud huff, Becca let a few more words fly in Mallory's direction before stomping out of the gym. Audible sighs of relief came from the three in the bleachers. Mallory stared after Becca, ensuring she actually left, before shaking her head and walking to the locker room.

"That was a bit disappointing. I'd like my money back." Valerie pouted as they stood and gathered their jackets before making their way out of the gym.

"You good?" Lina asked quietly.

"I think so. That was kind of crazy."

"You think Mallory's okay?"

Caitlin shrugged. "We'll find out."

"Humiliating," was all Mallory would say, over and over again.

Mallory was lying with her head on Caitlin's lap, Pepper nuzzled between her legs. Caitlin took advantage of the situation and let Mallory's ponytail loose. She ran her fingers through her dark brown hair, hoping the motion was as soothing to Mallory was it was to her.

"What did you say to her?"

"That she humiliated me."

"I got that part. What else?"

"I told her about you. About us. And that I never wanted to see her or hear from her again."

Caitlin's hand stilled. "You did? Seriously?"

Mallory cautiously flipped over, not wanting to disturb Pepper, and leaned on her elbows. She looked up at Caitlin. "Of course I did. She needed to know."

"I don't know that it's a *need*..."

"I do. I blocked her number so what did she do? Show up where she knew she could corner me."

Caitlin mulled it over. Becca's level of obsession was more clearly aimed at Mallory than it ever had been at her. She almost got jealous about that. Almost.

"We can't guarantee she won't do something like this again, you know."

"No, *we* can't," Mallory said with a wink. "I'm proud of you for taking the high road tonight."

"Believe me, I was dying to get on that low road with her. I have some things I'd like to say."

"Deaf ears, sweetheart." Mallory propped herself up and kissed Caitlin. "It would all fall on deaf ears."

# CHAPTER THIRTY

The Golden City didn't last long. Lina, Caitlin, and Mallory gave it a mostly valiant attempt, but ultimately Caitlin couldn't muster the same excitement her girlfriend and best friend had for the game. After several rounds, Caitlin kindly suggested they find someone to take her place. Unsurprisingly, they were excited to find a new opponent. It did *not* go over well when Caitlin jokingly suggested they ask Becca to be their third. That was the end of any mention of Becca, even those meant to be joking.

While the Vanderbilt girls continued their playoff domination, Caitlin busied her free time with job searches. No official word regarding Nicole Donovan's imminent return in August had arrived yet, but Caitlin wasn't in a position to wait. There weren't many job openings popping up in late winter, but she pushed to get her name and resume out there just in case. For a fleeting moment, Caitlin contemplated returning to River Valley, where there was almost always a guaranteed opening. Being at Vanderbilt had renewed her love for teaching. Maybe with the experience from Briarwood and Vanderbilt combined, River Valley would be more manageable.

That idea was sliced in half when Caitlin reached out to one of her former colleagues who, somehow, was still teaching English at River Valley. An emphatic "DON'T DO IT" followed by a long list of things that hadn't changed reminded Caitlin of her reasons for leaving. She cringed while reading the list, disheartened that the school remained under utterly ineffective administration. Well, strike that option off the list.

The entrance of March brought with it a resurgence of winter. It was a bitter day covered with dangerous-looking clouds when Caitlin made her way home from an interview. In her late-night scrolls, she'd found a position at a local liberal arts college that seemed to fit her combined teaching and therapy skills. It was idyllic, and she felt like it was also a longshot, but just one week after submitting her resume, human resources had called and asked her to come in for an interview. Caitlin had jumped at the opportunity then thrown herself into researching the school to be sure she wouldn't be caught off guard by any questions.

She pulled into her garage, humming to herself. She had a good feeling about that interview. Barb Brewster, the woman who ran the on-campus crisis center, was approachable and instantly warm but had an obvious undertone of firm control. Her personality seemed a perfect snapshot of how the center ran. A few other people, including someone from human resources, were present for the interview. Once Caitlin got over her initial nerves, she'd felt herself slip into a comfortable place and the answers had flowed from her mouth. She didn't want to jinx herself, but she was pretty sure she'd nailed it.

Whether or not she was exactly qualified for the position was a different matter, one she didn't belabor as she went inside and flipped on the lights. Pepper delivered an immediate pathetic cry, letting Caitlin know she was in fact starving and couldn't live another moment without a fresh bowl of meat crackers.

Cat fed and dinner in the works, Caitlin pressed play on a Mallory and Lina curated playlist. The two had collaborated on it, titled it "Approved Songs," then shared it with Caitlin without a word. If she didn't love them both so much, she would have told them to fuck off.

The knowledge stilled her movements as she chopped vegetables for a stir fry. Yeah, she loved Mallory. She wasn't in a rush to tell her, figuring that her actions spoke the words on a daily basis, but she knew it was bound to slip out sooner or later.

Likely sooner than later, she mused, as the sound of Mallory unlocking the front door echoed through the foyer. The key exchange had been an act of silent love, but also pure necessity with Mallory's challenging basketball schedule.

"It does not look good out there," she said by way of greeting before kissing Caitlin's cheek. "If the weather report holds up, we'll have off tomorrow."

Caitlin cheered, raising her chopping knife in the air. "Finally! I can't believe January and February let us down with no snow."

"I think this is going to end up being an ice storm, but that guarantees a day off. Snow's too iffy."

"Ah yes, the ice-encased world, your preferred habitat."

Mallory playfully jabbed Caitlin in the ribs. "You spend too much time with Valerie. This smells amazing, by the way."

Caitlin nudged Mallory's face with hers, looking for a real kiss. As she received it, the front door opened a second time and Lina bounded in, her movements akin to an excited puppy seeing its owners after a long day apart.

"Okay," she said, raising her hands in protest. "Do you two make out all the time or do I have the worst timing ever?"

Mallory tapped her chin, faking deep thought. "Seems like the answer is yes to both of your pressing questions."

"I'll take that. And I'll let you get back to your repulsive face-sucking once big shot here tells us how her interview went."

Mallory's eyes lit up and she smacked her hand against her forehead. "Why didn't I lead with that?"

"Probably because you were too excited to tell me about the promise of ice and how excited you are to be slip-sliding–"

"The interview, Caitlin. Now." Lina popped a sliced pepper into her mouth. "And then I'll leave you lovers alone."

Caitlin absently tapped the edge of the knife against the cutting board. "I have a good feeling about it. I like the woman who runs the center, and there was a good vibe all around the campus."

Mallory and Lina had matching anticipatory looks on their faces. Apparently she hadn't said enough.

"I may have slayed it," she added, lifting a corner of her mouth. She passed Mallory a bottle of white wine.

"That's more like it!" Lina exclaimed, pumping her first in the air.

Mallory wrapped her arm around Caitlin's waist and squeezed. "I know you slayed it, sweetheart. What's the next step?"

"Wait and see if they want me for a second interview. I should hear within a week."

Lina grabbed a couple of peppers, narrowly missing the descent of Caitlin's knife. "Keep me posted. I'll take my leave and let you two celebrate. Save me some leftovers," she called before shutting the door on her way out.

"I'm excited for you, Caitlin. This job sounds like a perfect fit for you." Mallory kissed the side of Caitlin's head before going to work on the corkscrew.

"You won't be sad about me not being at Vanderbilt?"

A low chuckle rose from Mallory's throat. "That has its pros and cons. I don't love the idea of you not being right across the hall all day, and while we've navigated working together pretty well so far, you know my history with dating people I work with." She poured each of them a glass of wine. "And once basketball season is over, we'll have more time together. I think it all balances out."

"Kind of like how I balance you out?"

Mallory smiled and sipped her wine. "Something like that, yeah."

Mallory's tongue pressed against the back of her teeth, her lips slightly parted and fully kissable. She was the picture of concentration, furrowed brow and all, and Caitlin was dying to disrupt her with a lingering kiss.

Alas, it was Mallory's move, and the Parcheesi board was in Caitlin's favor. Not wanting to be accused of breaking the rules or intimidating her opponent, Caitlin sat quietly, settling for observing the gorgeous woman across from her.

"You're staring."

Caitlin hummed. "Is that against the rules? I didn't notice that when you read me the refresher."

"It is if you're doing it to distract me."

As though summoned by a greater being, the ultimate distraction filtered through the speakers in Caitlin's living room. Mallory forgot about her staring girlfriend as stars lit up in her eyes at the sound of T. Swift's voice.

"You know, this song makes me think of you. It made me think of you before anything really happened between us, actually." She finally moved her piece, giving Caitlin control of the board.

Caitlin paused her turn and listened to the song. "Because I'm so delicate?"

"That's...not exactly a word I'd use to describe you."

After making a quick move, her only strategy at Parcheesi, Caitlin sat back and listened harder. "Mmm, yeah, you do have a bad reputation. I get it."

"You're impossible. Do I have to spell it out?"

Caitlin grinned. She may not be able to win board games against Mallory, but she had a decent track record at outwitting her. "No. I get it, babe."

"I'm going to be cheesy for a moment."

Caitlin inhaled dramatically. "My favorite time of day! Swiss or cheddar today?"

Mallory chose to ignore the joking dramatics, which she was learning was often for the best. "You get the song because you get me. People don't get me...but you do." She reached over and brushed her thumb over Caitlin's lips. "And that part of us doesn't feel delicate."

"Does that mean–"

"Nothing about us feels delicate," Mallory amended, knowing where Caitlin had been headed. "Nothing."

"I love you." There. It was out. Maybe it was blurted and unceremonious, but there it was. It had been rumbling around inside of Caitlin, and she wasn't willing to hold it back any longer.

Tears sprang into Mallory's eyes; not exactly the response that Caitlin was expecting.

"Is it cool that I said that?" she stage-whispered.

Mallory laughed and pulled Caitlin into a tight hug before kissing her through the light scatter of tears that had fallen.

"It's cool. I love you, Caitlin. I really do."

Caitlin brushed away the remaining wetness from Mallory's cheeks. "So these were happy tears?"

"Yes, and if you tell anyone–"

"I know, I know. Your reputation. I wouldn't dare. That was just so delicate, babe."

After kissing Caitlin tenderly, Mallory sat back with a thoughtful expression. "You know, I have to disagree with Taylor."

Caitlin quirked an eyebrow. "Mallory…don't say something you'll regret."

"I think this *is* for the best. You and me. Us. Isn't it?" She grinned, the cheesy romantic side of her ringing loud and clear.

The song ended and Caitlin leaned into Mallory's arms. "It is," she murmured, letting the feelings of love and comfort wash over her. She wouldn't have predicted it, but Mallory was proving to be everything she wanted and needed.

Delicate moments and all.

THE END, but really just the beginning

Bella Books, Inc.

*Women. Books. Even Better Together.*

P.O. Box 10543
Tallahassee, FL 32302

Phone: 800-729-4992
**www.bellabooks.com**